CU00829156

THE GOOD WIFE

GEMMA ROGERS

Boldwood

First published in Great Britain in 2024 by Boldwood Books Ltd.

Copyright © Gemma Rogers, 2024

Cover Design by Judge By My Covers

Cover Illustration: iStock

The moral right of Gemma Rogers to be identified as the author of this work has been asserted in accordance with the Copyright, Designs and Patents Act 1988.

All rights reserved. No part of this book may be reproduced in any form or by any electronic or mechanical means, including information storage and retrieval systems, without written permission from the author, except for the use of brief quotations in a book review.

This book is a work of fiction and, except in the case of historical fact, any resemblance to actual persons, living or dead, is purely coincidental.

Every effort has been made to obtain the necessary permissions with reference to copyright material, both illustrative and quoted. We apologise for any omissions in this respect and will be pleased to make the appropriate acknowledgements in any future edition.

A CIP catalogue record for this book is available from the British Library.

Paperback ISBN 978-1-80549-493-5

Large Print ISBN 978-1-80549-489-8

Hardback ISBN 978-1-80549-488-1

Ebook ISBN 978-1-80549-486-7

Kindle ISBN 978-1-80549-487-4

Audio CD ISBN 978-1-80549-494-2

MP3 CD ISBN 978-1-80549-491-1

Digital audio download ISBN 978-1-80549-485-0

Boldwood Books Ltd
23 Bowerdean Street
London SW6 3TN
www.boldwoodbooks.com

For Mum, because it's her second favourite book.

1

CHLOE

When I came out of the toilet into the washroom area, a curvaceous redhead stood at one of the porcelain sinks applying lipstick in the arched mirror. Her mouth frozen in a perfect O shape as she swept the wand over her Cupid's bow. A blood-red shade to match her gown, which looked as though it had been made especially for her. It clutched her small waist yet skimmed the roundness of her behind, reminding me of Jessica Rabbit.

Standing beside her, I ran a hand precariously over my sandy hair, straining to get it out of the clip it was pinched into. My husband, Tom, liked my hair up. He said it made me look classy and poised. I, however, did not. I had no desire to showcase the deep trivets of my collarbones in the black off-the-shoulder gown Tom had chosen for me to wear. My misgivings validated as, stood next to the ethereal beauty, I looked like a child in her mother's dress.

The redhead did not speak, although she smiled politely. I went through the motions of washing my hands, unable to fully tear my gaze away. In her hand, she held a raffle ticket, the number nine printed on a white stub. She glanced at it before tucking it into the plunging neckline of her dress.

'What's the raffle for?' I asked, vaguely remembering Harry Poulter, the CEO and owner of Middeon, handing tickets to the directors as they crossed the threshold of Glenthorne Manor, the location of the company dinner.

The redhead tossed her hair back, glossy waves bouncing across milky shoulders as she let out a chuckle. 'It's for me, darling,' she said in a smooth southern Irish accent before slipping her lipstick into a gold clutch bag and checking herself once more in the mirror.

'You?' I asked, lines creasing my forehead. It was strange, standing next to someone yet having a conversation with their reflection in a mirror. As though it wasn't quite real.

Her eyes ran the length of my body, leaving me exposed. 'You've never been here before, have you?'

I shook my head. It was Tom's first time too, a quarterly event that only the directors of the technology company were invited to. Tom had recently been awarded a promotion to finance director, heralded as a rising star by Harry. The youngest in the history of Middeon to make director at the tender age of thirty-six and the invitation was a big deal.

A three-course black-tie dinner at Harry's stately home in Turners Hill, a leafy village in Mid Sussex around fifteen minutes away from where we lived in Copthorne. I didn't understand what Middeon did – creating computer chips or something – but they were climbing the ranks in their field.

'Have a nice evening,' the redhead said, smoothing down her hair one last time and leaving me alone in the washroom, heels clacking on the tiles as she went. I grimaced, still none the wiser about the raffle. What on earth did she mean?

Bemused, I dried my hands on a plush towel and returned to Tom.

There were fourteen guests seated on a large oblong table in what could only be described as a ballroom. The walls were adorned with oak wooden panels and along one side floor-to-ceiling arched windows flooded the room with rays from the sinking sun. A huge chandelier hung from the centre of the ceiling and in one corner stood an ebony grand piano.

All of the directors were male, bar the human resources director, a stoney-faced-looking woman in her fifties who had arrived unaccompanied along with Graham Spectre, the technology director. Everyone else had their polished wives seated beside them.

I slid into my seat, trying to look as though I belonged despite being the youngest person in the room, bar Tom, by at least twenty years. I'd followed the rules all night: speak only when spoken to, don't slouch, chin up, shoulders back and hands in lap when not eating.

Tom frowned as I laid my napkin across my lap, irritated I'd left my seat, but the champagne we'd been given on arrival had gone straight to my bladder.

'I'm sorry, there was a queue,' I placated.

He smiled tightly, resuming his conversation with the wife of Jim Robbins, the marketing director sitting to his right.

I picked up my fork to finish the prime fillet mignon, three mouthfuls left to have before I reached my limit of ten. I knew he'd be counting too. He always was.

On the floor to my left, I noticed a ticket stub as I gathered in the skirt of my dress which had caught on the chair. I reached down to collect it under the pretence I was adjusting my hem. It was the number nine. A match to the woman's in the bathroom. Could it be the winning ticket? No one had mentioned the raffle or what prizes were available to be won. However, Tom had told me Harry was notorious for his grand gestures so I assumed whatever it was would be significant.

Next to me, Graham, a bulbous man with a raucous laugh which made me jump, hadn't noticed his ticket was missing. With the stub tucked into my clammy palm, I took a sip of wine, trying to locate Tom's ticket, spying it wedged underneath his glass. Deep in conversation, he didn't notice when I swapped the two. They must have been handed out when I was in the bathroom, was I supposed to get one or was it one ticket per couple?

Surveying the length of the table, I spied the mysterious redhead sat next to Harry Poulter. She threw her head back and laughed at something he'd whispered into her ear. Tom had told me Harry was widowed, but I couldn't imagine she'd be his latest squeeze. He was knocking on sixty with an enormous overhanging belly, a receding hairline and rosacea. I knew some women were attracted to powerful, not to mention rich men, but instinct told me she wasn't one of those.

'Are you enjoying your steak, darling?' Tom asked, interrupting my thoughts.

'It's delicious,' I said automatically, despite it being too rare for my taste. Red liquid pooled in the corner of my plate every time I carved a slice.

'Don't fill yourself up too much, you've got another course to go yet.' He smiled, although it didn't reach his eyes. His smiles never did any more.

Acquiescing, I laid my fork down, resting my hands in my lap, cheeks burning.

I watched his gaze flitter over to where mine had been seconds before, his lips parting. He'd always had a thing for redheads, unable to stop himself from commenting if there was an actress on the television, and *she* was exquisite.

Our plates were collected a few minutes later and dessert was served – a sliver of dark chocolate cheesecake. Decadence delivered on a tiny plate as the guests moaned in pleasure. I took a small bite, the first of the ten I was allowed, filling sticking to the roof of my mouth. It was a struggle to swallow and I dabbed at my lips with the ivory napkin, surveying the other guests and catching snippets of conversation where I could.

Tom had barely spoken to me all night, but I knew he was networking, trying to establish his place amongst the directors. I watched as he fiddled with his cufflinks, a sign of boredom as he listened to the wife of the marketing director I'd not yet been introduced to. She was in her mid-fifties with bird-like features, each finger had a ring on it, each wrist multiple bangles, jangling as she told Tom about a recent visit to the South of France.

Heads turned to the sound of a chinking glass. Harry Poulter pushed his chair back, his stomach straining against the buttons of his white dress shirt.

'Thank you, my wonderful guests, for your presence this evening. Now, as is tradition, the directors will retire to the drawing room for a glass or two of bourbon. Ladies, feel free to indulge in the bar set up in the library. We have an excellent mixologist who can make anything you desire.'

Everyone began to stand, chairs scraped backwards on the parquet floor.

'Come on, dear, let's get you a Bellini.' The woman whom my husband had been chatting to throughout dinner appeared at my side and nudged my arm as the others vacated the room – men in one direction, the wives in another.

Tom gave me a nod before following the crowd. The ticket stub I'd swapped no longer under his glass but now in his hand.

I stood on shaky legs, anxiety unfurling at the prospect of small talk with strangers.

'I'm Anita,' the woman introduced herself, linking her arm through mine and leading me towards the exit.

2

TOM

Graham clapped me on the back as we entered the dimly lit drawing room. Rows of books stood on mahogany shelves at the rear of the room where Harry was delving into an ornate drinks cabinet. It felt oppressive inside, but perhaps it was the company rather than the décor. The walls were papered with an intricate burgundy pattern, an attempt at cosiness but rather it seemed to close in on its inhabitants. A seating area of navy settees and armchairs were positioned around a teardrop coffee table and a couple of directors had already claimed their perches.

'Now for the good stuff,' Graham said, heading straight towards Harry, who was pouring bourbon from a large decanter.

I followed.

'Of course, Tonya, no problem, have a lovely evening,' Harry said to the HR director, who appeared to be making her excuses to leave.

'She always disappears early – not very sociable that one,' Graham whispered into my ear as she swept past.

It was clear she was outnumbered, the only female on the board, although I was sure Harry had deemed her attendance at these dinners were compulsory. She likely couldn't wait to escape the male camaraderie.

As Harry handed out glasses of bourbon to those without a drink,

Graham told me Tonya was unmarried, career-focused and not a woman to be trifled with.

I was half-listening when Harry's redhead slipped inside the room, catching my eye, and took her place next to him. I knew he wasn't married – was she his date for the evening? How had he managed to pull her? Unable to take my eyes off the beauty, Graham's voice faded out when she looked right at me, her full lips forming a smile. I jolted when Harry clapped his hands together and cleared his throat.

'Welcome, gentlemen, I do hope you enjoyed dinner. Let's raise a glass to another successful quarter.'

Everyone lifted their glass, amber liquid swirling as we all took a sip.

'Now it's raffle time!'

I watched as the six other directors looked on eagerly, Harry held court with complete focus from his team. Fishing in my pocket for my ticket, I frowned at the number. Didn't Harry give me number four when we arrived? How did I end up with number nine?

'The lovely Savannah here has picked a winner,' he gestured towards her as she held out the ticket stub before loudly pronouncing, 'The number nine!'

There was a low murmur around the room as the directors checked their tickets. My ears tinged pink on discovering I'd won.

Savannah scanned our faces, awaiting the winner.

'Here,' I said, waving the ticket.

'Ah, young Tom Beswick.' Harry waved me forward as all eyes fell upon me.

When I reached him, he shook my hand and passed me an envelope, which I knew, from Graham, contained a cheque.

'Excellent, excellent, congratulations, Tom. I'll leave you in Savannah's capable hands.' He motioned towards Savannah before focusing back on the room. 'Right, gentlemen, who's up for some poker?'

My heart hammered in my chest as Savannah slipped her arm through mine and guided me towards the door.

'Lucky bastard,' Graham muttered under his breath as we passed, grimacing at his raffle ticket. How much was the cheque for? Graham was hardly on the breadline and his reaction seemed a little sour, unless there was more to winning than I thought?

'Where are we going?' I said quietly, leaning in towards Savannah and breathing in her sugary perfume.

A smile danced on her lips and she squeezed my arm conspiratorially. 'You'll see.'

3

CHLOE

'So, what do you do...' Anita prompted, passing me a Bellini from the bar. Tiny age spots peppered the back of her hand. Her sparrow-like arms were slender, skin crepey from too much time spent in the sun.

'Chloe,' I inserted for her, 'and, well, I used to be an editor, but now... I guess I'm in between jobs.'

'I haven't worked for years – some of the wives do. Marcus's wife, Jill, she's a bereavement counsellor and there's Anton's wife, Victoria, she works at a rescue centre for abandoned dogs.' Anita paused briefly to adjust the strap of her navy dress.

'You're Jim's wife?' I asked, assuming as she was seated next to him. Jim had been one of the directors Tom had pointed out to me on our arrival. We'd smiled to one another as we found our place cards, but Tom hadn't bothered to introduce us. He'd been too busy summoning the waiter for a glass of Merlot.

'Yes, we've been married for thirty years, heaven knows why I still put up with him.' She laughed dryly, her crow's feet wrinkling, powder sitting in the lines.

'When is the raffle?' I sipped on my cocktail, hoping my tone sounded nonchalant. The drink was far too strong.

Anita didn't bat an eyelid before answering. 'It happens in the drawing room after dinner, so Jim tells me. They do the raffle, drink and play poker for an hour or so, leaving us wives to scheme in here.'

'What do they win?'

'Usually it's a cheque – a bonus if you like. If Tom wins, make sure he spends it all on you.' Anita clinked her glass against mine.

'I bumped into a redhead in the washroom, I don't see her in here?' I said, turning to look at the women in the room.

'Oh, that's Savannah, she's Harry's latest, but she doesn't socialise with us,' Anita said disdainfully, her nose wrinkling.

I wanted to press for more information, but before I could, a voice came from behind.

'Hello, newbie.' A gaggle of four women surrounded us, all with perfectly coiffed hair and floor-skimming dresses of silk and satin. My dress was black satin. Simple, classic, Tom had said, but I still felt underdressed.

'Hello,' I replied, heat rising in my cheeks.

'It's lovely to meet you – you're Tom's wife, yes?'

'Chloe,' I replied, not sure whether to offer my hand to shake or curtsey. Instead, I did neither, clutching my Bellini close as though it might ward them off.

'I see you've met Anita. I'm Jill,' the brunette with lipstick on her teeth planted a hand to her chest, 'and this is Hannah, Sara and Victoria.' Gesturing to the women next to her.

'Victoria is Anton's wife, works at the dog shelter,' Anita interjected.

Victoria smiled warmly; she looked the most approachable. 'Someone has to look after those poor mutts,' she said.

I smiled back and nodded politely at all of them.

'I'm going to struggle to remember everyone's names,' I admitted, knowing my cheeks were blazing.

'Oh, that's all right, you'll soon get to know us.' Hannah cackled, reminding me of the witches hunched over the cauldron in *Macbeth*.

'It's lovely to have some young blood,' Jill said, emphasising the word young. 'How old are you, dear?'

'Twenty-six,' I said, trying to make my voice sound confident.

'How long have you and Tom been married?' Sara asked.

'Three years.' It was starting to feel like the Spanish Inquisition.

'Oh, still in the honeymoon phase – remember that, ladies?' Jill laughed as they all nodded.

I thumbed the band of my wedding ring, grateful when Anita came to my rescue and interjected, complimenting Sara on her necklace.

The cocktails flowed and conversation quickly moved on to gossip. Who was up for the chop at Middeon, who had floored the management team with their sales figures for the first quarter and which director was sleeping with their personal assistant. By the time the men came to collect their wives, my head was spinning from the constant chatter.

'You must give me your number,' Anita said as Jim sidled up beside her, bringing with him the smell of cigar smoke. 'We have a WhatsApp group, I'll add you to it.'

I frowned as I imagined what those messages might include, the latest Mulberry handbag on sale or notification of a charity auction we all had to contribute to. No thank you.

'I don't have a phone.' I bit my lip, wishing the ground would open up. 'Well, I do, but it's a really old handset, it doesn't have any apps.'

'Hello, you.' Tom appeared, pressing his lips to the side of my head, arm curling around my waist.

I turned to look at him, his skin glowed and he smelt freshly washed, woody. Not his usual signature aftershave. Had he showered?

'For goodness' sake, Tom, get your wife a proper phone. How am I supposed to WhatsApp her otherwise?' Anita chimed with an exaggerated eye roll.

'Chloe hates technology, but perhaps between us we can work on her,' he leaned in conspiratorially, a charming smile danced on his lips.

Anita practically melted and I swallowed the rock in my throat. I didn't hate technology, but I hadn't had a smartphone for months, not since it was knocked into a sink full of dirty water. I'd been using an ancient Nokia handset of Tom's ever since but of course it wasn't something I could admit in present company.

We said our goodbyes and headed out to the sweeping gravel drive, where a herd of black Mercedes waited to collect us and escort us home.

Tom sighed as he got into the back with me, his legs splayed wide. The driver hadn't even left the grounds before he was unbuttoning his collar, sliding off the bow tie and sinking back into the leather seat.

'Well, that was fun.'

'It was,' I replied, although now I was keen to get home and out of this dress.

Tom took my hand and interlaced his fingers through mine. 'I won the raffle,' he said, digging out a cheque signed by Harry for five thousand pounds.

'Congratulations,' I replied, my brow furrowing in confusion as I thought back to my conversation with the redhead.

'I met Savannah in the bathroom, she picks the winner, doesn't she?'

Tom cleared his throat, swallowing, his Adams apple bobbed and I got the impression he was choosing his words carefully.

'Yes, she pulls the number out, in the drawing room.' He looked uncomfortable and began fidgeting with his watch as I studied him. There was more to it, I was sure, remembering his appearance in the library, the scent that clung to him not his usual signature aftershave.

'You did well tonight. They were impressed,' he said filling the silence.

I flushed, welcoming his praise. 'Thank you. Anita was friendly.'

Tom's face darkened slightly. 'Hmmm, yes, about the phone. Perhaps we can look at getting you something.'

I tried not to let the excitement bubble on my face. Tom kept saying he was going to replace the rubbish handset I was using, but whenever I asked, he always offered his. Expecting me to use it in front of him and then hand it back rather than getting me something more permanent. Maybe he'd relent if it meant getting pally with the directors' wives. Those circles he would surely approve of.

Back home, as I got undressed in the bathroom and removed my make-up, I was deliberately slow, still trying to process the night's events. Positive that a five-grand cheque wasn't the only thing my husband had won. Did the wives know it wasn't only money up for grabs in the raffle but potentially something sordid? Surely they wouldn't tolerate that.

When I emerged, as I'd hoped, Tom was already fast asleep, snoring quietly. I slipped into bed trying not to disturb him, relieved I wouldn't have to perform. Perhaps Savannah had exhausted him. Surprised to find I wasn't at all jealous; in fact I should thank her for saving me the trouble.

My marriage to Tom was no longer a happy one. We'd met when I was twenty-three, a whirlwind romance after he'd approached me in a book-shop. I was perusing the aisles, checking out similar titles to the book I'd been given to edit. Back then, I was the assistant to the editor at Oakley Publishing House, a small press in South London. Tom was in his lunch hour and asked me for suggestions on what hardback to gift his mother, admitting he'd only read one fiction book in his life and it was Stephen King.

He was charming, a little flirtatious, and I was bowled over from the outset. He had a strong jaw and eyes the colour of dark pools. Ten years older than me, Tom knew what he wanted and wasn't afraid to ask. We'd had dinner that night where he'd promised me the world and I'd believed him. Three months later, we'd flown to the Seychelles for a holiday that ended up being an intimate beach wedding neither of our parents attended.

Within six months, we'd moved out of his flat and he'd bought a house thirty miles away in a quiet Sussex village which meant the visits to my friends and parents became less frequent. Tom always had plans, making arrangements to fill up my time, leaving little for anyone else. How easy it had been for him to slowly isolate me. I'd been so head over heels, I'd missed all the warning signs, believing it was love which made him want to spend his every moment with me and no one else mattered.

When I'd finally cottoned onto it not being about love at all but about control, it was already too late.

4

TOM

I woke on Sunday feeling energised. My time with Savannah had been worth it and Chloe was none the wiser as to what I'd been up to while she'd been drinking with the wives. I'd pulled out the cheque written by Harry Poulter for five thousand pounds, brandishing it as my raffle prize, but she took little interest. My wife was getting harder to please nowadays. Didn't she realise how hard I worked to keep us in the life we'd become accustomed to? A little playtime with Savannah was hardly a crime, in fact for me it was the unexpected highlight of the evening.

Graham, the technology director, had given an indication of how the evening would go, the three-course meal, the cheque, although he hadn't mentioned Savannah's involvement in the raffle. He'd taken me under his wing as soon as the promotion had been made public, helping smooth the transition from financial controller to director.

I'd joined Middeon four years ago in a finance role, training clients in invoicing and budgeting software initially before moving into the controller role, intent on climbing the ladder as fast as I could. The promotion to director was a big deal and came with more benefits, namely a company-leased Range Rover and a larger salary.

Only the directors were invited to the quarterly dinners – another perk of the management team. Someone would win a monetary bonus in the raffle and, as long as they were discreet, the option of an hour with Savannah. A sweetener on top of the bonus, she'd enlightened me as we'd climbed the stairs of Glenthorne Manor.

I couldn't believe my ears, but the stirring in my groin as we'd ascended had been hard to ignore. Did anyone refuse? Would it be frowned upon to do so? I'd wanted to ask the questions whirling around my head but could barely speak as she'd directed me towards one of the bedrooms.

Savannah was ravishing and despite having never cheated on my wife before, debating whether to go through with it lasted around ten seconds as I watched her remove her dress. Chloe would never know and Savannah was too sexy to refuse. Curves in all the right places and downright filthy it had turned out.

I couldn't deny she'd left me wanting more, slipping her business card into my hand before I'd left the bedroom. It had all been over embarrassing quickly, caught up in the moment, although I'd told her I had to get back to my unsuspecting wife.

An escort. Who'd have thought it? Never before would I have entertained the idea of something so smutty. Savannah was a prostitute, albeit a high-class one, and paying for sex was something for losers as far as I'd been concerned. Afterwards, as I looked around the drawing room, necking another bourbon, my stomach hardened at how many of us she'd likely 'entertained'. Was Graham one of them? It seemed unlikely, given his reaction to my win, especially as he'd omitted to tell me the part Savannah played in the raffle.

I'd expected knowing looks and claps on the back, but no one batted an eyelid. Harry didn't mention it either. Had they all been in my position before? Was I likely to be the office gossip for the next month, or was Savannah right, was discretion the one rule everyone stuck to? If any of the wives discovered what Harry was offering, or even HR for that matter, it would be a catastrophic, the sort of headlines newspapers would pay a fortune for. So what happened at Glenthorne Manor stayed at Glenthorne Manor. I could get on board with that. Especially as Savannah had switched on a desire I didn't know existed and I knew I'd have to see her again.

Chloe was quiet over breakfast on Sunday morning as I laid out our plans for the day, ignoring the twinges of guilt that hit every time she looked at me. My parents were visiting for lunch, so I asked her to get the place ready whilst I picked up a leg of lamb from the supermarket. I couldn't deny Chloe was an excellent wife, loyal and well trained. She kept the house spotless, as I'd come to expect, and had learnt a lot on the cooking course I'd paid for. Once I'd convinced her I needed her at home, not spending all hours fawning over silly manuscripts. I intended to earn the money and she would look after everything else.

I had expected her to fall pregnant by now, to have a strong healthy boy to chase around, but it was yet to happen. Still, she was young and there was plenty of time for that. Chloe had been sweet and innocent when I met her and I knew straight away she was the perfectly pliable girl I could mould. My parents had reluctantly agreed when I told them I was going to marry Chloe, despite her not being privately educated like I'd been.

My mother had drummed it into me that no woman would really ever be good enough; she'd put me on a pedestal since I was a boy, expecting perfection and nothing less. She'd hated every girlfriend I'd brought home, finding fault with them all, but to be fair they had needed work, unlike Chloe who had been easy to mould. It pleased me that when they came to visit, Chloe was the flawless hostess even if occasionally, like this morning, she still needed pointers.

'Those aren't the clothes I laid out for you.' I'd frowned over the top of the newspaper when Chloe had entered the kitchen in leggings and a T-shirt.

'I can't clean in those clothes, they'll be ruined,' she'd replied, her snippy tone grating.

'Of course.' I'd smiled tightly, not willing to enter into an argument when my parents would be arriving in a matter of hours, and if I was honest my head was still consumed by Savannah.

'Right, I best get down to the supermarket and get some meat,' I announced after breakfast, getting up to slip on my shoes. The sun outside was glorious, perfect for an afternoon walk by the stream later on. Collecting my keys and phone, I presented my cheek to Chloe for a kiss before heading out of the door, keen to be alone so I could message Savannah.

5

CHLOE

My shoulders loosened as soon as the door clicked shut, as if all the tension had left my body without Tom's presence stifling me. Donning rubber gloves, I scrubbed the kitchen until my arms ached. Tom expected perfection and nothing less. I wouldn't give him the satisfaction of running his finger across a dusty surface and raising an eyebrow at me.

I moved from room to room with the mop and duster, plumping cushions and lighting scented candles. How had my life come to this?

I missed the hustle and bustle of working in London. The thrill of reading a manuscript by a new author I knew, deep down in my gut, would be a hit. I had loved my job and was still finding it hard to process how it ended two and a half years ago. How the edited manuscript of a successful author had found its way off my computer to an internet streaming site long before publication day. I'd been forced to resign soon after.

Tom was involved, I was sure of it. When his gentle suggestions I should leave my job for a more homely life were rebuffed, he'd found a way to sabotage my career. I'd had my suspicions. He was only too pleased to have me at home, playing the dutiful wife. I should have left, packed my things and dropped my wedding band on the table on my way out. But I had no one to turn to, nowhere to go, thanks to Tom.

My relationship with my mum was already fractious due to the speed with which I'd got married. Dad was laid-back about the whole thing, but Mum was heartbroken and had warned me I was making a mistake. She'd never warmed to Tom and thought he was smug. The wedding was the breaking point. I was their only child, yet my parents had not even been invited to the wedding. Tom had insisted he'd arranged it all as a romantic surprise, whereas I'd thought it was just a holiday, but now I saw it for what it was. A rushed wedding with no chance to back out, one that didn't allow my parents to be involved or object to.

My friends had pulled away too or inadvertently I'd pushed them away, my social circle dissolving into Tom's needs. They were tired of my unavailability, eventually giving up and ceasing contact altogether. They'd found Tom rude and aloof, too full of his own self-importance. He'd made no effort with them on the few occasions we'd socialised – on purpose I'd later realised. So he could have me all to himself. He loved me too much to share me. Showering me with expensive gifts – I could have anything I wanted except for independence. Tom wanted me to rely on him for everything and I was so blinded by love, I had no idea he was controlling me. It became too late to make my escape, I was in too deep.

I couldn't bear to turn up at my mum's door with only the clothes on my back and an apology for getting caught up in it all after how much I'd upset her. I'd been so sure I hadn't made a mistake like she'd said. Although I knew she'd never turn me away, I couldn't bear the humiliation of arriving on her doorstep asking if I could move back in, knowing she'd been right all along. It had been easier to stay, to make the best of it.

I'd never felt entirely trapped until the day Tom coldly told me the only way out of our marriage was if I was in a box. He hadn't physically hurt me. Not past a smattering of bruises on my upper arms from being gripped too tightly, but in the past couple of years, he'd slowly sucked the air from my lungs. It was easier to be compliant, keep him happy and go along with his plans and rules.

I'd become paralysed at the thought of making decisions for myself, to live without him handling everything.

I was used to Tom telling me what to do, despite knowing it wasn't a normal, healthy relationship. He chose the clothes I wore each day. At first, I'd thought it was romantic, but Julia Roberts in *Pretty Woman* it wasn't. He dressed me like a doll, took me for haircuts and manicures when I needed them, bought all my clothes and accessories. My own once bohemian style entirely replaced with one he preferred, a classy, well-groomed lady.

He controlled the finances too, checking bank statements to see what I'd spent, with his prior approval. Tom chose what we did at the weekends, where we went on holiday and improvements we made to our home. I didn't even have a driving licence or a car.

The only thing I'd found to give me a relief was running. Now I ran most weekdays while Tom worked – the only time I felt free. He used to say he loved my athletic body and the stamina I had in the bedroom. As long as I took my phone with me so I could answer when he rang, he was happy, but he didn't say it anymore, although he didn't stop me running.

To say Tom was OCD would be an understatement. He liked things just so: food placed in cupboards with the labels facing outwards, books on the shelf arranged by colour then size. His clothes had to be folded a certain way, hung in a particular order in the wardrobe. Everything had to be neat and tidy, but most of all precise. In the early days of our marriage, he'd given me a lesson on silver service and the positioning of the cutlery. We'd only been having a lasagne.

His demands were constant, but none more so than when the rule of ten became law.

'I've heard having only ten mouthfuls of any meal is the optimum amount of food to digest at any one time,' he'd said over dinner one night. 'You should try it.' It was a request couched as a suggestion and I felt I had no choice. So I did, ten mouthfuls of chicken casserole, which sounded like a lot, but it wasn't unless you loaded your fork up, which Tom frowned upon.

I'd assumed he was trying to help me. I'd gained a few pounds, the honeymoon period had worn off, before I began running, but I was happy and keen to make Tom happy too. It soon became a rule at every meal. Even if I was eating a biscuit, it had to be divided into ten bites. Mindful eating, he'd called it, doing it with me the first few times before the enthusiasm wore off. Like a disease, it spread to other areas of my life. I had ten minutes in the shower, ten minutes to do my hair, ten minutes to do my make-up. Every tiny thing broken down into slots of ten minutes. It had started as a joke but quickly became a way of life.

When I no longer had a job, during the weekdays when Tom was at work, once the house was spotless and all chores taken care of, if I didn't run, I went for a walk. If only to find a random stranger for some interaction on a park bench. I was lonely and missed my friends, my work colleagues. I missed aimless conversations and banter. On one such day while I was out, Tom called and asked me to get home in ten minutes because he had a package being delivered which had to be signed for. That sunny day, I'd walked three miles out of the village and despite jogging home I'd missed the courier. Tom was incandescent and a new rule was brought into play. At any one time, I couldn't be any further than ten minutes away from the house.

It shrank my world even further. I could go to the local shops and the park, visit the stream, but that was it. Any further outside the circle, I risked not being able to get back in time. I trained harder, pushing myself to go further, move quicker. Tom called numerous times whilst I was out, urging me back for one ridiculous reason or another, yet I always made it back in time. It was a tiny win, but I'd found a sort of escape. A way to push the boundaries of my world.

Today, however, there would be no running. I had to be the queen of entertaining my in-laws. The perfect wife Tom could show off to his adoring mother. I would have to smile sweetly and ignore her veiled attempts to pick holes in everything, as was her way. Hopefully, it would be one of the last times I'd have to go through with it, because maybe just after last night, I had a plan.

6

SAVANNAH

I was studying at the dining table when my phone rang. Being an escort wasn't exactly a nine-to-six job, so whenever I was free, I had my head in a textbook. It was my last year of university, working towards a bachelor's degree in law and trying to make sense of the legislation I needed to quote for a paper due to be submitted but I couldn't ignore the prospect of making money.

'Hello,' I purred into the phone as I answered a number I didn't recognise.

'Savannah, it's Tom, from Friday Night.'

I let the silence stretch out, I'd been anticipating his call.

'The Middeon dinner at Glenthorne Manor,' he continued. I could hear the desperation in his voice, to be remembered, as if any of them stood out. They were all the same: massive egos that required stroking.

'Tom, hi, how are you?' I said warmly, folding the page of the textbook so I wouldn't lose where I was.

'Great thank you, how about you?'

'Fabulous. What can I do for you?' It wasn't really a question, I knew why he was calling, his satisfied smile on Friday night popping to the fore-front of my mind.

'I hoped you might have... availability, this week?'

'Let me check my diary and I'll get back to you. On this number?'

'Yes, could you send a text if possible?'

'Of course,' I chuckled. 'I'll be discreet.' My voice silky smooth.

'Thank you.' I heard the anticipation in his voice before he hung up, the sigh of relief I wouldn't expose him whilst he played happy families at home.

I eased back into my chair, picking up the textbook. I'd check my diary in a while, certain I could make a space available. Tom had no idea of the rate yet and I was sure it would make him gasp but I was also sure he wouldn't refuse. I enjoyed the thrill of his wanting, the power I held. Men would lie and deceive and take risks to spend time with me. It made me feel beautiful and sexy to know I was desired more than the women they lived with or were married to, but it was their money I coveted. Once I had my degree, I would be closing my appointment book for good.

Introducing myself to Harry Poulter at the bar of his local golf club a year ago had paved the way for many of the bookings I had now and I owed a lot to him. Which was why I was only too happy to attend his quarterly dinners. I got paid five grand for my evening, which included my services for him and one other *winner*.

The key to success was to be everything their girlfriend or wife were not. So when they were meeting each other for a liquid lunch or organising charity functions, on top of studying I had to fit in gym sessions, making sure my arse didn't wobble when I walked. While they were knee-deep in housework, creating the perfect home for their workaholic husbands or changing the nappies of their offspring, I was getting waxed, plucked and manicured. That's all it was, an illusion. It helped if you enjoyed sex, which I did – obviously not with old, overweight men, although they were my bread and butter. But I could fake it as well as the rest of them.

The goal was to get my degree and find a firm where I could practice. It was why I'd left Ireland and moved to England at nineteen. Desperate to put some space between me and my overbearing mother and enjoy a little freedom. My father was a lush, drinking his wages away before my mother could pay the rent. Money had been tight and me and my brother Craig had been signed up to work as soon as we were old enough to help put food on the table. It wasn't the life I'd envisaged and I knew if I didn't leave, I'd be stuck in the same cycle my mother had found herself in.

When I'd arrived in the country, I'd worked eighteen-hour days in low-paid jobs to scrape together enough money for a room in shared accommodation. Existing on packets of noodles and crisp sandwiches whilst dreaming of bettering myself. Eventually, I was accepted by the University of Brighton and offered a placement on a foundation degree in law, but even with student loans and bar work there was hardly anything to live on.

That's when I met Natasha in a bar. I'd been serving her and her companion all night, catching snippets of a conversation that piqued my interest. When her friend stepped outside to take a work call, we'd got chatting and I'd asked her outright if she was soliciting for sex. She'd laughed and told me she was an escort and men paid for her company, not for sex. Even that idea was abhorrent at first, until she told me how much money she was making – like me, she was trying to pay her way through university. We'd bonded over the intensity of student life, the overwhelming amount of information one had to absorb and having barely enough to make ends meet. That was until she'd started escorting.

Natasha and I became friends, sometimes studying together and letting loose at the end of a tough week. Being a few years older, she took me under her wing. Giving me a crash course in escorting, sure I'd be a natural with my Celtic looks and bubbly personality. She passed a few easy clients over to me when she couldn't fit them in and it wasn't long before I was raking in enough money to give up my bar job, allowing more time for study. When I met Harry he introduced me to a more lucrative stream of income although I kept a few of my regular clients on.

Most of the men who secured my services were usually married and had given in to the middle-aged spread, so Tom was a welcome surprise. I couldn't deny I found him attractive. He had broad shoulders, a smattering of dark hair on his toned chest, a shapely jawline and midnight blue eyes which were particularly striking. He was clean, eager and, with a little coaxing, concise about what he wanted from our time together. I'd pulled out a few of my most popular tricks, which may have worked a little too well, given the speed at which he finished, but I was sure he was satisfied with his bonus.

He must have been, to call and want to book another session with me so soon. It looked as though I had a new client to add to my books.

7

CHLOE

Tom's parents, true to form, arrived precisely at midday; the apple never did fall far from the tree. I had the lamb already in the oven and we sat in the garden, enjoying the warmth of the June sun with a pot of tea and biscuits.

'Oh, Thomas, you really must prune that blossom tree,' Gwen said, her lips pursing at the drooping branches and scattering of pink blossom across the manicured lawn.

I wanted to tell her the smattering of colour was pretty, but I kept quiet. Tom would think it rude for me to disagree with our guests. More-so, it would be a cardinal sin to quarrel with his mother.

'I'll get someone in, Mother,' Tom sighed. 'Anyway, how was your week?' he tried to change the subject.

Gwen launched into a tirade about the opticians and the ghastly service she'd received from someone who didn't even look old enough to be employed, yet alone a qualified optometrist. It was same pattern at every visit, Gwen could always find something to complain about.

'I'm just going to check on the lamb,' I said, when she'd paused for breath.

Tom smiled and patted my behind as I got up. 'There's a good girl,' he said, as though I was a pedigree racehorse.

I smiled sweetly over gritted teeth and retreated to the safe haven of the kitchen.

Tom had his parents over usually once a month for Sunday lunch and they were long and laborious for both of us, although I'd only made the mistake of criticising his mother once. That Sunday, I'd spent all afternoon clearing up the smashed bottle of red wine from the kitchen floor, trying to bleach the red out of the cream grout until my hands stung.

Today, thankfully, lunch was well received, with only one snipe about how my parsnips could have been crispier.

Charles, Tom's dad, used the walk by the stream afterwards to berate Tom about how thin I had become. He usually kept his opinions to himself, drowned out by Gwen who was as overbearing with her husband as she was with her son. Tom had got his domineering ways from his mother yet he seemed desperate to please her as much as he was eager to be liberated from her grip.

'She runs, Dad, she's as fit as a fiddle.'

'Yes, well, the girl could do with more childbearing hips,' he snapped back as I strode ahead of them, pretending not to hear.

When they finally left, Tom took a large whisky into the lounge and I began loading the dishwasher, glad to be alone with my thoughts. Before they'd arrived, he'd been in a good mood and I no doubt had Savannah to thank for that. Now, he was likely contemplating his failure to impregnate me. The Beswicks were desperate for a grandchild, but when Tom had decided I should come off the pill a few months ago, I'd booked an appointment in secret at the doctors to get a coil fitted.

I'd known a few months after we'd moved into the cottage, when Tom had begun to change, that I didn't want to be the mother to his children, hence the coil, but I also knew I needed an escape plan. Tom wouldn't let me go easily. Marriage, as far as he was concerned, wasn't something he would fail at. Finding myself isolated, with no job, no income and no friends, I was trapped, but now Savannah had materialised like a gift. I just had to find a way to contact her.

Later that evening, I joined Tom in the lounge and we watched a police drama on the television. I was desperate to put on some comfier clothes. The lemon checked capri pants Tom had chosen kept riding up. He stroked my hair, his words slurring from the amount of whisky he'd consumed.

'I think you need a trim, my love, perhaps some highlights?'

'Sure,' I replied, obediently, hoping Tom would soon fall asleep on the sofa.

'I'll book you an appointment,' he said, patting my knee. 'Why don't you go and get ready for bed. Wear the red one tonight.' His eyes glinted like a wolf circling its prey.

I got up with legs like lead and made my way up the stairs on autopilot. The red negligee meant he wanted me to play the whore tonight. White was virginal, black was demure yet sexy. Red was often chosen when he was drunk; he'd be rough and I knew I'd be sore tomorrow.

I laid frozen beneath the covers, waiting for footsteps on the stairs, skin crawling.

'Come here, you little slut,' Tom slurred, undoing his belt as he entered the bedroom. 'Get on your knees.'

* * *

Once Tom was snoring soundly, I slipped downstairs to get some water and paracetamol, my head pounding from where he'd pulled my hair. His wallet was on the side with his keys and I considered unlocking the door, slipping on my trainers and running into the night. *Stupid Chloe.* What a mess I'd let my life become. Instead, I picked up the wallet, sliding out a twenty-pound note I knew he wouldn't miss to hide with my stash, and continued leafing through.

He hadn't even bothered to hide Savannah's business card, it was slipped in between some old receipts, as though he didn't have a care in the world. No need to worry about his wife finding him using the services of an escort and demanding a divorce. If I did, he'd only laugh at me, just as he had the last time I'd said I was leaving.

'Where will you go, Chloe? No one wants you, not even your mother,' he'd said, the words stinging. 'I'll find you, you won't be able to hide from me.' Sending shivers down my spine. That was the end of the conversation.

Memorising Savannah's number for fear of Tom finding it written down anywhere, I slotted the card back where I'd found it and returned to bed.

8

CHLOE

'What are your plans today?' Tom asked over breakfast. I'd made sure I'd got up early to set the table with granola and coffee. He had a ten-minute window to eat after his shower, so he could leave the house at half past seven to get to work in the rush-hour traffic by eight.

'I have some ironing to do and the driveway needs weeding,' I said, pulling ideas at random. Tom liked me to be busy whilst he was at work. Idle hands meant idle minds and a wife who thought too much didn't please Tom. I didn't tell him how I had long showers, taking my time to get ready. When Tom wasn't around the ten-minute rule went out the window. I read the paper over lunch and went for a run before dinner if I didn't get a chance in the morning. 'Do you need me to run any errands?' I asked, hoping I might have an excuse to venture into the village.

'I need another bottle of whisky, whatever you can get that's single malt. Glenfiddich if they have it.' Tom straightened his tie. 'And pick me up some of those crackers I like, the sour cream ones.' It wasn't a question, more of a command.

'Of course.'

When he left, I stood naked in front of the mirror in the bathroom before my shower. Last night, Tom had bitten my left breast and angry purple bruises had sprung up. I was sure he hadn't meant to go so far, to hurt me, but there was a first time for everything. Refusing to waste any more of my tears on him, I got in the shower, the water as hot as I could stand it. Today I would contact Savannah and set the wheels in motion.

Once dressed, I checked my stash, unscrewing the knob on the bed post in the third bedroom and fishing out the money wrapped in a tiny plastic bag, wincing as I slipped it into my bra.

The walk into the village was the same route we'd taken yesterday, by the stream. The water sparkled in the morning sun and wildflowers filled the banks, bees buzzing from buttercup to buttercup collecting pollen.

I smiled at a female dog walker with a bouncy cocker spaniel as I passed, debating whether to say hello, but her fleeting eyes looked away. I wanted a dog, some company at home, but I wasn't going to ask Tom. He'd find a way to use the animal as leverage. He wasn't capable of love, not in the normal sense, and I couldn't bear the thought of it being treated badly if he came home in one of his moods.

The woman behind the checkout was chewing gum at a furious pace as she scanned the whisky and crackers, although she was slow to total up. My phone rang in my pocket, but I couldn't answer it in time as I was paying. Outside, I rang my husband back. He was the only person who called me.

'Where are you?' he asked, his tone prickly.

'I'm at the shop, I've bought the crackers and whisky,' I said, trying to appease him.

'Ah yes, I see, the transaction has just come through on my phone. Could you get me some stamps as well please.'

'Sure,' I said, turning around to go back in.

'What's for dinner tonight?' he asked.

'Quesadillas.'

'No, I don't think so. How about that chicken pie you do.'

'Okay,' I replied, mentally checking if I had the ingredients at home. 'How's work?'

'Oh fine. I've booked you an appointment for your hair tomorrow with Laura, ten o'clock.'

'Thank you,' I replied, touching my hair, which had almost reached my shoulders. I guessed it would be back to the bob.

Offering a swift goodbye, Tom hung up and I queued up again for stamps and leeks.

There was only one useable phone box in the village, painted a beautiful forest green. The other one had been stripped and turned into a mini library where people took their used books for others to read. It was a treasure trove and I'd borrowed many since we'd moved, missing the days as an editor where I read for hours. Now the opportunities were few and far between, Tom demanded my full attention. Before I discovered the phone box, I longed for something to fill my days, but the main library was too far to get to on foot.

The one time I'd risked going further without Tom, catching a bus to visit the library, he arrived home with a surprise takeaway lunch only to find the house empty. I hadn't been able to make it home in ten minutes when Tom called and when I did arrive, he made me eat the cold congealed noodles in ten large bites.

The phone box was at the end of the small high street and I slipped inside, closing the door behind me, wrinkling my nose at the musty smell. The crappy handset Tom had given me so he could keep in touch had itemised billing and I couldn't risk making the call from that. Even if I withheld my number, he'd give me the third degree about who I was calling. Fishing change from my pocket, I dialled Savannah's number. She answered after four rings, her voice sultry but obviously put on.

'Savannah speaking.'

'Hi, this is Chloe, we met last Friday at the Middeon dinner, in the bathroom. I'm Tom's wife.'

There was a short pause.

'Hello, Chloe, how can I help you?' Savannah said stiffly.

'Would you be able to meet me for coffee, tomorrow maybe?'

'I don't get involved in other people's marriages, Chloe.'

'I have a proposition for you,' I replied, forcing my voice to sound more confident than I felt.

'Interesting, and what might that be?'

'There's a coffee shop in Copthorne, on Star Lane. Do you know it?' I replied, ignoring her question.

She chuckled dryly. 'I can't say I do,' she said. 'I've never been to Copthorne, but I have a satnav, I'm sure I'll find it. I'm free at two.'

'Two will be great. I'll see you then,' I said, feeling my knees buckle with a mixture of fear and relief.

9

SAVANNAH

I couldn't deny I wasn't curious at what Chloe wanted to discuss. I'd only ever had one call from a wife before and it wasn't pleasant. I'd let her rant and rave, tell me how disgusting she thought I was, before I kindly asked her not to call me again and blocked her number. Strangely, I never saw that client again. Maybe Chloe had called because she wanted to discuss a ménage à trois? Now that would be interesting. It would be my first couple, but if the price was right, I'd consider it. Chloe was fresh-faced, attractive, petite and willowy, her look classic like a blond Audrey Hepburn.

I had classes to attend in the morning but I was meeting Tom at four tomorrow afternoon at the Airbnb I rented for work in Brighton. In fact, once I'd had coffee with his wife, I'd be heading there to prepare for his arrival. He'd been quite reserved on our first meeting at the Middeon dinner, but I sensed depravity lurking. Tomorrow, he might let his hair down and the prospect intrigued me.

The squeak of a tap jolted me from my thoughts. I had the local councillor in the bathroom, who would emerge shortly and request I cover him in baby powder before rocking him like an infant while he nuzzled my chest. It took all sorts, but he was an easy client; I barely had to get my hands dirty. Plus it paid the bills, so I couldn't complain.

10

TOM

Tuesday afternoon at four o'clock. That's when I'd see Savannah again. She'd messaged me whilst I was deep in budget planning. Needless to say that went out of the window almost immediately when my phone beeped and the name Seth popped up. I'd saved her under Seth in my contacts in case Chloe looked at my phone, but, true to her word, Savannah had been discreet. The message read as though it had come from a colleague, instructing the files requested were to be delivered to an address in Brighton by four o'clock on Tuesday afternoon.

We hadn't discussed a price, but I'd banked Harry's cheque, my bonus prize from Friday, and I couldn't think of anything else I'd rather spend it on. I paced my office, reading the message over again, imagining Savannah's long red talons gliding over the screen, aware of the stirring in my groin, relieved the office door was closed and I'd told Bella to hold my calls.

Savannah had made me wait almost twenty-four hours before confirming my booking. I'd started to think she didn't want to see me again, and perhaps I hadn't performed as well as I could have on Friday, but damn it, the woman was a goddess. I could hardly control myself. I'd not been with anyone else since I'd met Chloe, committed to my marriage, but as soon as I saw Savannah, attraction had bubbled instantly.

I'd been consumed by the memory of Friday night ever since. The curves of her behind, the porcelain flesh of her hips I'd grabbed as I'd plunged deep into her. She was nothing like Chloe, who lately had started to resemble a greyhound when naked, all bones and sinew.

Every minute of the weekend had been torture, wondering when I'd see her again, especially Sunday lunch. Having to sit through my mother blabbering on about her eyes, not to mention my father berating me as Chloe was yet to conceive even though we'd only be trying for a few months. I'd have to take her to a fertility clinic, get her tested. There had to be something we could do. My parents expected a grandchild and I wanted a son. Perhaps Chloe needed to stop running, eat a little more. Yes, that had to be the problem and it was easily fixed.

I'd sensed she'd been distracted lately, not as attentive as usual. Perhaps she was bored – if that was the case, all the more reason to have a baby, it would be a good filler for her days. Motherhood would suit her well, as long as she didn't forget to put me first, of course.

My mind slithered back to the redhead. I'd be counting the minutes until I tasted her again. It looked as though Bella would have to shift a meeting, but that wouldn't be an issue. I'd tell her something important came up. An appointment I had to attend, one I simply couldn't get out of.

11

CHLOE

When Tom arrived home, I was still out on the cobblestone driveway. Slowly working my way back up to the front door, sun beating on my back and my fingers raw with a bucket of pulled weeds beside me. He climbed out of the car with a grin on his face, brandishing a bunch of pretty pink roses.

'For my beautiful wife,' he said, giving me a kiss on the cheek as I stood to brush myself down.

'Thank you, they're lovely,' I replied, taking them from him. 'Good day?'

'Yes, not bad for a Monday actually. Is the pie in the oven? I'm starving.'

'I'll put it in now,' I said, following Tom into the kitchen. I'd made the pie once I'd returned from the shops and popped it in the fridge before I'd started weeding.

Tom scowled.

'It will only take half an hour,' I reassured him. 'Why don't I open a bottle of red wine and we can sit on the patio?'

'Are you done with the driveway?'

'Nearly, but I can finish it tomorrow,' I suggested, the muscles in my back complaining.

'Easier to get it done now, isn't it? We can enjoy a glass over dinner.'

Tom loosened his tie and unbuttoned the top of his shirt as I tried not to grimace.

I deliberately left the flowers in their wrapping on the side in a small act of defiance and returned to the driveway, resuming the position on my hands and knees.

* * *

'I've got an important meeting tomorrow, I need the blue pinstriped shirt,' Tom said later, as he shovelled in the last of the chicken and thyme pie.

I was on my eighth mouthful and struggling, a rock in my stomach as I imagined the conversation I would have with Savannah over coffee.

'Chloe, are you listening?'

My eyes shot upwards from my plate at the sharpness of his tone.

'Yes, it's already in your cupboard. I ironed it yesterday.'

'I've been thinking,' Tom said and my heart automatically sank. 'We should make an appointment at a fertility clinic, try to ascertain why you aren't pregnant yet.'

A bolt of ice struck my spine and I instantly sat up straighter, laying my fork down.

Tom looked at the discarded cutlery and raised an eyebrow. He had been counting. I picked it back up again.

'You could probably do with putting on a few pounds, perhaps all this running isn't good for you.'

I bit my lip and ignored the pricking of tears. Running was my escape, mentally and physically. I hadn't managed a run today and I was already tightly coiled like a spring. I couldn't let him take that away from me too.

'I'll find somewhere, book an appointment,' I said, smiling.

It was so Tom to assume I was the problem in the baby-making department. His sperm was good, strong stock, how could he possibly be at fault. Of course he was right to some extent, the fault lay with me – but it was because of the coil. I couldn't see another doctor, an internal examination would show I'd had a coil fitted and the game would be up. I'd have to come up with something.

'I'll leave that to you then. Are you looking forward to your trim? It's getting a bit long, isn't it?'

I nodded, nine mouthfuls, one more to go.

Tom picked up his empty plate and stood by my side, waiting for me to finish my tenth mouthful. My throat closed up as I chewed the shortcrust pasty, which was difficult to swallow with a dry mouth.

'Oh come on, you can finish the rest,' he said impatiently, watching as I forced down the last of the pie, clearing my plate.

'Let me take that,' he said, palm outstretched.

Tom was in a chivalrous mood, rinsing and loading the dishwasher as I wiped down the sides before we sat on the patio with a glass of red wine, watching the sun dip beneath the hedges.

'So I'll be a little late tomorrow, my meeting might overrun,' Tom said, clearing his throat and frowning at the blossom tree. I tried to hide my relief, whenever Tom worked late it felt like a reprieve.

'Okay. I'll make quesadillas; they don't take long to cook.'

'Sure,' he said, although his mind was elsewhere. He ran his index finger around the rim of his glass.

My back ached from rushing to finish the weeding before dinner and I shifted uncomfortably in the iron chair, feeling the sting of sunburn on my shoulders.

'Would you mind if I had a bath?' I asked, knowing he usually liked company for evening television viewing.

'No, go ahead, perhaps we'll have an early night. Let's make a baby,' he said squeezing my hand. I had to resist the urge pull it out from beneath his.

'Okay,' I said, forcing a smile before retreating upstairs.

12

CHLOE

I stared at the pink roses neatly arranged in the glass vase we'd had as a wedding present. My back still sore from yesterday's weeding, but at least Tom was gentle last night, requesting the white negligee. Although he'd made me sit with my legs up against the headboard in an undignified pose for thirty minutes afterwards while he perused his phone. Apparently assuming the position after sex increased the chance of fertilisation. If only he knew.

Like me, Tom seemed especially jittery this morning, he hadn't eaten much at breakfast and I guessed it was to do with the meeting he had later. He'd laid out a yellow sundress and white cardigan for me this morning to wear to the hairdressers – an appointment I wasn't especially looking forward to. Laura, the lady who always did my hair, thought the sun shone out of Tom's arse. She didn't fully understand the implications of being a 'kept' woman and was forever romanticising what it must be like being married to Tom. She had no clue but most people didn't. Tom had a way of charming even the most sceptical of characters, everyone thought he was wonderful.

I stretched at the kitchen counter, flexing my aching muscles before lacing up my trainers. I should be able to get at least five kilometres in before I had to get back and shower. I had lots of nervous energy to get rid of, twitchy about my upcoming chat with Savannah.

It was cloudy outside and I ran down by the stream, dodging dog walkers and toddlers on their scooters before heading around into the woods on the opposite side. The trail was shaded and muddy, never fully drying after a shower. Although gloomy, it was well used and I ran on autopilot, using the time to think about what I was going to say to Savannah. What my game plan was to get her onside.

Running released the tension I'd been holding and I'd discovered a long time ago it was much better therapy than screaming into a pillow. I managed five kilometres in record time and got to the salon at five to ten, wearing the sundress, despite the clouds, still a little pink-cheeked.

'Chloe, hi! Right on time, do you want to take a seat?' Laura led me to the chair by the window, which I hated. Nobody liked being on display to passers-by with half their head wrapped in foil. 'The usual?'

'Tom's suggested some more highlights,' I said listlessly.

'Gentlemen do prefer blonds, so they say.' She winked and I smirked, Tom was no gentleman.

Three hours later, once I'd text Tom, gushing how much I loved my new hair, despite being desperate to grow it, I joined Laura at the desk, reaching inside my bag for my purse.

'No, no, Tom's already paid, would you like to book in again?'

'No, it's fine, thanks. Tom will nudge me when I need to come in.'

'Goodness, he's so attentive, you better hope no one steals him.' She cackled, throwing her head back, her wild mane shaking.

Snorting at Laura's comment, I took a slow walk down the high street, checking my phone to see if Tom had called. I guessed he'd read my text, therefore knew where I was and I hoped he wouldn't call while I was with Savannah. It would be embarrassing to have to excuse myself and rush outside to answer. He'd tell from my voice something was wrong. Thankfully, Tom hadn't given me any tasks to do before he got home, so there was nothing to rush back for.

I had an hour to kill before Savannah arrived, so I grabbed a cheese roll from the bakers and ate as I walked, ten bites be dammed. The phone box library had the latest Jane Fallon in it and I popped it in my bag, knowing I'd devour it in one sitting. My stomach swirled with angst ahead of meeting Savannah. Was she expecting me to go at her guns blazing for sleeping with my husband? No doubt she was wondering what my proposition would be. Would I have the guts to ask and what if our conversation got back to Tom? It was a risk I'd have to take.

13

SAVANNAH

I made a point of getting to the quaint coffee shop ten minutes early, securing a table at the back, out of earshot. My lecture this morning had been intense and my brain still felt wired from all the information I'd consumed, so it was nice to slow the pace down a little. It amused me I'd taken time over what I'd chosen to wear for our meeting, wanting to go smart but casual, as if Chloe was competition. It was ridiculous. I'd never compete for a man and I didn't want one who cheated on his wife with an escort, no matter how high-class. Tom was a client and all I was interested in was his money.

The waitress came over, scruffy in a dirty apron, and I ordered two cappuccinos. If I was fucking Chloe's husband and being paid handsomely for it, the least I could do was buy the coffee.

I checked my messages while I waited. Harry had been in touch, confirming an appointment, as well as Ricardo who owned a string of Italian restaurants across Sussex.

The door jangled and in walked Chloe. She'd had her hair lightened since I last saw her and it was shorter too, a cute little bob which suited her elfin features.

I raised my hand and she smiled politely, making her way through the coffee shop until she reached my table at the back.

'I bought you a cappuccino,' I said, in way of greeting, gesturing for her to sit. It was important I took control from the outset. I had no idea how the meeting was going to go. Was she about to berate me for my choice of profession, throw her coffee over me or what? I had to admit I was intrigued, especially as, if anything, in person she appeared nervous rather than outraged.

'Thanks for agreeing to meet with me,' she said, a slight tremble to her voice.

'What was it you wanted to discuss?' I replied, wanting to get straight to the point.

'Savannah – is that your real name?' she asked, and I raised an eyebrow, the corner of my mouth creeping upwards.

'I couldn't possibly comment.'

'Of course, sorry, I just wondered, you know, if it was a stage name. Whereabouts in Ireland are you from?'

'Waterford, but I've lived here since I was a teenager. Any more questions?' I asked wryly. Did she think I was going to open up, that we'd bond over the hardships we might have faced growing up? What did she plan to gain from meeting me?

'Sorry, I'm jabbering.' Chloe wrung her hands together, pink blotches appearing at her collarbone.

'I'm guessing you're here about Tom,' I said, keeping my voice soft and non-threatening.

'I know what happened at the dinner. I know you two have had sex.' She paused, taking a sip of her cappuccino, hand trembling.

It was my own fault, I'd been so flippant in the washroom, letting the cat out of the bag. Usually I was the height of discretion, but I guess her age had thrown me off guard. So young to be the wife of one of Harry's directors. I hadn't realised who I was talking to.

'He came back from the drawing room freshly showered with a five-grand cheque. It doesn't take an idiot to work it out.'

I breathed deeply, waiting for the demand to come next, or begging – she looked like she was one who might. *Please stop screwing my husband, I love him, we were perfectly happy before you came along.*

What she said next made me nearly choke on my drink. Her big blue eyes locked onto mine, imploring as she spoke.

'I want you to make him fall in love with you.'

14

CHLOE

Savannah cleared her throat, trying to mask the shock etched on her face.

'I'll pay you,' I said, trying to keep the desperation out of my voice, 'just let me know how much it would cost.'

'Hang on, am I hearing this correctly? You want *me* to make *your husband* fall in love with me?' Her tawny eyes narrowed and she snorted, chuckling to herself.

'That's right.'

'Why?'

I swallowed hard, unsure how much to say, but I had to get her onside. She was my chance for escape.

'Because he won't let me leave him. If he falls in love with you, he'll have no reason to make me stay.'

Savannah took a second, letting my words filter in, eyeing me curiously.

'Does he hurt you?' she asked.

I shook my head. 'No. He's controlling, but he doesn't hurt me... exactly,' I admitted.

Savannah frowned, lines appearing in her flawlessly smooth forehead.

'Well, I can't say I'm not a little surprised,' she said, leaning back in her chair and draining her cup.

I picked at my cuticles under the table, waiting for the verdict, desperately hoping she'd be the answer to my prayers.

'The thing is, Chloe, what happens once he's fallen in love with me – if he does, of course. I don't want him.' She wrinkled her nose as though I'd offered her cast-off clothes.

'Well, you can ditch him, but I would have left. Even if he comes after me, I'll know he's had an affair. It's grounds for divorce.'

'Having sex with an escort is grounds for divorce anyway without having to pay someone to solicit the affections of your husband.'

'I know.' I shook my head, feeling the burn in my chest. I was losing her. 'He's told me the only way out of our marriage is if I'm in a box,' I muttered, forcing myself to meet her eyes as she contemplated my words before speaking.

'Sounds like a catch,' she said, her Irish lilt rich with sarcasm.

I stirred my cappuccino, the spoon clinking against the porcelain.

'I'm meeting him this afternoon.'

'Really?' I said, my voice too high, a glimmer of hope on the horizon that he'd already made plans to see Savannah. My gut instincts had been spot on.

'How much are you offering?'

'How much will you charge me?' I countered, having no idea where I'd get the money from to pay Savannah.

'Five grand,' she said flatly, laying her hand down on the table, 'and that's a bargain.'

I swallowed, my mouth dry, where would I lay my hands on such an amount? I had about five hundred in my escape fund.

'I can get you that,' I lied, uncertain if I could. 'Half upfront and half on completion,' I said, surprising myself at my new negotiating skills.

'Okay, you have a deal. I'll meet you here on Thursday, same time, to make the first payment.'

It gave me two days to try to come up with another two thousand pounds, but I hoped it would be worth every penny.

'So, let me get this right.' Savannah wiped the corners of her mouth with a napkin. 'I need to convince him to leave you, for me.'

I nodded, unable to contain my knees knocking together under the table.

'I have to say, this is the strangest conversation I've ever had.' Savannah gave a dry laugh before placing ten pounds on the table and getting to her feet.

'Thank you,' I said, looking up at her, the tightness in my chest evaporating. She still looked polished without the evening gown. Even in jeans, pumps and a classic white shirt, Savannah was truly stunning. Tom didn't stand a chance.

'Don't thank me yet. You owe me the two and a half grand whether he goes for it or not.'

'He will,' I replied, and watched her stride out of the coffee shop before smoothing clammy palms down my thighs and finishing my cappuccino.

15

TOM

The day dragged, the morning booked solid with meetings that could have been emails. Chloe sent through a text once Laura had finished her hair and I was looking forward to seeing it. I hoped it was neater, a few highlights were necessary to brighten it up as it was looking a bit drab and straggly. I smiled inwardly, not many men would take care of their wives as well as I took care of mine.

Bella brought in lunch, although my stomach was churning too much to eat. In a matter of hours I'd be with Savannah, sampling her delights. She'd be the only sustenance I'd need. I'd received a message this morning, clarifying payment. Five hundred pounds for an hour! I had no idea if that was the going rate, never having paid for sex before. She wasn't cheap for sure, but no doubt worth every penny.

'Tom, how are you doing?' Harry Poulter walked into my office without bothering to knock, but as he was the CEO, I could hardly complain. The man had promoted me and let me into his world, which I had a feeling was going to be beneficial in more ways than one.

'Good thank you, Harry. How about you?'

'Yes, yes, the wheels are still turning. I need to have a chat with you about something.' He sat down heavily in the chair opposite my desk, breathing laboured like he'd been climbing a flight of stairs. 'Middeon has been put up for sale.'

My face fell as I tried to take in the revelation, but Harry hurriedly continued.

'Nothing to worry about, but I'm getting long in the tooth and looking to retire. I'd much rather be playing golf nowadays than stuck behind a desk.'

He unbuttoned his collar, easing his tie down a fraction, frowning at my horrified expression. A new owner would surely mean a shake-up, was my promotion safe or had Harry put me directly in the firing line? Last in, first out. My stomach clenched as I waited for him to mop his forehead and put his handkerchief away.

'As I said, it's unlikely there'll be any changes and for now we must carry on. It's business as usual, but I do need your help with something.'

I opened my mouth to acquiesce, but no words came out. What about management restructures? They always happened with a takeover. How could Harry assure me my position wouldn't be up for the chop?

'We need to look at redistributing the entertainment budget. For transparency, we have to open the books. Clearwater are overseeing the sale and it mustn't look to them like we've had too much fun, eh,' he chortled.

'Okay,' I said slowly, my brain firing, 'it shouldn't be a problem, we have some money left in the marketing budget. I'll have a chat with Jim, see what we can siphon through there.'

'Attaboy.' Harry got up and slapped me on the back before coughing. The man looked like he was going to have a heart attack any minute and I pushed aside fleeting thoughts of what Savannah got up to with him. They put my teeth on edge. 'Golf this weekend?' Harry said as he walked towards the door, having dropped his bombshell and leaving as though nothing had happened.

'Sure, although I'm not very good,' I admitted.

Harry bellowed with laughter. 'Oh we do love a good whipping boy, Tom. Come, I can always get you some private lessons if you're terrible.' Harry cleared his phlegmy throat and I had a sudden urge to lather my hands in antibacterial gel. 'I'll get Bella to put it in the diary. Do you know The Grange?'

I shook my head.

'Lovely little nine-hole course with a well-stocked bar. Saturday morning all right?'

'Sounds great.' I mustered a smile, despite my reservations. I had to play the game and integrate myself by whatever means necessary, even if golf was the dullest sport to be invented.

Once he'd left, I asked Bella to schedule a meeting with Jim as soon as he could fit me in and opened the budget spreadsheet to see where I could sneak in some of Harry's overspending. The quarterly dinners cost a fortune, not to mention the extras. It would be a difficult conversation for Harry to have with a prospective buyer if they wanted to drill down on what exactly he'd been spending the profits on.

When at last it was three thirty, I said goodbye to Bella, suggesting she take an early day. Her eyes lit up and she thanked me profusely, wittering on about having to take her dog to the vet. I cut her off, telling her I was in a rush but to enjoy her afternoon. Today I'd proven to be a good boss and a good husband despite what I was about to do.

I jumped in the Range Rover and keyed the address Savannah had given me into the satnav, my hands already clammy with anticipation. In less than ten minutes, I was out of Crawley town centre and on the A23 heading to Brighton.

The traffic was busy, but I arrived outside the apartment on time. It was a stone-coloured modern built block overlooking a large park. Not quite walking distance to the beach, but the seagulls could be heard searching for their dinner, a reminder of the seaside location.

I gazed up at the glass-front balconies and expensive rattan suites. Could the higher-up apartments have a sea view? They must cost a pretty penny, but the address Savannah had given me was number 2, on the ground floor. She had to be raking it in to afford one of these by herself, but at five hundred pounds an hour, I was hardly surprised. Thank goodness for Harry's raffle money. I shook the image from my head of Harry with his greasy hands all over her.

'Hello, you.' She opened the door smiling broadly, wearing a white silk robe tied tightly at the waist. Tiny impressions of lace underwear were suggested through the flimsy fabric.

I swallowed as I took in her beauty. The angle of her jawline, the fullness of her lips. She'd lined her eyes in black, the tiny flicks at the outer corner made her look like a sixties film star.

'Hello again,' I said as she pulled back the door to allow me inside. The apartment had high ceilings, the front glazed showcasing a relaxing view of the green space. Blinds were pulled back, letting sunshine stream into the room. At the rear, through patio doors, there was a large terrace surrounded by frosted-glass waist-high panels. The décor of the open-plan living space was cream and elegant – exactly what I'd imagined. There was nothing seedy about it. 'Nice place.'

'Thanks, but it's not mine, it's a business rental.'

'Makes sense,' I replied, casting my eye around. 'Do you live in Brighton?'

Savannah turned her back on me, leaving my question unanswered as she walked to the kitchen which had glossy cabinets. My eyes followed her behind, mesmerised.

'Would you like a drink?' she asked.

'Just the one please, I'm driving.'

Savannah poured small whiskies from a crystal decanter for us both, leaning against the counter and taking a sip. She traced her eyes over my body, leaving me exposed. Everything she did was seductive – how she spoke, her sexy accent, not to mention how she moved. I was entranced and my groin pulsated as I stared at her.

'We need to go over some rules first.'

'Okay,' I said, my mouth dry. Was this really happening?

'I use condoms at all times, for every type of penetration. I don't do sadomasochism or violence. I like my skin unblemished. Payment is upfront, and contact is only by the mobile number on my business card. I do not like clients turning up unannounced.'

I nodded in agreement.

'If there is something you want to try, we can discuss it first but have to mutually agree.'

'Understood.'

'Would you like to take a shower?' she asked.

'Sure.' My forehead creased. Was this normal practice? I'd go with the flow, not wanting to advertise it being my first time.

Necking my drink, I followed her to the bathroom, where a white fluffy towel and a variety of mini Molton Brown men's shower gels had been laid out for my use. Savannah leaned in and turned on the rainforest shower and I had to resist the urge to shove her inside the glass door and take her then and there.

'I'll be in the bedroom to your left when you're finished.'

'Thank you. Oh, here you go,' I said, pulling out a white envelope filled with five hundred pounds cash. I wanted to be quick in the shower, the clock was ticking and I expected value for my money.

'Wonderful, thanks,' she said, slipping it into her pocket before leaving and closing the door behind her.

I raced through the shower at top speed, taking a moment to admire my reflection in her large mirror once out. Wrapped in a towel, my damp torso was toned with a little chest hair. Just enough but not too much. I slicked back my wet hair and tried to tuck my erection into the folds so it wasn't too obvious.

It shouldn't matter what Savannah thought. I was paying her after all, but I couldn't help feeling I was about to be judged as I left the bathroom. That disintegrated when I entered the bedroom to find Savannah laid back on the enormous four-poster bed in an alluring pose, robe gone. She modelled a pastel green lace bra and thong, her red hair fanning out over the cream sheets.

'Come here,' she purred and I climbed on top of her, towel discarded on the floor. 'I see you're more than ready,' she said, stroking my back and glancing down between my legs.

I grinned, the urge to be inside her overshadowing any embarrassment. 'I am.'

'Now,' she whispered into my ear, 'why don't you tell me what you'd like.'

16

SAVANNAH

Tom wasn't bad, albeit a little vanilla, surprising as from Chloe's description I'd thought he'd be rougher or at least exert control. He did go on top and enjoyed watching himself in the mirrored wardrobes during sex. He was easy to please and I licked and sucked and stroked, delaying the inevitable until he couldn't take any more. I was sure he would have some kinks, they all did, but that would come with time. I rarely orgasmed when I was with a client, too focused on their gratification to worry about mine, but Tom's incessant asking if I had meant I had to fake it.

'Would you like a cigarette?' I asked as we lay, damp with perspiration, entangled in the sheets.

'You know what, I think I would,' he said, and lay back with his hands behind his head, looking like he deserved a gold star for his performance.

I rolled over to reach for the bedside drawer and he stroked my naked behind.

'You really are beautiful, you know that?'

'Am I?' I asked, coquettishly, rolling back over and passing him a cigarette and lighter.

'Stunning,' he breathed.

'Does that mean you'll be back for more?' I teased, holding my cigarette between my lips for him to light it.

'Definitely.' He lit both and blew a cloud of smoke into the air, frowning at the clock on the wall. It was five past five.

'You don't have to rush off,' I said, 'tell me some more about yourself.' Normally I ran like clockwork with clients, but if I was going to get Tom to fall for me, I had to be a bit more flexible. It felt like playing a role, which was something I was used to yet I thought I'd be able to pull Chloe's plan off. Men were so easily manipulated with sex and Tom would be no different. I hoped it would be easy money.

Tom smoked his cigarette and talked about his job at Middeon, not mentioning Chloe.

'How did you meet Harry?' Tom asked, the name sticking in his throat. Inwardly, I smiled, so he was the jealous type.

'At a bar.' I flicked my ash into the ashtray and pulled the sheet up to cover my breasts. 'He bought me a drink and we got talking.'

I'd made it sound more innocent than it was. In truth, Harry was drunk and pawing me relentlessly. I'd left after one drink, pushing my card into his hand. He'd called me a day later and, a little while after that, the enterprise of the Middeon dinners was born. The money had come in handy, my landlord had upped the rent on my flat in Crawley due to the rising interest rates and the Airbnb I used for clients wasn't cheap.

The conversation stilted, Tom still basking in the afterglow. He didn't seem interested in my past, other than asking me where I was from. The accent always did that. He never strayed towards my profession and I got it: while clients were here, they liked to pretend they were the only one. Tom was no different, although I had no idea how I was supposed to make him leave Chloe. It was one thing that men wanted me for sex but despite their indiscretions, their marriages always remained impervious. But for five grand, I'd find a way.

'You can take another shower if you want to,' I offered, 'before you go home.'

His face darkened at the mention of home.

'I guess I had better, if you don't mind.'

I shook my head and got up to put on my robe. I wasn't seeing another client today and intended to have a long soak in the bath while the sheets went in the washing machine. I couldn't determine how interested Tom was, but I had to be led by him. Rushing things would rouse suspicion.

It wasn't until Tom was dressed and ready to leave that he pulled me to him by the door and kissed me passionately, gripping my waist, fingers digging into flesh. I was shocked by his ferocity, not to say I wasn't used to it from the others but Tom had been reserved up until now.

'I want to see you again,' he whispered into my hair.

'I'd like that.'

'When?' he said, urgency in his tone, unwilling to release me from his grip.

'Thursday? Same time.'

'I'll be here,' he replied, entwining his fingers into my hair before kissing me again. He opened the door and left without a backward glance. I leant against it, forehead resting on the walnut door, a smile dancing on my lips. Maybe I could pull this off after all.

17

CHLOE

I waited anxiously for Tom to return home, biting my cuticles, knowing he would scold me when he saw what I'd done to them. The pretty French manicure ruined. All afternoon, I'd pictured him and Savannah together, surprised not to feel a twinge of jealously. Tom, after all, was my husband, but I hadn't been in love with him for a long time. All I wanted now was my freedom, although I had no idea how I was going to pay Savannah for it and I only had two days to come up with half the money.

I busied myself making sure the house was spotless. Once it was, I cooked and shredded the chicken for quesadillas, prepping the vegetables and making a large salad, which I stored in the fridge. They wouldn't take long to assemble and pan fry once Tom was home and I was sure he would be ravenous, having worked up an appetite.

My heart fluttered in my chest when, around five to six, the Range Rover pulled onto the drive. I smoothed down my sundress, checked my reflection and rushed to the door to open it for him.

'How was your day?' I said, holding out my hand for his satchel.

'Long,' he said sullenly, not bothering to ask how mine was or comment on my hair. Had his meeting with Savannah not gone well?

'I'll start dinner,' I said, setting down the satchel by the coat stand and walking into the kitchen.

He followed behind tutting. 'I thought you said it would be ready?' he grumbled.

'It's all prepped. Quesadillas, remember, they take minutes to cook. Shall I make you a tea?' I tried to inject as much cheer into my voice as I could muster, but Tom was clearly in a mood. He hadn't told me when his *meeting* had finished, so how could I have had his dinner on the table for his return? But it was typical of Tom, blaming me for something out of my control. 'Or a bottle of wine?' I suggested, hoping it might take the edge off.

'Quit fussing, would you, I've just walked in the bloody door.'

Chastised, I turned my back to load the tortillas before placing them in the pan to fry.

He didn't speak again until we were sat at the table, our steaming plates in front of us.

'Did you book an appointment at the fertility clinic?'

'No, I'm sorry, I forgot.'

His fork clattered to his plate, making me jump. 'For fuck's sake, Chloe, do I have to do everything around here?'

'I'm sorry, I'll do it tomorrow.' I fought the urge to snap, but I knew it would enrage him further.

'This is dry,' he complained, tossing a half-eaten tortilla onto his plate and pushing it towards me. 'You eat it, you need to put on weight.'

I'd been nibbling at mine, my stomach tight with anxiety, counting my mouthfuls. I'd only managed seven small bites, unable to relax with Tom's prickly demeanour. It was like sitting next to a bomb, waiting for it to go off.

As if reading my mind, he added, 'You have three mouthfuls left, I want to see you cram everything in.' His eyes sparked, the corner of his mouth turning upwards as though I was sport to watch.

'I can't, I'll be sick.'

'I want you to eat it,' he said each word slowly, impactfully.

Lowering my eyes to the tortilla in my hand, I crammed it inside my mouth. There was so much, I could barely close my lips to chew. He sniggered as bile rose up in my chest and I gagged, struggling to swallow, but refused to be beaten.

'Now mine, two bites left,' he instructed, revelling in my torment.

'Tom, please?' I whispered, furious at myself for begging, for sounding weak.

'If you want to carry children, Chloe, you need to be strong and healthy. That's what you want, isn't it?'

I nodded, feeling the onset of tears burn my eyes. He could be so cruel for no other reason than pure entertainment.

'Go on then.'

Stifling the urge to vomit, I stuffed in Tom's half-eaten tortilla, managing to consume it in the two bites I had left. Indigestion fired in my chest and I knew it would cause me havoc later.

'Perfect,' he smiled and leant over to ruffle my hair as though I was a child. 'You haven't said thank you for your haircut,' he said, his tone now as light as a feather.

'Thank you,' I complied, trying to keep the bitterness out of my tone. I hated the man I'd married or rather what he'd become. A tyrant who had to hold all the power, all the time.

'Fetch me the paper, would you, I haven't had a chance to read it yet.'

I got up obligingly to get it for him and left him reading at the table while I loaded the dishwasher. My neck mottled with utter loathing for the woman I'd become.

* * *

'What's wrong?' Tom asked later as he sat in front of the television watching a David Attenborough documentary on whales.

'Nothing,' I replied, shifting in my seat next to him, not bothering to glance up from the Jane Fallon book I was already halfway through.

'No, really, what is it? You're like a robot these days, you barely speak.' He sighed, irritation radiating off him in waves. Was he trying to pick a fight?

'I just wish I had a bit more of a social life. I miss my friends,' I said, the words spilling out of me as trepidation climbed my spine. The look on his face told me I'd said too much.

'They abandoned you, remember? When you moved here.'

I didn't point out he'd made them feel so unwelcome when they'd visited they had decided not to return. The phone calls and emails fizzled out when I frequently cancelled on plans I'd made to see them. Tom always needed me at home or to do something. He had a habit back then of surprising me with days out or tickets for something when I'd arranged to see them, feigning he hadn't remembered I was busy and sulking when I didn't want to cancel. I always gave in.

When my iPhone was dropped into the dirty washing-up water, along with it went my phone number and all my contacts. Tom only had my mother's number, which he'd put on the crappy handset he'd given me, along with his. I only had two contacts, but still I was too proud to call my mother. Tom had pushed us apart slowly but surely. My marriage was a mess I'd have to get out of myself.

'You have me, you don't need anyone else,' he said, resting his hand on my knee. I squirmed beneath his touch. 'It's why we need to get you pregnant, give you something to focus on.'

'I just miss life that's all – friends, family, work. All I do is stay here and clean, run errands for you. I don't talk to anyone and I have nothing for myself,' I blurted, unable to control my flaring temper.

'What's this then,' he snapped, yanking the book out of my hand and tossing it to the floor, the cover bent backwards and now forever creased. 'You know, you're so ungrateful. I work hard to give you everything – this beautiful cottage, the best clothes, your hair and nail appointments. You don't have to work. Most women would kill for a life like yours.'

I glared at him. *You want me to be chained to this place like a prisoner.*

'When you're a mother, you won't be able to work anyway, you'll be too busy bringing up our child.' He scowled at the television. 'In fact, on that note, perhaps you should go and get ready for bed. I'll be up shortly. Wear the red.'

18

TOM

'Ungrateful bitch,' I hissed as I poured myself a large whisky after Chloe headed for the stairs. I'd make her wait, I was in no rush to sleep and didn't overly feel like having sex with my wife who lay there like a sack of potatoes in comparison to Savannah. But still, I had a high sex drive and it was a release for the pent-up aggression churning inside me. Not only at Chloe's ingratitude but at the sexual frustration I was already feeling at not being able to see Savannah for two days.

Savannah was like a Ferrari to Chloe's Ford, and although my wife was attractive, she didn't hold up well against a goddess. I stroked my chin, remembering Savannah's milky nipples standing to attention as I caressed them, arching her back as I slid into her, wet with anticipation. The memory so arousing, I grew hard.

I could see myself burning through the bonus in a matter of weeks. No matter. There was more where that came from as long as I did what Harry needed. Recoiling at the image that popped into my head every time I thought about Harry, Savannah squashed beneath his bulk. What if I could ensure Savannah was exclusively mine? That no other man got his grubby mitts on her. It would be expensive, given she charged five hundred pounds an hour. But what if I could have it all, a doting wife at home – one who perhaps needed a little direction to get back on track – and a nymph to play with as and when I chose?

I swirled the Glenfiddich around my glass before gulping it down, enjoying the burn. The idea excited me. Yes, I could have it all if I wanted, and why shouldn't I? I deserved it. Chloe was just having a blip, perhaps it was time to widen her circle, under my watchful eye, of course. I wanted the pliable girl I married, one who wanted to please me, not the sullen one she had become who seemed to run on autopilot day in, day out. Also there was the added bonus that allowing Chloe a little freedom would increase the opportunities to see Savannah undetected.

My mobile rang, jolting me from my thoughts, and at first my heart leapt at the possibility it could be Savannah, but, alas, it was my mother.

'Hello,' I answered, a little abruptly.

'Oh hello, darling, sorry to disturb you.'

'You aren't, I'm watching television. Everything all right?'

'Yes, we're fine. I just wondered if I could send you through our shares statement, we can't make head nor tail of it,' she chuckled.

'Of course, send it through and I'll call you tomorrow once I've had a chance to take a look.'

'Thank you. How have you been?'

'We're good, Chloe is booking an appointment at a fertility clinic tomorrow so she can have some tests,' I said, sure that would please my mother.

'What a fantastic idea, it's not uncommon nowadays for women to need a little extra help.' I could hear her smiling down the phone and Dad shouting in the background before she spoke again. 'Dad said have you got someone in for the blossom tree as he could stop by and prune it for you.'

'No, it's fine, I'll sort it,' I said. Since my parents had retired, they were always keen to offer any help that would involve a visit to the cottage, something I had to regularly sidestep otherwise their presence would be constant.

'Okay, my lovely boy, well goodnight and I'll speak to you later.'

'Bye,' I said, hanging up the phone and rolling my eyes. Sometimes they were so needy and being an only child meant I bore the brunt of it. At least the inheritance would be mine alone and it would be hefty. I was intrigued to see what shares they held and how much they were worth.

David Attenborough signed off in his comforting tone and I shut off the television before the ten o'clock news came on. The world was a depressing place and the news seemed to highlight it. Pouring myself another whisky, I leaned back in my chair, closing my eyes to relive my afternoon again. Another five minutes would be fine, then I'd go upstairs and do my duty, imagining it was Savannah I was inside.

19

CHLOE

I laid in bed stewing, waiting for footsteps up the stairs. As I fumed, I plotted how I could raise funds for Savannah. A loan was not an option. We only had a joint account, so Tom could see all transactions that were made. I could open a new account with my passport and a bill and turn off paper statements, but there was always a chance a letter would come through the door or via email. Tom had access to all my passwords and without a smartphone I couldn't get online easily. Plus I hadn't seen my passport since the last holiday we'd had to Malta. Tom always kept anything important locked away.

I wasn't about to rob a bank, or a shop, and I couldn't ask anyone to lend me the money. Tom was too smart. If I asked him for money, he'd want to know exactly what I wanted to purchase and, if deemed acceptable, he'd buy it for me.

There had to be another way. My eyes roamed the dimly lit bedroom, the red satin straps rolling off my shoulder. The fabric made me itch, or was it wearing the red which made my flesh crawl?

I had clothes in abundance. Tom often came home with a new outfit, always classy, always smart. I didn't own a single pair of jogging bottoms or loungewear. Tom couldn't stand them, he said they'd make me look slovenly. He abided my running gear only because he rarely saw me wearing it. When I ran, it was always during the day while he was at work and I showered and changed before he got home. All of the clothes-selling apps were online, so I wouldn't be able to sell them on Vinted or eBay. Although there was one option I hadn't already considered.

'Turn the light off,' Tom snapped as he walked in, jolting me from my thoughts.

I leaned over and switched off the bedside light, preferring not to have to look at him either.

'Roll over onto your front,' he commanded, a slight slur in his voice.

I did as I was told, squeezing my eyes shut and forcing my mind to my happy place.

* * *

I frowned at the blouse Tom had picked out for me to wear the following morning, left on the wardrobe door. I'd seen him peruse the rails while he cleaned his teeth. I used to challenge him, occasionally wear something else out of defiance, but it always put him in a bad mood and I couldn't be bothered with the arguments when he came home.

The blouse was a horrid salmon colour and high-necked, it looked like something his mother would wear, and he matched it with sand-coloured wide-legged linen trousers which were starting to get a bit loose around the middle. I knew why he'd chosen the blouse. Last night, he'd left fingerprint bruises around my neck where he'd gripped me so tight from behind as he'd orgasmed.

Shuddering at the recollection, I ignored the insipid outfit, dabbed a little concealer on my neck and put on my running clothes, keen to get out into the fresh air, desperate to wipe the memory of last night and set my mind and body free.

Tom had been monosyllabic at breakfast, but at least he hadn't given me a list of things to do while he was at work. I knew I had to call the fertility clinic, unable to work out how I'd get out of an appointment. There would be hell to pay if I hadn't made some progress by the time Tom got home.

Before I left, I rooted through my jewellery box. The idea had come to me last night. In the beginning, Tom loved to lavish me with gifts of jewellery – expensive rings, earrings and necklaces laced with precious stones. I thought at the time it was because he struggled to show his emotions, having always been a little reserved. He'd said he enjoyed spoiling me, but now I saw he was just reeling me in, trying to buy my affections.

Selecting a diamond promise ring and gaudy emerald earrings I never liked, I slipped them into my running belt and headed for the village. Tom paid little attention to what jewellery I wore. He preferred small studs and I had those in abundance, it was unlikely he'd realise the ring and emerald earrings were missing. The nearest pawn shop was five miles away, but I figured I could run there and catch the bus home. It would be a risk but worth it.

The run wasn't as pleasant as the picturesque bank along the stream. Instead, I was dodging people on pavements and trying to keep my balance on an uneven grass verge alongside a busy A road.

I arrived at Hamilton Pawn Shop in under an hour, a hot sweaty mess. My muscles tight with anticipation as I pushed open the door and placed my jewellery on the counter. I wanted to be in and out as quickly as possible although it was doubtful I'd see anyone I knew. Tom was busy at work and even if he popped out, he wouldn't go near this side of town and he'd never frequent a pawn shop in a million years.

The man behind the counter smiled, looking me up and down. 'Been for a jog, have you?'

I nodded, still a little out of breath.

Picking up the ring, he narrowed his eyes at it. 'What have we here then,' he said, not sounding dissimilar to Fagin. The shop was musty, a cloying smell of sweat lingered in the air, which I was sure wasn't coming from me. 'Hmmm,' he murmured, raising his magnifying lens. I wrinkled my nose at his fingernails which were in need of a good cut and clean.

'It's 18-carat gold,' I said. 'The diamond is one carat, I believe.'

'It's half a carat,' he corrected me, putting it back down on the counter and picking up an earring. He didn't look at me when he spoke, his focus on the emerald stone. 'I'll give you eight hundred for the ring.'

I rolled back on my heels, face falling. 'What about the earrings?'

He shrugged. 'Two hundred.'

'That's not enough.' I sighed, more to myself than to him.

The man pushed the jewellery back across the counter towards me. 'Take it or leave it,' he said.

'I'll take it,' I said, trying to throw off the feeling of deflation. A thousand pounds was better than nothing. It meant I had fifteen hundred in total, but how was I going to get another thousand pounds by tomorrow?

'Got any ID?'

I pulled my debit card from my running belt and slid it over to him.

'You not got a passport or driver's licence?'

I shook my head as he looked me up and down.

'I'm not supposed to accept this as a form of identification.'

'Please,' I begged, hoping the owner would take pity on me.

He waited a few seconds before answering.

'All right, as you're so pretty.' He smiled, revealing yellowing teeth, and I moved away, repulsed.

While he did the necessary paperwork, I wandered around the display cabinets. He had a treasure trove of all sorts of items. How many desperate people visited his shop every day? How many of them, like me, looking to escape?

'All done. Cash, I presume?' he called.

'Yes please.' I returned to the counter to watch as he counted out twenty fifty-pound notes. Rolling up the bundle, I zipped it inside my belt, checking it was secure. 'Are you open tomorrow?' I asked.

'Sure am.'

'Thanks for your help,' I said, smiling politely, while kicking myself at not having brought more items with me, but my plan was to return tomorrow to raise the extra thousand pounds I needed.

I bought a bottle of water from a newsagents further down the parade of shops with the twenty-pound note I'd slipped from Tom's wallet on Sunday and glugged it before setting off again.

My muscles ached and my stomach was in dire need of food, but with my mind elsewhere, I ran past the crowded bus stop, heading for home, a shower and lunch. Halfway down the busy A road, my phone rang. I pumped my muscles harder, desperate to reach the end where a bridleway veered off and it would be quiet enough to talk without cars zooming by.

'Where are you?' Tom asked instead of a greeting.

'I'm out, running.'

He took a second to respond, listening.

'Sounds busy,' he said and I jogged further away from the traffic.

'Just boy racers with their huge exhausts.' I laughed, hoping it didn't sound too forced.

'There's a man coming to prune the blossom tree in half an hour. You'll be home to let him in, yes?'

'Uh-huh,' I said, picking up the pace and praying the man would be late. I'd never make it home in half an hour unless I ran flat out and I wasn't sure I had the energy.

'Good. I'll see you tonight.'

'Bye,' I panted, putting the phone away and breaking into a sprint.

20

SAVANNAH

By midday on Wednesday, Tom had already messaged me twice. The first was a lame:

I can't stop thinking about you.

The second was a delightful picture of his erect penis that looked to have been taken whilst he was in the toilet. It was progress, although not much of the romantic kind. If any other client had sent me messages like that, they would have been given a warning, then blocked immediately if they carried on. But Tom was different. He had to believe I felt something for him.

Send me one

The third message flashed up on the phone as I was taking my second shower of the day. My morning client had a thing for water sports and it usually got quite messy. I consistently overcharged him as the laundry afterwards was ridiculous, but he kept coming back. My stomach ached from the litres of water I'd consumed that morning, but I couldn't spend all day on the toilet. I had a busy afternoon to get through. I needed to race back to the flat in Crawley, get some shopping in and return an item of clothing I'd bought online before coming back to Brighton, where I'd try to squeeze in some study before my last client. So I didn't really have time for a text exchange with Tom.

Once out of the shower, I typed back a hasty reply.

That will cost you extra ;)

My message was hardly going to reel him in and I had to remember the end game – five grand from his wife. That was if she came through, but it was hardly any effort to get started. Putting on a pair of lacy shorts, I positioned myself on the bed, laying on my side, and took a shot of my legs, twisting myself around to make sure I got my backside and underwear in the photo too.

His response came seconds later.

That will help me get through the day.

I smiled to myself. It was all going swimmingly. Tomorrow afternoon, I'd have two and a half grand from Chloe as part payment to seduce Tom. What must her marriage be like if she was desperate enough to enlist the help of her husband's escort to escape it? Tom seemed normal, if not a bit highly strung, but you never knew someone until you lived with them. I had to imagine he must be pretty awful for Chloe to contact me.

My only concern was not getting stuck with him. What if he turned out to be a psycho? However, I'd managed to get shot of a few unsavoury characters in my time with the help of a retired police detective – another client of mine – and the threat of a restraining order. It was part and parcel of the job, oddballs came with the territory, and I was much choosier over who I booked now. I could usually wheedle out the weirdos from our first encounter. If anything, Tom was shy and a bit meek at the Middeon dinner and there had been nothing alarming on Tuesday. I was sure I'd be able to handle him.

21

TOM

I'd masturbated in the office toilet when Savannah sent me her photo. I'd wanted more but wasn't going to request an intimate shot yet, especially as I had no idea if Savannah was joking when she mentioned there was a cost involved. Back when Chloe and I were dating, I'd managed to get her to send me a photo of her breasts. She'd sent me a demure shot of her in a pink polka dot bra, like something a teenager would wear. She was too chaste then to show even a hint of nipple, but Savannah wasn't. She would be filthy if that was what I wanted. Savannah would gladly do all the things Chloe wouldn't entertain.

'Jim's free now,' Bella called through to my office.

'Thanks, Bella, could you pop out and get me a coffee when you get the chance please?'

'Sure,' she said, gathering her handbag immediately.

I pulled out my wallet and handed her a ten-pound note. 'Get one for yourself too,' I said, before leaving for Jim's office.

Jim had a large corner office, overlooking Crawley's busy town square. People hustled and bustled around the shops from the early morning until late afternoon. Their constant movement would drive me mad and I was glad I had bought a house out of town. Copthorne village where we lived was quiet but not so remote. We were ten minutes from Crawley, close to

Gatwick Airport, the industrial estates, a shopping centre and a plethora of restaurants and pubs. It was out of the way, allowing us to keep ourselves to ourselves, yet forty minutes from London by train and closer, in the opposite direction, to Brighton Beach. The main pull had been it was far enough from Chloe's old life she didn't keep in touch with anyone. I'd made sure of that.

'What can I do for you, Tom?' Jim said, catching me staring out of the window, probably wondering if I was coveting his office.

'I've sent you the budget spreadsheet. I just wanted to run some things past you. Harry needs us to spread some of his entertainment budget and I've found some ways we can filter it through marketing.'

'Harry and his bloody spending.' Jim sighed, rubbing his forehead. He was receding, the hairless skin shiny beneath the overhead lights. Did he know Middeon was up for sale? If he did, I would have expected him to mention it, but I wasn't going to be the one to let the cat out of the bag.

'I know,' I agreed. 'How did Ian get around it?' Ian was my predecessor who'd departed Middeon, leaving the vacancy open for Harry to promote me.

'I don't think he did. In fact, I think he was averse to Harry's ways, if you catch my drift, that's why they parted company. He got a compromise agreement.'

I grimaced. So Ian not doing what Harry wanted had got him paid off and shoved out the door? I swallowed and loosened my collar. I wasn't surprised, it was accountancy fraud, and perhaps I should have thought twice before being such a yes man.

'Okay, show me where you've plugged it,' Jim said, opening the spreadsheet. 'I still need some budget for the Mitel Chip. Advertising doesn't come cheap.'

Over the next twenty minutes, despite my reservations, I showed Jim where I'd squirrelled away most of Harry's overspending. Jim hadn't spent his allocated budget on website design or software, but with a few tweaks we could make it look like he had.

'The software trial we had for Ulysses we didn't continue, we have an invoice chain we can use. Also, we can create some payments for the graduates who came in, they did some web creating as part evidence for their dissertations.'

'You are one hell of a smart fucker, Tom,' Jim chuckled dryly. 'I knew there was a reason he made you director.'

I smiled at the backhanded compliment. At least Harry would be happy and I'd get to keep my job, until the company was sold at least.

'Your wife, she mentioned to Chloe a WhatsApp group at the Middeon dinner,' I ventured.

'Oh that, God she's always giggling at something one of them have sent her.' Jim rolled his eyes, but I could see the warmth in his face. It was obvious he held deep affection for her. I tried to mirror him.

'I'm going to get Chloe a new smartphone, she's been using an old handset since she dropped hers in the sink when she was washing up. I'll message you later with the number. Perhaps you can pass it on to Anita?' I said, glad I'd remembered his wife's name mid-conversation.

'She'll love that, initiating another wife into the fold. Beware though, Tom, don't say I didn't warn you. The bloody thing will be pinging all the time.'

I smiled tightly. I could always mute it. 'Excellent. It'll be good for Chloe to get better acquainted with everyone.'

When I returned to my office, a lukewarm coffee awaited me beside a handful of change. Bella's takeaway coffee cup had been discarded in the bin.

'Sorry, I should have waited, I didn't think you'd be so long with Jim,' she explained, her face flushed.

'No worries, we got chatting. Thanks,' I replied, closing my office door. Bella was great, but if you engaged in conversation with her, it went on forever. Pretty much like every woman I'd ever met. Except Chloe, but she'd been trained well. She better have made it home to let the man in I'd paid to prune the blossom tree.

I checked the camera doorbell to see she'd arrived home ten minutes ago. Red and sweating, she'd glanced at the camera as she'd opened the front door, not dissimilar to a rabbit caught in the headlights. Where had she been to have only just got back from her run?

22

CHLOE

I got home five minutes before the gardener arrived to prune the blossom tree. A small victory despite my aching muscles and headache from not having eaten. I'd pushed my body to its limit with a ten-mile round trip on an empty stomach and now it was turning on me.

The gardener was around my age, in his mid-twenties, and I was embarrassed about my appearance when I opened the door. My face still tomato red, hair plastered to my head. He politely declined a cup of tea and I showed him to the garden, leaving to let him get on with it. Back in the kitchen, I made a sandwich, tearing into it ravenously. I longed for a shower but would wait until he was gone.

Instead, I counted the money retrieved from my running belt and added it to the stash in the bed post. Fifteen hundred pounds, yet I still needed another thousand to give to Savannah tomorrow. Did I have enough jewellery and could I trust she'd be able to pull it off? What if she told Tom my plan?

Hearing the sound of the strimmer floating up the stairs, I laid every piece of jewellery I had out on the bed, trying to estimate their worth and whether Tom would notice they had disappeared. I couldn't even feign a break-in, not with the two cameras Tom had set up at the front and back of the cottage.

I settled on an antique-looking amethyst ring, a white gold rope necklace and diamond set hoops that my mum had given me for my twenty-first birthday. I didn't want to pawn them, but I knew they'd be valuable and my desperation outweighed sentimentality. Yet still I teared up as I ran my fingers over the diamonds, heartbroken at the thought of selling them.

Leaving the selection in the jewellery box for the time being, I trudged downstairs and leafed through an ancient copy of the Yellow Pages for fertility clinics in Sussex.

I was on the phone to one when the gardener came in to ask for a glass of water. Droplets of sweat peppered his brow, which he wiped away with a tanned forearm. His blond hair slicked back.

'Here you go,' I whispered, passing him a large glass as I held on the line for the receptionist to come back to me with an appointment.

'Thanks,' he said, our fingers brushing as he took it out of my hand, raising it to his lips and chugging it back. He flashed me a smile and put it in the sink as the fizz of attraction filled my chest, catching me off guard.

'Mrs Beswick, we could offer an initial consultation for you and your husband next week. Wednesday at three o'clock, would that suit?' The receptionist's plummy voice broke the spell.

'That would be wonderful, thank you,' I replied, hanging up while mentally calculating when my next period was due. If I was bleeding, surely I couldn't undergo an examination which would reveal the coil I'd had fitted. However, I was still a couple of weeks away.

'I'm done.' The gardener appeared at the back door, his gloved hand leaning on the frame, making his T-shirt ride up.

'That was quick.' I smiled, stepping outside to join him. He'd done a fantastic job, the blossom tree pruned back and shaped, no longer looking wild.

'I'll carry this to the van,' he gestured towards a flattened bag where the trimmings lay.

'Oh, sure,' I said, holding the side gate open for him. 'I'm sorry I didn't catch your name.'

'I'm Ben.' His smile was dazzling, forming cute dimples in his cheeks.

'Chloe,' I replied.

He paused for a second, then carried the branches out the front to his van, returning with the empty bag.

'Last one,' he said, stepping past me. So close I could smell woodchips. 'Please let your husband know I'll send him an invoice through on the email he gave me,' Ben said on his return.

'Thanks for coming out to us so quickly,' I said, as though I was talking to an emergency plumber. Pruning a tree was hardly life or death and internally I winced.

'Any time,' he replied. 'Here's my card.' He held it out to me and I took it before waving him off and locking the side gate.

'Well, that was a revelation,' I muttered to myself. It had been so long since I'd found anyone attractive, I was sure Tom had broken that part of me. I smiled to myself all the way to the shower.

* * *

'Surprise!' Tom called out as he walked through the door later, handing me an iPhone box with a red bow stuck on the front.

'Really?' I beamed at him as he kissed my cheek, for once a genuine smile on my face.

'Yes, really. It's about time we got you a new phone. I've preloaded it with some apps, and any others you want, just request them and I'll approve,' he said, without a hint of irony. It didn't matter that he was treating me like his teenage daughter who wasn't allowed on social media, I had a phone! I had the internet at my fingertips.

'Thank you,' I said, standing on tiptoes to throw my arms around him. He squeezed my behind and nuzzled my neck, his five o'clock shadow getting caught on the frills of my collared blouse.

'Perhaps I should have bought you one a while ago,' he mused, 'had I known you'd be this grateful.'

'The man came to prune the tree,' I said, leading him to the garden.

'Yes I saw.' His eyes narrowed. 'He's done a good job,' Tom said begrudgingly. 'Despite all the flirting,' he added after a long pause.

My smile faltered. 'What flirting?' I said, my hands on my hips.

I raised my eyes to the camera positioned over the back door and saliva rushed into my mouth. He'd watched my exchange with Ben.

'Don't be so coy, Chloe, you were practically whoring yourself,' he snapped, his mood souring fast.

'I wasn't,' I replied, sounding pathetic.

To my relief, Tom threw his head back and laughed before gripping my shoulder tightly. 'Too bad you're stuck with me forever, right.' He yanked me towards him, kissing the side of my head, his fingers digging into my collarbone as I tried not to wince.

'I'm not going anywhere,' I said, snaking my arm around his waist and forcing a smile.

'No, you're not,' he agreed, eyes twinkling.

23

TOM

'I'm playing golf on Saturday,' I announced over dinner. Chloe had cooked lamb chops with mint sauce – my favourite. An obvious attempt at distraction from her fawning all over the gardener this afternoon. It had been embarrassing to watch via the camera and of course, had I known he was going to be young and attractive I would never have solicited his services. Unfortunately there was no profile picture on his Facebook business page, only a logo but at least it reaffirmed to Chloe I was always watching. Every now and then she needed a little reminder that when I'd said until death do us part, I'd meant it. Realistically I didn't have to worry about Chloe playing away, she didn't work, or go out with friends. How would she meet another man? I could see everything she did on the phone I'd bought too. I was always one step ahead.

'Okay.'

'Harry has roped me into nine holes.'

'You hate golf,' she said, spearing a new potato with her fork. What was she on, three or four mouthfuls? I hadn't been keeping count, but she was programmed to stop at ten.

'I know, but you've got to do what you've got to do to get ahead,' I said stiffly, prodding at a runner bean.

'I booked an appointment at a fertility clinic in Chichester. Next

Wednesday at three o'clock. I've given them your email address to confirm the appointment,' Chloe said.

'Good girl. I'll get Bella to put it in my diary.'

'Do you mind if I get the bus into Crawley on Saturday, if you're going to be playing golf?'

'To do what?' I asked, my eyebrows hitching up my forehead. Her request was unusual, Chloe rarely went out by herself past the village.

'I wanted to buy some running leggings and I was going to get a provisional driving licence form from the post office.'

I frowned at my plate and laid down my fork. 'Chloe, you know you won't be able to learn to drive.' I chuckled. 'You'll be hopeless. I'll take you anywhere you want to go,' I said, reaching out and patting her hand. I couldn't let Chloe loose on the roads, all that independence would be no good for either of us.

'But what about when we have a baby, I'll need to be able to drive then.'

'We'll cross that bridge when we come to it,' I replied. 'And don't sulk,' I added, seeing her face fall at my rebuttal. 'Come on, five mouthfuls left.' I nudged her hand, even though I had no idea if it was five mouthfuls, and she continued eating.

Chloe was getting ideas above her station. I needed her here, where I could keep an eye on her. A baby would be the perfect anchor but I felt irked.

'I'll be home around six tomorrow, I have another late meeting. How about I bring home takeaway so you don't have to cook. What do you fancy – Indian or Chinese?'

'I'd love a Chinese,' Chloe said eventually and that was that. Driving licence forgotten.

* * *

The next morning, I gave Chloe a list of things I wanted her to achieve. She wouldn't be cooking dinner, after all. The house was always spotless, but it would be good for her to get some spring cleaning done.

- *Put in the dry cleaning*

- *Wash down the patio and outdoor furniture*
- *Defrost the freezer*
- *Change the sheets*

Chloe had got the iPhone out after dinner last night and the glowing screen had her attention for the evening as I watched her pore over the internet like a heroin addict on methadone. Little did she know I'd uploaded spyware so I could see everything she looked at. With Chloe entertained and with no need to worry what she was doing on her phone, I was able to think about my forthcoming meeting with Savannah.

Although as soon as I'd sent Jim Chloe's number, the messages from Anita started. Chloe had already been roped into a bake sale for a children's charity Middeon supported and had made plans to meet Anita for coffee in the village on Friday. I didn't mind, she could hardly get up to mischief with a woman in her mid-fifties.

With Chloe's day taken care of, I headed off to work with a smile on my face, looking forward to seeing Savannah later, knowing I would be visual-ising it all morning. Perhaps I could get her to send me a photo, or even a video. A little taster to whet the appetite.

24

CHLOE

As soon as Tom left, I raced around the house. The list he'd given me was time-consuming enough, without having to get to the pawn shop and back in time to meet Savannah for coffee. I didn't want to risk spending any cash on a cab and I couldn't use my card; Tom would want to know why I'd gone into Crawley when the dry cleaners was in the village. Anxiety swelled in my chest and I forced myself to breathe through it.

Before I got dressed, I emptied the freezer in the kitchen, putting the contents into the larger one we had in the garage. I switched it off, left the door open and gave it a spray with the de-icer, plugging the base and surrounding tiles with a layer of towels to soak up the melt. First job done. Upstairs, I whipped the sheets off of our bed, shoved them into the machine on an hour wash cycle and put fresh ones back on.

The outdoor furniture and patio could wait, it would be a nice day and they would dry quickly. Tom wouldn't be back until six so that gave me plenty of time to do it later when I got back from my coffee with Savannah. I cleared away the remnants from breakfast, collected the jewellery, put on my running belt and got out the door.

There was no way I could run to the pawn shop and back. Yesterday had taken it out of me and already a mile in my calf muscle was pinging a complaint so I planned to run there and catch a bus back.

I tried to block the pain out as I ran, concentrating instead on what I needed to do today. I was, confident I would get all my tasks done as long as Tom didn't add anything else. I was surprised he'd been so relaxed about me being on my phone last night. It hadn't stopped chiming since Tom had given Anita my number. It was like I'd been enrolled into the wives' club, which tragically was what the WhatsApp group was called. There was a constant flow of memes, gossip, photos of purchases, recommendations for Botox clinics and the like. It was all so superficial and uninteresting to me, although I appreciated Anita's kindness in reaching out, and despite our differences, it was nice to talk to another female when the only person I communicated with was Tom.

I wanted friends, but I didn't fit in amongst their designer lifestyles and none of them would be able to help me find a way to leave Tom. Savannah was my only hope and I was a thousand pounds shy of her first payment. Praying Hamilton Pawn Shop would be my saviour forced my tired muscles on.

Arriving just as the door was being unlocked, the man from yesterday seemed surprised to see me so early.

'Back again?' He chuckled, and I'd already given the game away. Anyone who came to a pawn shop at opening time had to be desperate.

'I am,' I said confidently, unzipping the running belt and placing the jewellery on the counter.

'Hmmmm.' He examined the three items for a long time with a perfect poker face, not giving any indication whether he wanted them or not.

Eventually, he pushed the amethyst ring back across the counter.

'That's tat, not worth anything.'

My heart sank.

'I'll give you four hundred for the hoops, and two fifty for the necklace.'

'I need a thousand,' I said, embarrassed to feel the sting of tears hit my eyes.

'Then I'd be out of pocket,' he said, smiling to reveal a gold tooth amongst the yellowing teeth I hadn't noticed yesterday.

I hung my head, trying not to cry.

'You're a runner right?' His eyes glazed over my body.

I bit my lip to stop it trembling.

'Well, you must be pretty fit.' His words were coated, they had texture. As he uttered them, his lip curled up into a smirk and he gestured towards the office behind the counter, the door ajar. 'I'll give you a grand, I'll take all the jewellery.'

I took an involuntary step back as the proposition repulsed me. A physical reaction to his words. Cheeks flaming, I shook my head.

'I'll be quick and it'll solve all your problems.'

My throat seemed to close, a precursor to a gag, but I found myself rooted to the spot. Thoughts inside my head spinning out of control. The idea was disgusting, but I was short for the money and I only had a few hours to get it. If I didn't pay Savannah she wouldn't go ahead with the plan and I couldn't escape my husband. Did I have a choice?

25

SAVANNAH

I spent all morning at home studying the equality law module, yet my mind kept wandering to how I could get Tom to leave his wife for me. I hadn't had a real relationship in years, so I'd been out of the game for quite some time. I knew how to seduce, but to encourage feelings strong enough for someone to dissolve their marriage was something else entirely.

Perhaps Chloe could give me more of an insight this afternoon when we met. She seemed meek and, from what I saw at the dinner, obedient. Maybe Tom liked that, but I was sure it was something I could never pretend to be. On the other hand, Tom might be drawn to the opposite, someone who was direct and in control. That would be an easier mask to wear and one I was used to. I had a different one for each client. I was a pro at being whatever they needed me to be. It was something that couldn't be taught and a skill I'd have to use to my advantage with Tom. Either way, I'd be getting two and a half grand, which was a tidy sum and not to be sniffed at.

What I really needed was a sugar daddy, but that wasn't Tom. I'd been working on Harry Poulter for quite some time, but he loved his independence too much. It was a nut I might be able to crack eventually. Perhaps I had to wait until he was a bit older and fatter when the interest of the other girls who entertained him waned. For now, Chloe's proposition was too good to resist for such little work. I'd have her money and the money Tom was paying to see me, so in effect it was double bubble.

A YouTube yoga video to stretch my muscles and a long soak in the bath helped me think over our afternoon meeting at the Airbnb. It was time to find out what Tom wanted. Perhaps I'd be able to unravel him and work out what made him tick. It started with the sex of course, there was a psychology to it. Half the fun was trying to figure out what initiated their fantasies and predilections, discovering who required or relinquished control and why their desires sometimes bordered on the perverse.

Clients enlisted the company of escorts for all sorts of reasons – bored with their wives or partners, or sometimes they might have a special kink they couldn't express at home. Occasionally it was loneliness which pushed a man to pay for an hour with an attractive woman who would listen, if that's what he wanted. Love, though, I knew little about love.

26

CHLOE

'So?' The man behind the counter winked at me, grinning inanely and my flesh crawled.

'I'll take the £650,' I said, my voice mouselike.

'Oh well, your loss.'

He counted out the notes as he'd done yesterday and pushed the ring back across the counter. I took both and turned on my heels, desperate to get out of the shop as fast as I could.

Turning left out of the door, I kept walking until I reached the bus stop, my heart pounding. Unable to believe I'd considered that creep's proposition, only for a second, but I had considered it.

What had Tom reduced me to? I was a shadow of my former self, a confident woman who'd had a loving upbringing. I'd excelled at school, gone on to achieve a master's degree in English Literature and got a successful job in publishing, yet now I was unemployed, my career ruined, a kept wife who was no more than a prisoner in her marriage. Someone so desperate for money to escape I'd considered selling myself. It hadn't come to that but I had sold my twenty-first birthday gift from my parents and my heart sank at having been made to do so.

The bus stop yesterday had been crowded, but thankfully today there was no one waiting but me. I sat on the kerb to still my quivering legs and mentally counted all the money I had. It came to two thousand, one hundred and fifty pounds in total. Three hundred and fifty pounds short, but there was no way I could get the money before this afternoon when I was due to meet Savannah. I'd have to hope she'd accept what I had, with the promise of more to come.

Within five minutes, a bus rumbled around the corner and I got on, sitting at the front. I'd be back in the village in around fifteen minutes and could walk home from there. My mobile phone bleeped, a message from Anita's number, not the 'Wives Club' group chat this time, suggesting a spa day. She seemed keen to befriend me and I was looking forward to having coffee with her tomorrow. Anita was a fountain of information at the dinner, and it would be interesting to gain insight on the lives of the directors' wives. Tom was only too happy for me to get to know them better, believing they posed no threat to the bubble he'd created for us.

Despite the initial excitement when Tom had given me the phone, I'd rarely used it. I was so out of the habit and reluctant to search anything on the internet as Tom had to be able to see whatever I looked up. There was no way he would have given me a phone without some sort of trace on it.

Shit, what if it had recorded my steps or location and Tom found out I'd visited a pawn shop? My stomach lurched at the thought. Surely the phone wasn't that technically advanced? I'd tell him I'd run to town, got cramp and caught the bus back. Perhaps next time I was somewhere I didn't want Tom to know about, I could leave the phone at home or switch it off. Although if I did and he rang, that would cause an even bigger problem. I couldn't win. All I could do was hope he was too busy at work to be checking up on me.

I hopped off the bus and took a slow jog home. The freezer had defrosted, so before I showered, I cleaned it and switched it back on. Tom had left a long summer dress out for me today, which wasn't too bad, although the shade of pink did nothing for my skin tone. I hated that I never got to choose what I wore any more, but it was another way for him to maintain control.

Fuck him. He was hardly husband of the year; he was screwing an escort. I'd wear what I damn well liked. Hanging the dress inside the cupboard, I put on some white jeans and a coral off-the-shoulder fine-knit jumper with a matching floaty scarf to hide the tiny bruises on my neck.

Feeling empowered, I applied my make-up with care, taking double my allotted time. I still had my pride, and although I couldn't compete with Savannah in the beauty stakes, I knew I wasn't unattractive. Ben, the gardener, had seemed interested at least.

At one o'clock, I walked past the stream into the village, carrying four shirts and a suit Tom wanted dry cleaned. Once I'd dropped them off, I shopped for the ingredients I needed for the lemon drizzle cake I'd offered to make for the bake sale.

By the time I reached the coffee shop, selecting the same seat at the back as Savannah had chosen, it was ten to two. I smoothed down my hair as though I was waiting for a date, butterflies fluttering in my chest.

Savannah arrived on time, looking immaculate, her face freshly painted. She too wore white jeans, paired with red wedges and a red blouse. Was it all for me or for my husband? I'd already ordered two cappuccinos whilst I was waiting and Savannah picked hers up immediately, taking a sip.

'I'm sorry, I don't have all of it,' I said instead of hello, pushing a crisp white envelope of cash across the table.

'Go on, dive right in,' she quipped, the corners of her mouth upturned. 'How much are we talking?' she added, resting her palm on the envelope.

'Two thousand, one hundred and fifty,' adding quickly, 'I'll get the rest to you.'

Savannah pursed her lips but slid the envelope into her sage green slouch bag.

'There's one condition,' I said, taking off my scarf and leaning across the table.

'Oh?' she replied, eyes glistening at first until she noticed the bruising.

'I need to know how it's going, if you're making progress.'

Savannah nodded conciliatory.

'I have a condition too,' her gaze solely focused on my neck, 'I need to know everything about Tom.'

27

TOM

At four o'clock, I rang the buzzer at the entrance of Savannah's rental having sat outside for ten long minutes, forcing myself not to turn up early. She let me into the foyer and was waiting for me at her front door, wearing a midnight-blue Chinese-style long dress with buttons at the collar, a demure choice I whole-heartedly approved of. Her red hair cascaded over her chest in bouncing waves. She took my breath away.

'Hello, handsome,' she said, kissing me on the cheek with painted lips.

'You're exquisite,' I said, pulling her into an embrace, the bulge in my trousers instant.

'Would you like a shower?'

I nodded, already unbuttoning my shirt.

'Take your time, I want you to tell me afterwards exactly what you want. What fantasies do you have, Tom Beswick?' She grinned, nibbling the tip of her fingernail. 'I can't wait to find out.'

I raced through the shower, desperate to get back to her. There was something I wanted to do, that I'd been thinking about. The question was, would Savannah let me?

'Do you have a donation for me?' she asked as I emerged from the bathroom in my boxer shorts.

'Yes, of course,' I replied, handing her the envelope.

She took it, giggling as she pointed at the erection I was unable to conceal. 'I'm guessing you already have something in mind?'

I nodded.

'Can I tie you up?'

I saw a flicker of something in her eyes. Fear maybe? It made me harder.

From underneath the bed, she slid out a large black bag and fished out two red satin cords, passing them to me.

'Take off your dress.'

Savannah did as I asked, slipping the dress over her head to reveal a lace bodysuit in the same colour.

'Kneel here.' I pointed to the space at my feet, on the carpet at the base of the bed where a white rug lay.

She licked her lips and got into position, allowing me to tie each of her wrists to the opposite poles of her four-poster bed. I reached into her box of tricks and pulled out a blindfold, slipping it on her. Finally, I took off my boxer shorts, releasing the pressure of the fabric. I was rigid, pulsating with arousal, all fingers and thumbs trying to get the condom on.

'Open your mouth,' I said, entwining my fingers into her hair.

When she did, I eased myself into her, feeling her wet tongue slide down my shaft, knowing I wouldn't be long. As she took me into her mouth time and time again, I was already close to climaxing, pushing myself deeper and deeper until I came, legs shuddering. My heart felt ready to burst out of my chest, it was hammering so hard.

'Your turn,' I said, laying down on the carpet, pulling the gusset of her suit to one side and finding her sweet spot with my tongue. She bucked upwards, the cords taut against her wrist as she writhed with pleasure, orgasming as I put my thumb inside her.

Once we were finished, I untied her and she rubbed at her wrists.

'That's rare for me, I never come when I'm with...' She seemed to be about to say 'a client' but thought better of it. My ego inflated. Chloe was the bore in the bedroom, not me. She didn't like to be restrained, when I'd tied her up once before she whined constantly which led to me losing my erection.

'Drink?'

'I'll take a beer if you've got one.'

She nodded and went to retrieve them, her rear a gorgeous sight.

We slipped into bed, drank beer and smoked, chatting about the past couple of days. It was more natural this time. For a second, I thought I was with Chloe, the easy way we used to chat about everything. In the beginning when she was like a little chirping bird which needed its wings clipped. Rather than irritate me, I enjoyed conversation with Savannah, even the tone of her voice was like syrup.

'I want to kiss you,' I said, wrapping my hands in Savannah's red waves and pulling her towards me.

We kissed long and deep, our hands exploring each other's bodies, taking our time. Then bizarrely, with a tenderness I rarely felt, I made love to Savannah. Something I hadn't done with Chloe for years.

28

SAVANNAH

My afternoon with Tom was enjoyable. He left at five and I was pleased he'd finally let himself go. He liked restraining and he liked control, but it didn't make him a monster. I wasn't so naïve as to believe I was seeing the whole picture. Things always went on behind closed doors, Chloe herself had said as much. She'd told me over coffee about Tom's control, the cruel way he behaved and the negligees he made her wear depending on his mood which had led to the bruising on her neck. I'd driven from Copthorne back to Brighton apprehensive about his visit, although there had been no red flags during the time we'd spent together.

Before Tom had left, he'd booked in for next Tuesday at four and while I'd washed sheets and packed up my things ready to go home, I'd come up with a few ideas on how I could up my game. Getting him to fall hook, line and sinker was going to be a challenge, but I sensed I'd be able to reel him in.

Chloe had demanded updates and on the days I was due to meet Tom, I'd try to fit in a meet with her if my appointments allowed it. She didn't want me to contact her by phone, it was important there was no trace between us. If Tom found out, the plan was over and I wouldn't be getting the rest of the money. She told me she'd had to pawn jewellery to raise the funds. Chloe had no money of her own and everything she spent in the joint account was scrutinised by Tom. I asked her why she didn't work and she told me Tom wouldn't allow it.

I found the whole set-up crazy. Why would someone let a man dominate their life, their choices. Not me, after I'd witnessed my mother be submissive to a drunk my whole life. I'd never let anyone infringe on my freedom, but Chloe said she'd been worn down by years of coercion and now it was easier to follow Tom's lead. I couldn't get my head around it.

Was I safe during my meetings with Tom? I had the upper hand currently, but what if that changed? I couldn't deny I had been pleasantly surprised, unlike most men he seemed to know his way around the female body and it wasn't going to be an arduous task to continue the charade but what if he was just pretending? What if his mask was about to slip?

29

CHLOE

'What are those?' Tom stared at my white jeans, which were now grubby from cleaning the patio furniture. Splashbacks of dirty water peppered my calves.

'I didn't want to clean in that dress,' I replied, thinking on my feet.

Tom set the Chinese takeaway down on the table and I got bowls and cutlery out from the cupboards. Despite his derision at my outfit, he seemed in a good mood, whistling as he emptied the bag of food and began digging in.

I'd hurried back from meeting Savannah for coffee and got so caught up fulfilling Tom's list I'd forgotten to put the dress on before he got home. He would have seen me leave the house in my jeans on the cameras anyway if he checked, but thankfully he changed the subject.

'I was thinking of taking Harry for dinner on Saturday,' he mused.

'After golf?' I asked.

'Yes, what do you think? I could get a table at South Lodge in Horsham, I'm sure they could squeeze in three.'

I agreed, although the thought of an evening entertaining Tom's boss filled me with dread. Nothing but sheer perfection would be expected and Tom would be on edge.

'I want to impress him. Show my gratitude for the promotion.'

'I'm sure he knows how valuable you are,' I replied, daunted at the prospect, but Tom wasn't listening. His mind elsewhere as he selected a second spring roll.

Harry and I hadn't spoken past a brief introduction at the Middeon dinner. He'd come across as loud and brash. The type of man who got what he wanted and then some. I'd shrink in his presence, but as long as I played the dutiful wife, Tom would be happy.

'I'll ask him tomorrow and let you know to book a table,' he said eventually.

'How was your meeting?' I asked, a minute later, watching as Tom's lip curled upwards.

'The project is coming along nicely,' he said without batting an eyelid. I hoped he was right.

Tom said he had work to finish off and I was allowed to go to bed early without him. I left him downstairs, engrossed in his laptop. Upstairs, I laid on my side, unable to concentrate on my book. Had I been too open with Savannah today, hoping she'd take pity on my situation? Maybe I had, but she'd gone for it, so it worked. It still left the problem of how was I going to raise the rest of the money if she delivered on our deal? It occurred to me all I needed was Tom to visualise a life without me, one where Savannah slotted into my place, and I'd be free.

My finger hovered over Mum's mobile number in my phone. It would be wonderful to hear her voice, to try to gauge if I could return home. We hadn't spoken in over eight months – the last time, a stilted yet polite conversation, all the while Tom breathed down my neck. When I clicked to call, an automated voice told me the number would not connect. Had she changed it? Or had Tom deliberately entered in a wrong number, changed a digit? I wouldn't put it past him. We were practically estranged now, but dissolving all contact with my mum would be the ultimate goal. He'd know I'd have no backup plan, nowhere to flee to.

Clicking on the internet app, I typed her name in, but a long list of Shirley Woodwards came up, none of them my mum. I knew the address; my parents still lived in my childhood home, but they'd got rid of their landline years ago when they both bought mobile phones. I could write a letter, Tom couldn't stop me contacting her that way. I'd be able to explain how I'd got caught up in everything but now I was sure I'd made a mistake. Whether she'd respond would be another matter and what if a letter arrived at the weekend and Tom saw it? He'd insist on reading it first if he gave it to me at all.

If I visited her, I'd have to go into Crawley and get the train to South London. If Tom needed me or checked where I was, I wouldn't be able to get back in ten minutes, breaking one of his rules. No, it was better to plan. Write to my mum first and maybe ask her to come and pick me up. Tom couldn't physically force me to stay if she did.

I buried my face into my pillow. What would my future hold if Savannah couldn't make Tom fall in love with her? A lifetime of obedience and misery, a financially comfortable but ultimately loveless marriage with a man who could be cruel for the fun of it. I'd be coerced into bearing him a child, one he would train not to answer back, to sit up straight. As soon as he realised he wasn't the number one priority, he would resent his kid and perhaps turn his cruelty on our child. And what if I raised a monster like him? There would only be one way out of my prison and the thought didn't bear thinking about.

30

TOM

I waited until Chloe went to bed and ordered Savannah some flowers. I'd had a strange feeling in my gut since I'd left her apartment. I couldn't put my finger on it but the urge to see her again was prevalent. Perhaps I'd gain some insight on the relationship Harry had with her during golf. If I was brave enough to bring the subject up.

In the box where I had to type a message, my fingers flicked across the keyboard.

I enjoy spending time with you.
   T

Was it too much? Maybe, but I couldn't help myself gravitating towards her like a moth to flame. In a fleeting moment of guilt, I ordered Chloe a bouquet too. Next week the doctor would likely tell her she was the reason we couldn't conceive and she might need a bit of a boost. I'm sure they'd give her some hormones to inject and she'd be as right as rain. I mean, people had babies every day, how hard could it be! It wasn't as if I was the problem.

At least tomorrow was Friday. I had a slight concern about Chloe and Anita getting chummy, as some of those wives were like vampires. Sucking the life out of their husbands and the money from their wallets. I'd heard the chats around the boardroom when the coffee was flowing before a meeting started. Harry and Graham, and of course Tonya, seemed to be the only ones fortunate enough not to be tied down.

Instead, Harry was lucky to be one of Savannah's regulars. But I'd find a way to make her exclusively mine. Did Harry have her on a retainer, and if he did, could I match it? The thought of her with other men turned my stomach, their paws all over her. The things they might make her do.

I poured myself a whisky as a fleeting thought crossed my mind. I'd got Harry out of deep shit in the finance department, maybe a little recompense wouldn't be out of the question. I'd gauge how the golf went first, no point in diving straight in.

Logging into my emails, I saw my mother had sent her shares statement through. My parents held over a hundred and fifty grand in Berkshire Hathaway shares. I rubbed at the bristles on my chin. Holy shit. I had no idea they had made such a significant investment. Perhaps Harry wasn't the route to go down if it turned out Savannah was expensive to keep. It was good to have options.

31

CHLOE

I woke up with terrible hay fever, my eyes itchy and nose streaming. Thankfully, Tom had told me when his alarm went off that he was going in early, so there was no need for me to prepare breakfast. I'd rolled over and gone back to sleep for another hour, rising at half past seven. Outside, glorious sunshine streamed through the windows, lighting up the house.

Tom had left me a note and my heart sank when I saw it propped up on the kitchen table, fearing it would be a list of chores. But it was a reminder about my coffee with Anita and one request – to pick up the dry cleaning. I poured myself a strong coffee and took some antihistamine on the patio, longing to enjoy the weather despite my eyes.

I checked the fridge on the way to the shower, to make sure I had everything for Tom's dinner. He'd picked out a long flowing skirt and vest top for me. I tried it on, added a belt and swapped sandals for Converse. Changing my hair from a straight bob by twisting then clipping my fringe back. It was nice to look different. I put on dangly earrings I knew Tom despised, admiring my reflection in the mirror. Tiny acts of defiance got me through the day.

I hoovered and polished and took a slow stroll by the stream into the village to collect Tom's dry-cleaning. The only thing ruining my good mood was the thought of a pompous dinner with Harry Poulter tomorrow evening. At least Tom would be out and I'd have Saturday to myself.

When I got home, I wanted to write a letter to my mother. I wasn't meeting Anita until one so had the rest of the morning, yet I was anxious about putting pen to paper, not sure how much I should reveal but I needed her help.

'Oh hey.' A figure tapped me on the shoulder in the queue at the newsagents, where I was picking up Tom's newspaper.

I turned around to see Ben, the gardener, grinning from ear to ear. My cheeks flushed instantly.

'Hi,' I said, matching his smile with my own.

'How are you doing?' he asked.

'I'm good, you?' I replied, unable to take my eyes off his bronzed arms, wrapped tight at the bicep in a navy T-shirt.

'*Financial Times*, eh?' He pointed to the paper I was holding.

'Oh no, that's Tom's,' I said, his name catching in my throat.

'Of course,' Ben said politely.

Fearing I was losing him, I blurted, 'Are you local?'

'Yeah, I live just behind the pub, in there most Fridays.'

So, Ben lived behind the Rose and Crown. He hadn't referred to it by name, but it was the only one in the village.

The man behind the counter gestured me forwards and I paid him for the paper, turning to bid Ben goodbye as I left the shop.

'You should stop by sometime, I'll buy you a drink,' he shouted down the street as he emerged from the newsagents.

'I might,' I called back, shielding my eyes from the sun with my hand.

Ben turned in the opposite direction and I slipped into the dry cleaners, glad he wouldn't see how flushed I was.

Had he been flirting with me, despite knowing I was married? The idea made my stomach fizz. He was gorgeous and closer to my age than Tom was, but I didn't believe he would be interested in me. Tom had said no man would, yet I couldn't help but feel a little lighter after speaking to Ben although the thought of popping to the pub for a drink with him was preposterous.

The lady behind the counter took my ticket and returned a minute later passing me Tom's shirts and suit. Draping them over my arm, I made my way home, a spring in my step.

When I got there, I saw a bunch of flowers had been left on the doorstep. Tom had sent me roses, the card a flourishing script.

Just because...

It had to be the Savannah effect. He had a guilty conscience; if it was at all possible for Tom to feel guilt, it was his way of making it up to me. Although how he levied a bunch of flowers against infidelity with an escort was beyond me.

I took them inside and rooted around for another vase before sitting down to write to my mother.

The letter was hard and initially my words wouldn't flow. How much should I tell her? Perhaps it was too soon to go into details of how unhappy I was. Our first letter should be about reconnecting, so I wrote how much I missed her, that my phone had been broken, and the contacts saved on it lost. I asked how my father was, whether he had his cholesterol under control and if they'd finally got their double glazing replaced. Before I looked up, I'd written a page and barely mentioned Tom at all or how small my world had become, how it lacked fun and friends, that there wasn't much laughter or joy.

Trying not to think too hard about it, I folded the letter and put it in an envelope. It wasn't as though communication with my mum was forbidden. There was nothing untoward in the letter, even if Tom saw it. Despite that, I still felt apprehensive as I posted it on the way back into the village to meet Anita. It wouldn't please Tom I'd contacted my mother.

32

SAVANNAH

I enjoy spending time with you.

I laughed at the handwritten message on the card.

I enjoy spending the money I earn from spending time with you.

I'd been surprised to answer the door to the courier this morning – a huge bunch of roses clutched to his chest. I rarely had visitors that I wasn't expecting. Thankfully, it was after Ricardo had left, otherwise it might have been awkward. Tom was taking a chance sending them to the Airbnb, but it was the only address he had for me.

They were gorgeous and I put them in the sink, looking forward to taking them home and arranging them in my new green John Lewis vase. I had to be doing something right with Tom, although it wasn't unusual to receive gifts from clients. Normally it was something they wanted me to wear or a bottle of perfume purchased in duty-free by the frequent travellers. Ricardo had even brought me a bottle of Limoncello from his restaurant once.

Admiring the pretty stems, I was pleased to be on the right track. I slipped my robe off my shoulder to expose the top of my breast and took a selfie draped across the sofa. A cute thank you note to accompany the photo. I wasn't seeing Tom for another four days, but it was important I was at the forefront of his mind.

As I clicked send, another message came through requesting the pleasure of my company tomorrow night and I accepted, checking the clock to see how long I had to get dressed before Jim Robbins arrived for his late lunchtime appointment.

Middeon had been good to me, most of the 'raffles' led to new clients and Jim was no different. Whenever he left, his head seemed heavy with a sense of shame at his misdemeanour, a little more broken with each visit. I had no doubt he was devoted to his wife. I was merely a vessel for pleasure, which was perfectly fine with me.

It was about time Harry put me on the bankroll, but he could be prickly and it wasn't a subject I was about to broach, especially when he earnt me so much money as it was.

33

CHLOE

I flinched as my phone rang in the beer garden of the Rose and Crown where I'd been sat with Anita for half an hour, chatting.

'Hello,' I answered in a deliberately cheery tone. I had to keep up appearances in front of Anita.

'Hi, darling, didn't mean to interrupt but wanted to check your flowers arrived.' Tom's voice oozed charm, likely knowing he was being overheard. It was so obviously for Anita's benefit, I grimaced. He had access to the doorbell camera; he knew full well they'd been delivered.

'I did, thank you, I messaged you.' I smiled at Anita, giving a slight eye roll, which felt rebellious.

'It's probably me, I haven't checked my messages. Anyway, I'll let you go, see you at home.' Tom said goodbye and hung up.

'Sorry about that,' I said to Anita, who immediately waved me away.

'Oh it's fine. Jim would love to check up on me if I let him.' She smiled wickedly. 'So, tell me, how long have you been married?'

'Three years,' I said, forcing a smile. I told Anita how we'd met in a bookshop and married three months later.

'A whirlwind romance then. If you don't mind me saying, Tom seems a bit stiff to me.'

I laughed out loud at Anita's observation. 'Yes, he can be a little reserved, but that's accountants for you.'

We moved on to talk about the other wives. Victoria, Anton's wife, was clearly her favourite and she spoke highly of her.

'I do socialise with the others, of course, but Victoria and I are friendly. I'll have to bring her next time, especially if there's alcohol involved.' Anita raised her blood orange gin in a toast, holding on to her sun hat at the same time.

We'd ended up in the pub after not being able to get a table at the coffee shop. The beer garden was busy, but we had managed to secure a picnic bench in the shade which suited both of us. Tom wouldn't have to know I'd been inside, he wouldn't be overly impressed with his wife drinking without him. He'd always sneered at the 'spit and sawdust' pub the village offered, not up to his kind of standards although it suited Anita and I just fine. In between us lay a bowl of chips which we dug into. I was surprised, fully expecting Anita to be on keto or some such diet she was so trim.

'I have a personal trainer, comes to the house three times a week. You should see him, he's bloody gorgeous.' She leaned in conspiratorially when I asked how she looked so fantastic at fifty.

At that moment, Ben stepped out onto the decking wearing sunglasses and carrying a tray of pints to a group of men near the door. It had occurred to me I might bump into him and I'd kept an eye out although I'd assumed he'd be working.

'You know him?' Anita raised an eyebrow after following my gaze.

'Oh he's a gardener, did some work at the house this week.' I averted my eyes.

'Handsome,' she said, teasing me, the bracelets on each arm jangling.

'I guess,' I admitted, ignoring the urge to glance back in his direction.

Our talk turned to Middeon and how Jim had worked there for over twenty years. She knew Harry well and didn't particularly like him.

'The man is slimy, I always feel like I need to wash once I've been in his presence.'

I agreed. 'Tom's just trying to find his feet at director level and unfortunately Harry's the man he needs to impress. I think we're taking him to dinner tomorrow,' I said, wrinkling my nose.

Anita groaned on my behalf.

We spent another hour soaking up the rays. Anita had another gin, I had a lager and lime – something Tom never liked me drinking in public because he didn't think it was a lady's drink. Whenever the sun shone, I always had an urge for it, remembering afternoons in the garden as a teenager, slurping from my dad's. It turned out Anita was much more down to earth than I'd imagined. She made me laugh with her outrageous comments that were never politically correct. She was a breath of fresh air and over time I could see myself potentially confiding in her.

Before we left, Anita used the ladies' room and I loitered by the bar, heart leaping into my throat when Ben came in from outside.

'I was going to offer to buy you a drink, but I guess you're leaving.'

'Yes, we're off now,' I said, glancing at the door to the toilets expecting Anita to materialise any minute.

'Another time,' Ben said, hopefully.

'That would be nice,' I said, the words out of my mouth before I could stop them.

'You have my card.' A boyish smile played on his lips, and he nodded goodbye as Anita sidled up beside me.

'More work in the garden?' she said, voice dripping in sarcasm.

'Of course, what else?' I replied, unable to hide my blush.

34

TOM

'So how was your coffee with Anita?' I asked when Chloe had finally prepared dinner, she'd been slow tonight and I was ravenous by the time it was served.

'We couldn't get a table at the coffee shop, so ended up in the pub across the road.' She let out a girlish giggle, wrinkling her nose, which made her look like a pig ready for slaughter.

'Ah, that explains it,' I said, shooting her a pointed look. Chloe wasn't slow, she was half-cut. 'If that's the sort of thing you're going to get up to with Anita, I may have to intervene.'

'We only had two drinks and it was only because we couldn't get into the coffee shop,' Chloe blurted.

I raised an eyebrow and she lowered her gaze to her plate. I reached for the salt and knocked her wine over, the contents spilling over her chicken.

'Oh sorry, darling, I'll clear it up when you're finished,' I said, doing my best to look remorseful.

Chloe glanced at me, then down at her plate.

'Come on, you're only halfway through,' I encouraged as she slowly picked up her fork, her previous spirit extinguished.

I savoured every mouthful of the spicy chicken, enjoying it all the more as I watched Chloe as she struggled to chew and swallow hers floating in

Chardonnay. It served her right, I wouldn't have my wife going out and getting drunk in the village while I was at work.

After dinner, I locked myself in the en suite bathroom, enjoying a pre-shower treat as I gazed at the photo Savannah had sent me earlier. God, what was happening to me? Sneaking off to masturbate to a picture. The need to satisfy the urge I had to be inside her again was overwhelming.

Chloe's sullen mood and waif-like appearance in her negligee was more of a turn-off than turn-on and I couldn't even be bothered to try to impregnate her tonight, too caught up in thoughts of golf with Harry tomorrow. The plan was to stay for lunch after nine holes. Harry had agreed to dinner and we'd arranged to meet again later that evening at South Lodge.

When Chloe began snoring lightly, I rolled onto my side and checked the app on my phone to see what she'd been searching for. She wasn't on any social media and other than looking up clothes, stretches for running and various dinner recipe ideas, there was nothing much to note. She had typed her mother into a search engine, no doubt after trying to call her and realising the number I'd put in didn't work. I'd wait until she mentioned it and feign surprise at my faux pas.

Her messages to and from Anita and the wives group chat were dull and uninteresting, women's stuff and the poxy charity bake sale on Sunday she'd been roped into. Chloe was hardly a mystery, she didn't have the intelligence to keep any secrets from me. The woman was an open book and it was easy to know what page she was on. Like the stupid flirtation with the gardener, obvious from the moment she'd opened her mouth.

When we'd moved into our love nest, she'd drawn the line at having cameras inside, although I could easily put them in if I wanted to. But it seemed the external ones were all I needed. Any time anyone approached the house, to deliver a parcel, to visit, or if Chloe left, I'd know about it via an alert on my phone.

Whenever she did leave the house, the Find My location app would tell me where she was if I chose to check up on her. Any bank transactions using the joint account card would flash up too. Chloe was under my watchful eye all of the time; she couldn't go anywhere without me knowing about it, nor would she dare.

35

SAVANNAH

Chloe's face when I walked into The Pass, South Lodge's Michelin star restaurant, on Saturday evening, clutching Harry's arm, was a picture. Tom, whose eyebrows jumped to his hairline on my arrival, was seated beside his wife at a corner table set for three when we were shown into the restaurant. Our waiter swiftly added another place setting, pulling out my chair for me to sit.

Harry had been a few minutes late when I'd picked him up. He'd wanted me to drive, so he could have a drink, and I didn't mind. Harry liked to drink a lot, and sometimes after we'd been out for dinner or to the theatre, when we got home, he couldn't perform. I still got paid of course.

Tonight's brief had been classy and I'd worn a black lace dress which emphasised my figure but didn't show a lot of skin – at the front anyway. It was low at the back and Harry loved to trace his fingers across my bare skin when we were seated. Showing the world I was his, for the evening at least.

'You've both met Savannah, haven't you?' Harry said to Chloe as Tom stood chivalrously until I sat, thanking the waiter.

Chloe's eyes were like saucers and I cut in before she could answer.

'I don't think we've been introduced,' I said, reaching across the table to shake her trembling hand.

'Chloe,' she said, her Bambi-esque face recovered quickly with a warm smile. She wasn't a bad actress unlike Tom, who despite his best efforts I could see was seething.

Harry and Tom dominated the conversation and Chloe, opposite me, generally only spoke when she was asked a direct question. The dinner was an eye-opener. Tom ordered for her, including what she had to drink. Patting her hand in a condescending manner whenever her sentences seemed to run on too long. He nudged her to finish her pudding, despite it being obvious she wasn't enjoying the cloggy texture of the baked cheese-cake and when the waiter came to top up our wine, he put his hand on top of her glass, not allowing her to have any more.

It was a side of Tom I hadn't seen. Chloe had said he was controlling and she wasn't wrong. At one point, as Harry was circling my upper back with his finger and whispering filth into my ear that couldn't be overheard, Tom leaned over and kissed Chloe's bare shoulder, mirroring Harry's affection, yet she physically flinched. It was only a split second, but I caught it.

'I need to use the ladies' room. Chloe, come and keep me company,' I said as though it wasn't up for discussion, loitering by her chair as she glanced at Tom for approval, not getting up until he'd given her the nod. 'You hate him, don't you?' I whispered once out of earshot.

She waited until we were washing our hands and checking our respective reflections in the mirror to answer. Taking me back to the time we'd first met.

'I do.'

'Leave him,' I said, a little flummoxed why she would stay with a man she had so much disdain for.

'He'll find me. I told you,' she said flatly. 'He knows everything I do before I do it.'

'He must be tracking your phone. Switch it off when you're out.'

'I will,' Chloe said, gripping the edge of the sink so hard her knuckles were white. 'How is the plan going?' she whispered.

'Well. I think,' I replied. 'I can't give you details here.'

'When are you seeing him again?'

'Tuesday.'

'Okay, can we meet before?' Chloe asked.

'Sure – 2 p.m., same place.'

I tried not to snigger as Tom's eyes bulged for a second when the waiter left the bill. He swiped it up from the table quickly and I was sure he was regretting taking Harry to dinner. Harry liked wine – expensive wine – and he would normally drink a bottle to himself. Although I wasn't lucky enough for him to be so sozzled I wouldn't have to perform, as he requested oral sex outside his house in the car when I drove him back. Lasting for ages because of the alcohol, until my jaw ached. It was worth it when he handed me an envelope containing a thousand pounds.

'I'll get Faye to arrange another dinner soon, I'll let you know the date,' he said as he got out of the car and waddled to the front door. The Middeon dinners were easy money, although I wasn't expecting another to be organised so soon. Usually they were once a quarter, but Harry had left before I got a chance to ask.

I got back to the flat, removed my make-up and sat in bed with a cup of tea when a message came through from Tom.

It was torture sitting so close and not being able to touch you.

It was exactly what I was hoping for. I hadn't missed his longing glances, his eyes clouding every time Harry touched me. I contemplated for a while about what to reply with.

I felt the same. I can't wait to feel your hands on me again.

Hopefully that would be what he was expecting. It must have been as, less than a minute later, Tom sent through a picture of him holding his erect penis.

All for you.

I chuckled to myself. Why men sent dick pics I could never understand. They were hardly attractive and I didn't know any woman who appreciated the arrival in their inbox. If anything, it was a turn-off. Yet still they did it.

At least Tom was thinking about me and not Chloe. Did he even love her or was she just a possession to him, a toy he could use and abuse? I couldn't fathom why they were together, but things were heading in the right direction, which meant it was only a matter of time until we both got what we wanted, for Chloe it was an escape from her controlling marriage which suddenly seemed far more important than my financial gain.

36

CHLOE

Tom had left on Saturday morning in new golfing clothes he'd ordered online – a ridiculous diamond-patterned polo shirt and blue trousers. I could tell he wasn't looking forward to golf with Harry, but instead of giving me a list of tasks he'd handed over five crisp twenty-pound notes and told me to buy something classy for the dinner at South Lodge.

In the early days of our marriage, I'd bought a top with a plunging neckline, which had promptly gone in the bin. Tom had said it wasn't suitable and he didn't want other men to see things that should only be for him. I'd argued at the time, but he'd sulked. Over the phone, Mum had said it was a red flag, but I'd dismissed her, he was just paranoid about me receiving unwanted attention, he wanted me all to his self, ignoring the warning signs. How naïve I'd been.

I'd caught the bus back from Crawley with my purchase – a new black dress I'd found in the sale. I'd got off at the village in the faint hope I'd bump into Ben again, but he was nowhere to be seen, so I'd walked the rest of the way. When I'd got home, I'd stashed the remainder of Tom's money in the bedpost, acutely aware I had another two and half thousand pounds to pay Savannah, peeling off the sale sticker so Tom would think I'd bought the dress at full price and I'd spent all the money he'd given me. I'd also picked up a couple of items of cheap jewellery in case Tom looked in my depleted jewellery box.

Tom had approved the dress when he'd arrived home and we'd later got a taxi to Horsham to meet Harry for dinner. I'd struggled to maintain a calm exterior when Harry had arrived with Savannah on his arm, my heart had leapt into my throat as I'd watched her walk into the room. She commanded attention wherever she went.

Tom sat rigid in his seat, his concentration fully on her, which had allowed me a moment to compose myself. It was more his nightmare than mine and I had no doubt Savannah would pretend not to know me.

Thankfully she did and the dinner went as planned, although how Tom was going to pay for it, I didn't know. The wine alone was extortionate, but he'd seemed satisfied when we were alone in the taxi making our way home that he'd impressed Harry. During some of the dull work talk, I'd noticed Tom stealing a few glances Savannah's way, but she'd acted cool, there as Harry's date and nothing else. So Harry used Savannah's services too? How many of the Middeon men did she have in her pocket?

Seemingly all het up, Tom didn't wait until we were upstairs before he'd launched himself on me minutes after coming through the door, roughly pushing me onto the table and wrenching my dress up. Thrusting violently with his eyes squeezed shut until he was finished. No doubt wishing it was her. It was over quickly and I was instructed to go upstairs and lay in bed with my legs raised again until he came up. He was determined we would have a baby – a notion I'd have to get Savannah to dispel. With the appointment at the fertility clinic looming, it felt like time was running out before I'd be exposed and the thought terrified me.

Sunday was a lazy sunny day with a hint of a breeze. Tom washed his car, then we would take a walk into the village in the afternoon to pick up some groceries. Tom decided as the weather was so nice we'd have a barbecue, which meant I couldn't attend the charity bake sale. Anita stopped by in the morning to collect my lemon drizzle offering I'd whipped up. On Tom's instruction, I pretended to have an upset stomach. She commented how pale I looked as I gave her a weak apology.

Tom used the opportunity to charm her, carrying the cake tin to her car and slipping her fifty pounds in donation towards the children's charity.

Later, I prepared a salad and flatbreads as Tom stood at the grill – a sacred spot no one was allowed to fill – to cook what he'd bought. He left me to scrub it afterwards while he enjoyed a beer in the sun. Once finished, I joined him, concluding the Jane Fallon book and wishing I was as brave as some of her characters. They plotted revenge against their cheating spouses – a stark contrast to my complicities, although I was confident Savannah would be able to work her magic. She seemed a woman of many enviable talents.

Since the Middeon dinner, Tom had been different: grumpy and distracted at home, as though he wished he was elsewhere. Would he feel able to go public if he got together with Savannah, what with her history amongst his peers at Middeon? I hoped it wouldn't be a stumbling block. As soon as he was ready to leave, I wouldn't stand in his way, happy to exit my marriage and let the solicitors deal with the financial side.

Everything was Tom's, as he so often reminded me. He'd say I had nothing without him and when he was feeling particularly cruel, he'd add that I amounted to nothing without him too, as though my sheer existence depended on being his wife. I'd believed him for so long, but he was wrong. I could be by myself. I could stand on my own two feet and although the thought terrified me, it excited me in equal measure.

I couldn't wait to reconnect with my family and friends, to hopefully fall in love again someday and learn to trust another man, one whom I could envisage having a family with in the future. I wouldn't let the scars Tom left stop me. I could have the blissfully idyllic ending I'd read in the books I'd worked on at Oakley Publishing. Tom would be a thing of the past, a blip in an otherwise happy existence.

37

TOM

We had a management meeting on Monday morning to discuss an upcoming investment opportunity in a Japanese software programme and afterwards Harry asked me to remain behind.

As the other directors filtered out of the room, Harry slapped me on the back. 'I took a look at the budget sheet this morning, Tom, great work.'

I'd mentioned it during the laborious nine holes on Saturday, trying to gauge whether what I'd managed to do with the figures might generate any financial gain for me. But Harry hadn't even looked at my email, promising he'd get to it on Monday morning.

He'd dominated the conversation during our round, first enlightening me with a general history of golf, then moving on to how to swing and what club to use as we made our way to each hole, clearly revelling being the teacher. Then he'd mentioned Marcus, the business development director, and how he was having a mare with a sexual harassment grievance Tonya had received from one of his sales managers. It was being investigated, but Harry rebuffed it as no more than horseplay in the office.

'With no witnesses, the lass hasn't got a leg to stand on,' he'd said before the conversation switched to our rising share price and whether he could get around insider trading rules. I'd barely got a word in edgeways.

The man was an enigma and at times I questioned how he'd managed to wrangle his way to own a technology firm. One to one, he was more like Del Boy selling his knock-off wares down the local market.

'Jim's happy?' he asked, nudging me from my thoughts.

'He's fine, he's still got budget for advertising, which is what he wanted.'

'Great stuff. You're on your way up, Tommy-boy, the sky is the limit.'

'If the new owners keep me on,' I said.

'Of course they will, they'd be mad not to,' Harry retorted, although his words didn't fill me with confidence.

As he turned to leave, I chanced my arm.

'I wonder if I may ask a personal question, Harry?'

'Go ahead,' he replied. Intrigued, he fingered his cufflinks while he waited for me to speak.

'Savannah... are you in a relationship with her?'

Harry threw his head back and roared with laughter, echoing around the empty boardroom. 'You aren't the first to fall under her spell, Tom, and I'm sure you won't be the last.'

I frowned, was that a yes or a no?

Harry continued to chuckle at my bewildered expression. 'No, I'm a free agent and Savannah can do what she pleases, but attached to her is a hefty price tag, and don't get me wrong, she's worth every penny, but don't get out of your depth. I'm not sure your one hundred and twenty thousand a year will be enough to keep her interested.'

He left the boardroom, still laughing to himself as I clenched my fists in annoyance.

I wasn't some john, an appointment slot in her calendar. It was more than that, we had a connection. She was attracted to me, I could tell. Not much of a surprise if her clients amounted to no more than old men with age spots and overhanging beer bellies. But Harry's words troubled me. Had I misread the signs from Savannah? Did she send photos of herself to all of them?

At lunchtime, I left Bella typing up a report and went for a walk, keen to be free of the office and the thoughts of Savannah roaming around my head. As I passed the busy shops, I paused at the window of Agent Provocateur to admire a cream camisole and French knicker set with black lace edging, imagining Savannah's head on the mannequin in the window. Within minutes I'd bought it, having a punt at her size, intending to give it to her tomorrow. I had to set myself apart from the other men she saw, perhaps then she would consider being mine alone.

38

CHLOE

Keen for an update I loitered outside the coffee shop on Tuesday afternoon, walking around in a tiny circle until I saw Savannah pull up across the road in a red Audi A1, the radio blaring. She stepped out of the car in a cream blazer and navy trousers, looking every inch the model in oversized sunglasses. I waved and hurried across the street.

'Aren't we going for coffee?' she queried.

'I was hoping you could take me to your house, where you entertain.' I chewed my lip and rolled onto the balls of my feet.

'It's not local, I rent an Airbnb in Brighton and, to be honest, it's not convenient right now, your husband is visiting later.' Savannah ran her tongue across her front teeth and gestured towards the coffee shop. I followed her lead, a little deflated.

I waited until we were seated and had ordered before speaking.

'So, have you made any progress?'

'It's early days, but he's interested.'

I leant back in my chair, as the waitress delivered our drinks.

'Why don't you tell me what makes Tom tick?' Savannah said.

That was easy. 'You can play to his ego, he's pretty vain and likes to think he's powerful and in control all the time.' I wrapped my hands around my mug. 'He seems... dissatisfied at home, like he wants to be elsewhere.'

'That sounds positive, he's been texting a bit. Was my presence at the dinner on Saturday a surprise?' Savannah smirked.

'Definitely, he stiffened in his seat every time Harry touched you. He's a jealous man, so I'm not sure how that's going to play out with your other clients.'

'I can deal with that. Anything else?' Savannah sipped at her coffee, remnants of her coral lipstick left on the rim.

'He wants a baby,' I admitted, biting my lip.

Savannah frowned.

'Well, I don't really think it's him, it's mainly his parents putting pressure on him. An heir to the throne kind of thing.' I rolled my eyes as though it wasn't a big deal, although the appointment tomorrow at the fertility clinic was giving me major anxiety.

'That might be a stumbling block,' Savannah said, piercing me with an icy stare.

'Not just for you,' I muttered.

The conversation stilted as we drank our coffee. We couldn't be more different Savannah and me. It struck me how odd it was, I was sitting less than a metre away from the woman sleeping with my husband. Someone I'd paid to steal him away from me.

'Are you good for the money?' Savannah's voice broke the silence.

'I will be,' I replied, projecting an air of assurance.

'Haven't you run out of jewellery yet?' She chuckled and I had the urge to slap the smile off her pretty face. It may be a joke to her, but leaving my husband consumed me. I wanted to get back to the Chloe I remembered, one who made her own decisions and did what she wanted. But I needed Savannah's help, I reminded myself, even if that meant suffering her jibes.

39

SAVANNAH

Tom arrived brandishing a gift bag from Agent Provocateur, urging me to look inside. I expected some tacky crotchless number, electric-blue lace or the like, and was stunned when I pulled out a gorgeous silk camisole.

'You're full of surprises,' I said, kissing his cheek.

'Do you like it?' His eyes were wide and expectant, almost childlike.

'I love it.'

He wrapped his arms around me in an embrace, squeezing me tight and pulling my face to his.

'Try it on.'

He tied me up as before, kneeling, leaving me in position while he showered. I could foresee it was going to be a regular thing, a prelude to the sex that would come later. Maybe Chloe didn't enjoy oral, although I doubted it would matter to Tom. Unlike with me, it was obvious Chloe's enjoyment wasn't high on Tom's agenda. However, he made an effort to try to please me. After he'd climaxed and I'd been untied, he was gentle, caressing my bare skin, stroking and exploring with his fingertips.

'Do you ever consider giving it up?' he asked as we lay wrapped in the bedsheets, his hand resting on my thigh.

'And do what?' I asked, already imagining myself stood in court, trying to get a jury onside, but those dreams I wouldn't share with Tom. They were private and why I was working so hard every spare minute I had to make sure I got my degree.

'I don't know – anything,' Tom said, his brows knitting together.

'I'd love to,' I said, keeping to the plan. 'Perhaps I'm waiting for a rich man to whisk me away from all this,' I teased, spinning my finger around.

'Well, I'm not rich,' he began, but I nudged his bare chest, interrupting him.

'Are you making me a proposition, Tom Beswick?' I giggled, fluttering my eyelashes. He brushed my hand away sharply and sat up, cheeks muddying. He didn't like it when I baited him.

I sat up too, trying to recover the mood, kissing his shoulder and slinking an arm around his waist.

'I can't stop thinking about you,' he breathed into my hair a minute later, sending shivers down my spine. 'I can't stop thinking about you... and the others,' he added bitterly.

'Maybe there doesn't have to be any others,' I purred, turning my face to kiss him passionately. My spirits soaring as I knew he was on the edge, I was so close, I could smell the rest of Chloe's money, but I couldn't rush it.

There was no more talk after that, just skin against skin, and I'd be lying if I said I didn't enjoy it.

Tom left just after five, and I knew I was slowly reeling him in, making him believe we could be something, the two of us. Slowly, slowly, catchy monkey, my mum used to say, but Tom was on the hook and I had the green light to up my game.

40

TOM

Chloe was waiting for me when I got home, dinner already on the table. I found her presence irritating. Like a fly, I wanted to swat her away.

'Don't forget we have the appointment at the fertility clinic tomorrow,' she said, passing me the salt without me having to ask. She sounded like a nag, and with Savannah on my mind, having a baby with Chloe didn't feel like a priority right now, even with my parents on my back.

'I don't need a doctor to tell me you're the problem,' I snapped, projecting my frustration.

Chloe recoiled and seemed to shrink into herself.

We didn't speak for the rest of the meal. I couldn't wait to get away, she was suffocating when all I wanted to do was be alone and relive my afternoon with Savannah.

Unfortunately, she was the dream and Chloe the reality. How could I have married Chloe when Savannah existed? But we didn't have a future. It wasn't as if I could settle down with a woman who used to be a prostitute. I'd be a laughing stock. Harry's reaction had proved that. He saw how Savannah had got under my skin and he was trying to prevent me embarrassing myself.

I nursed a large whisky, listening to Chloe clatter around in the kitchen, clearing away a dinner I'd barely touched. Every noise she made was jarring, jolting me from my memory of the afternoon. Couldn't she do it any quieter? Or was she truly trying to irritate me?

I scowled, pushing back into the chair, determined to relax.

A second later, my mobile buzzed in my pocket.

'Oh for goodness' sake,' I snapped, having forgotten to change it from silent.

I reached in to see who it was. Seth flashed up on the home screen and my insides liquified.

Thinking of you...

A second later, a video came through, Savannah's cherry red fingernails weaving their way down the delicate curve of her stomach towards a tiny strip of dark hair. I watched, open-mouthed, as she played with herself, whispering my name. Growing harder with every passing second. The sounds of Chloe stacking the dishwasher, banging the plates together floated through from the kitchen and I reached inside my trousers, practically pulsating.

The video ended and I played it again, twice, jerking off until I came inside my boxer shorts.

'Tom, do you mind if I have a bath?' Chloe called as I swiftly rearranged myself, uncomfortably warm and sticky.

'Sure,' I managed, voice croaky.

As soon as she ascended the stairs, I cleaned myself up in the downstairs toilet as best I could before returning to finish my whisky.

You are something else...

I sent the message to Savannah.

A few seconds later, her response came through.

You better believe it.

Savannah had me possessed, and what we were doing, it was exhilarating. I couldn't possibly let her go. Not now, not ever.

41

CHLOE

'Stop fidgeting,' Tom barked at me from the driver's seat as we made our way to the fertility clinic in Chichester.

I couldn't help it, I'd barely been able to get off the toilet all day, feigning an upset stomach to Tom. I'd told Anita the same thing when she'd called for a chat. Nerves always did that to me, hit me straight in the gut.

'I'm just nervous,' I said apologetically.

Tom sighed. 'There's nothing to be nervous about, I'm sure it'll be a chat today, an initial consultation. Although hopefully it won't drag on for weeks, Harry wasn't too happy about me missing a board meeting this afternoon.' He drummed his fingers on the steering wheel as we queued along the A27.

I'd googled fertility treatment last night whilst in the bath, trying to ascertain what to expect without specifically searching as to whether my coil was about to be discovered. Tom was bound to be able to see everything I did on the phone. It was another way to watch me.

I gazed out of the window as we crawled along, hoping if we were late they'd have to reschedule us. Although Tom's mood would be insufferable if they did. My thoughts strayed to the letter I'd written to Mum. Had it been delivered yet? I tried to imagine her reaction at reading it – would she be pleased I'd got in touch?

Despite Tom's instruction, I wrung my hands, blood pressure rising rapidly. It was all too much. The fertility clinic, the anxiety of my deal with Savannah and how I was going to pay her, not to mention waiting for a response from my mum.

'Just breathe,' Tom said as we finally pulled into the car park.

'You know I hate needles,' I replied, the blood draining from my face as Tom held the car door open for me.

'Oh for goodness' sake, pull yourself together,' he hissed, pinching the skin of my upper arm as he wrenched me from the car. He'd made me wear a sleeveless dress, despite the stubborn clouds and northerly wind. I shivered as a gale blew, turning my legs to ice. I didn't even have a cardigan.

I let Tom steer me to the reception desk, where he checked in while I gave a vacuous smile.

We were kept waiting fifteen minutes as Tom scowled at his watch. Eventually, Doctor Carrick, a man in his early fifties, came out to greet us and we were led into an office, painted in soothing blue tones. He gestured for us to sit down in front of the desk.

'Mr and Mrs Beswick, let's get straight to it,' he said warmly. 'How long have you been trying for a baby?'

'About a year with no success,' Tom answered for both of us, exaggerating how long it had been.

'Okay, any previous medical history that might determine the cause – diagnosed low sperm count or endometriosis?'

'None we're aware of.'

'Have you tried during ovulation? I only ask, as quite often couples are not aware of the dates they should be especially trying to conceive.' Doctor Carrick steepled his fingers, the tips wedged beneath his chin.

'We're having regular sex, at least four or five times a week,' Tom said unabashed, maintaining his professional composure, whereas I wanted to shrivel up and die at the intimate questions.

'Good, good. I have some initial forms for you to complete, medical history, et cetera, that will allow us to get a better picture. They will need to be handed back to reception, along with your identification documents.'

Tom patted the inside of his blazer pocket which held his wallet containing his driving licence. 'Did you bring your passport?' he asked, turning to me.

I stared back at him, narrowing my eyes. Tom had taken my passport for 'safekeeping' when we'd moved in the cottage, it only came out whenever we travelled and he always looked after it.

'No, I, I didn't think I needed to,' I stuttered, looking first at Tom, then at Doctor Carrick.

Tom's eyes darkened and I saw the flex of his jaw.

'Ah, apologies, the receptionist should have told you to bring them when she booked you in, but she's new. It's fine, we can check Chloe's on the follow-up appointment,' Doctor Carrick interjected, dispelling the tension.

I expected Tom to relax, but he remained poker straight in his seat.

'So what happens now?'

Doctor Carrick launched into the various options that potentially could be viable for us, depending on the results of tests to see if there was an obvious reason we hadn't been able to conceive. It wasn't going to be cheap unfortunately, he continued, privately investigative tests were costly. Tom had rebuffed my initial suggestion of fertility treatment via the NHS, declaring it too slow, exactly why I'd mentioned it.

'Tests?' I asked, trying to still the tremble in my knee.

'We request a blood test and a pelvic ultrasound scan to assess your ovarian function and examine your uterus, fallopian tubes, ovaries and cervix. As for Tom, we would ask for a semen sample for analysis – however, that depends on the last time intercourse was had.'

Doctor Carrick's question hung in the air unanswered. My mouth was dry and I found it difficult to swallow. Tom had said there wouldn't be any tests today, it would just be a consultation. Fear coursed through me and I wrung my hands together, stomach churning. I needed the toilet again. Trapped with nowhere to run, my deception was about to be exposed. When Tom found out, he would be livid and the punishment didn't bear thinking about.

42

TOM

I cleared my throat. It was only yesterday I'd had sex with Savannah, yet my mind went blank as to the last time I'd done the deed with Chloe. Was it Saturday, after the dinner? I wasn't sure, it hadn't been memorable, but I knew I damned well wasn't about to admit to cheating on my wife.

'I'm afraid I have to get back to work, I have a meeting, my apologies,' I lied. 'I assumed it would be an initial consultation only. We can come back to complete the tests another time.' It was more of a statement than a question, but I was a paying customer.

In my peripheral vision, I saw Chloe deflate, tension ebbing away from her body. It was only a blood test and a scan, yet she was acting like a cornered mouse. How would she be able to get through childbirth if she couldn't gather her nerves now. I looked at her, incredulous. What sort of mother would she make?

'That's no problem, Mr Beswick, if you can complete the forms and we can check your identification. I'll get Gail to book you in for tests next week.'

We said goodbye to Doctor Carrick, who handed Chloe some leaflets on what to expect during the testing process. Once we'd filled the forms in, Gail, the incompetent receptionist, booked us in for the following Monday, adding that we were to abstain from sex for forty-eight hours prior to testing.

'Do you have to go back to work for your meeting?' Chloe asked when we were on our way home.

I gripped the steering wheel tighter, watching as the blood drained from my knuckles. 'I can do it on TEAMS, I don't need to go into the office,' I told her despite the meeting being fictional. I didn't want any test to come back with insubstantial results after my dalliance with Savannah yesterday. 'Anyway, you were the one shaking like a leaf, you would have thought you were about to sit in the electric chair,' I said, delighted to be putting the boot in. 'I thought you'd be grateful.'

'I am,' she quickly replied, resting her hand briefly on my thigh. My skin seemed to itch beneath her touch.

'Perhaps you can show me how grateful you are later,' I said, smirking, but Chloe looked out of the window. Miserable cow.

Was it a good idea to go through this charade? Saddle ourselves with a baby when it was Savannah I lusted after?

I shook my head, propelling the thoughts from my mind. My parents expected a grandchild and not one from a whore. I knew if my mum were ever to meet Savannah, she'd sniff it out in seconds. The woman was like a bloodhound. No, Chloe was my wife and she would bear my child. Savannah was a bonus, someone to play with, a mistress at best.

* * *

Back at home, after I'd been in the office for my fictitious meeting, Chloe reheated a lasagne in the microwave she'd previously made and frozen. Putting it in the oven for another ten minutes to crisp up the top while the garlic bread cooked. I opened the wine and tried to look at my wife in a new light, mentally listing what it was I liked – no, loved – about Chloe. She was pretty, well spoken, obedient, loyal – too many good qualities to walk away from, plus the last few years of moulding her would be wasted.

'Fancy a glass of wine and an early night?' I said, rubbing her behind as she served the lasagne.

'Sure,' she said sweetly, kissing me on the cheek.

'So if we have a boy, what should we call it?' I asked as we ate, wanting to indulge in the fantasy.

'It's a little early to be talking about that,' Chloe said, helping herself to some salad.

'Go on, suggest one,' I said, trying not to find her avoidance irritating.

'Umm, Ben,' she uttered, stopping me in my tracks.

Fire erupting in my belly, I jumped to my feet. 'Like the fucking gardener?' I shouted, swiping my arm across the table, sending the contents into Chloe's lap.

The fucking bitch. I knew she had a thing for him.

Her face was frozen in a silent scream as she remained like a statue, steaming-hot lasagne and red wine puddling in the lap of her dress. She began to cry, but I was too angry to listen to her pitiful whimpers, instead swiping my car keys off the side.

'Clean this shit up,' I shouted, pointing a finger into her face before tearing out the door.

43

SAVANNAH

Tom turning up unannounced was irritating. I'd not long said goodbye to a client and was about to get in the shower before going home to hit the books. I needed to write up some notes from my ineligible scribbles in class this morning before they left my mind.

'I'm sorry,' Tom said as I swung the door open, 'I just needed to see you.' He stepped inside the front door without invitation. I'd buzzed him in and used the precious few seconds to tidy away the toys my previous client had been using. I'd sterilise them later.

'What's happened?' I asked, faking concern.

'Just a bad day,' he replied, a vein pulsating in his forehead.

'I was about to get in the shower, do you want to join me?'

His face lifted and I grabbed a condom from the bedroom drawer on the way.

We stepped inside the large rainforest shower and washed each other, enjoying the feel of soapy hands across skin. Our fingers delving too low, seeking pleasure. It was the first time Tom had been rough, gripping my flesh and squeezing my breasts like he had frustration to expel. Slipping on the condom, he turned me around and pushed me up against the tiles, entering me from behind. A few quick thrusts and he was done, but at least he had the grace to look bashful, his eyes unable to meet mine.

'I take it you needed that?' I laughed, despite my cheek feeling tender after being squashed against the tiles. Usually I'd complain but I was thinking of the bigger picture.

'I did.'

Afterwards, we sat on the terrace with a bottle of beer, shielded from the wind by the glass panels. It was strange, being so stripped back with him, no make-up on, wet hair tied back. He nursed his beer, staring into the bottle as if answers could be found there.

'I didn't bring any money,' he eventually said.

'I think we're past that, don't you?' I didn't relish the idea of giving my services away for free, it certainly hadn't been part of the plan but I felt I was close to sealing the deal.

'What do you mean?' Tom asked, and I gave him a knowing look.

'I like you, Tom,' I said, the lie feeling strange in my mouth.

'I like you too,' he replied, reaching for my hand.

I let the revelation sit for a while, trying to ascertain what Tom was thinking.

'But I don't know how we do this,' he said, and I deflated. It wasn't going to be as easy to get the other half of Chloe's money as I'd thought.

'I'd give it up, you know,' I said after another lengthy silence, 'for you.' I drained my beer and placed it on the rattan table.

'Would you?' Tom raised his eyebrows as though he suspected I was lying.

I locked eyes with his. 'I would.'

Tom frowned, leaning forward in his seat, as though I'd made his life irrevocably harder, and maybe I had. I was messing with Tom's life, leading him up the garden path. But then I remembered Chloe's money and how he treated her.

I'd watched my dad belittle and berate my mother over the years until I couldn't bear it any longer. I begged her to come with me to England, but by then she'd become institutionalised in her marriage, saying that she was too old to leave and start afresh someplace new. I could see the same thing happening to Chloe if she didn't get away from Tom.

44

CHLOE

I'd made sure I was in bed when Tom arrived home, despite it being before nine. It had taken ages to clean up his mess. The congealed lasagne stuck to the tiles like glue. I'd carried most of it in my lap to the bin, thighs burning. Lifting the hem up like I was a farmer's girl collecting apples in the length of my dress. I'd mopped and scrubbed on autopilot, blood seething. I'd simply uttered the name Ben as I'd been put on the spot and it was the first one which came to mind when Tom had asked.

His massive overreaction sent shockwaves through me. His temper was unpredictable but usually there was a build-up, I'd get a warning at least before he started throwing things. Was he getting worse, his violent outbursts escalating? Did he now view me as an obstacle in his way to being with Savannah? If that was the case and he wouldn't consider a divorce, what other plans did he have for me?

In bed, I'd let the tears fall, mainly borne out of anger and self-pity. I couldn't live like this any more. Perhaps I was better off dead.

I stiffened as Tom climbed in beside me, but thankfully he stayed over his side, ignoring me as if I wasn't there. I had nothing to say and he wouldn't apologise, he never did. Nothing was ever his fault. How could I have gone from loving him so much to hating him with a passion?

* * *

In the morning, Tom left before I got up. I'd ignored the alarm, bitterly remembering his outburst last night; my ruined dress and the scalds on my thighs. He could fix his own breakfast. I'd half expected him to appear at my bedside when the minutes crept past seven and I hadn't ventured out from beneath the duvet. But at half past he left as usual. I'd listened to the front door closing and the Range Rover pulling off the drive before slipping back to sleep.

Waking with a start, I saw it was past nine and leapt out of bed to pack a bag, annoyed with myself for falling back to sleep. I'd take the essentials, nothing more. If Tom was at work, he wouldn't be able to stop me leaving. My deal with Savannah no longer mattered, I'd had enough and couldn't wait a minute more. Last night had been my breaking point.

Who knew what Tom would do next, especially with the fertility tests booked in for next week, and I wasn't going to live in fear. I looked a fright, red, puffy eyes from all the crying I'd done last night. I was pale and drawn, but there was no time to rest.

Racing through the house, I filled a bag with clothes, toiletries and the paltry stash of money I'd saved. I only had a hundred pounds, but it would have to do. I searched high and low for my passport or anything with my name on – wedding or birth certificate – but Tom had hidden them well. It wasn't until I had my bag ready in the kitchen about to leave when there came a tap on the front door, sending an initial jolt of panic through me. It couldn't be Tom, he'd use his keys.

I pulled it open to find Anita on my doorstep holding a fruit basket.

'You sounded so wretched yesterday I thought I'd bring you this,' she said, handing the beautifully wrapped wicker basket to me.

'Thank you,' I replied, stepping back to let her in. Politeness overruling my necessity to get out of the cottage.

'How are you feeling?'

'Better, thanks,' I said, leading her through to the kitchen and gesturing for her to take a seat at the table. A quick coffee would be fine. Tom wouldn't be back for hours.

'Going away?' Anita asked, staring pointedly at my backpack resting on the chair with clothes spilling out of the top.

I stood at the kettle with my back to her, head bent low, gripping the counter. I didn't have the strength to lie, to carry on with the facade that was my marriage.

'I'm leaving Tom,' I said, the words spilling out of my mouth like lava, uncontrollable, as were the tears that followed. Huge wracking sobs that came from nowhere, the stress of the past twenty-four hours taking their toll.

Anita sat me down swiftly and took over making us a coffee, pulling a tissue from the sleeve of her cardigan like a magician.

'I knew you weren't happy,' she said, sitting beside me, her hand resting on my arm.

'How?' I asked, believing I'd hidden it so well.

'You practically flinch every time he speaks. I've been there, darling, before Jim, my first marriage. The signs were there from the moment I saw the two of you together. Has he hurt you?'

I looked into Anita's eyes, the depths of her empathy obvious.

Yes, Tom had hurt me. He'd controlled and belittled me, he'd frightened me, but had barely laid a finger on me. Did that count?

'I'll drive you wherever you want to go right now. I know a fantastic divorce lawyer, he's not cheap but—'

I cut Anita off. 'I have nothing,' I said, throwing my hands up in the air, 'no money, no bank account. Tom's name is on everything. I don't have a leg to stand on.'

Anita appeared momentarily ruffled, repositioning her cardigan.

'I'm sure there's something we can do.'

'I just want to walk away, I don't care any more, about the house, or possessions.'

'But it's not fair, half of it is yours, my dear.' Anita raised her eyebrows, outrage plain on her face.

'Thank you for your offer, but it's better if you go. I don't want to get you involved. Tom will know. It's easier if you pretend we haven't had this conversation.' I knew Tom would see me leave on the camera, the same as he would have seen Anita arrive, but I was desperate and while he was at work was my best chance of escape. If I was lucky, he'd be busy in meetings and I'd be on the train to my mum's before he even realised I was gone.

Anita squeezed my arm again before pulling me in for a hug. She smelt like peonies, her touch maternal, reminding me of the age difference between us. Reluctantly, she agreed to leave, telling me I could call her if I needed to, day or night. I thanked her, grateful for a friend. The only one I had.

After five minutes had passed, I switched off my phone and hurried out of the front door, leaving our steaming coffees behind. I didn't look back, heading for the path by the stream which would take me into the village. From there, I could get a bus to Crawley station and catch the train to London. In another hour or so, I'd be gone, free from Tom and free from my marriage.

45

TOM

I was in the middle of a meeting when the door camera went off; an alert popped up on my home screen. I placed my mobile on my thigh under the table and discreetly opened the app to reveal the clip of Anita standing there with a fruit basket. God, that woman couldn't leave Chloe alone. I scowled, ruing the day I'd given Jim Chloe's number. I closed the app and ignored the next alert, half an hour later, expecting it was Anita leaving.

Tonya was still wittering on about the vacancies she had to fill and how agencies charged an arm and a leg for providing applicants. I was struggling to maintain focus.

'Jim, can you get involved on the marketing side, there must be Twitter or Facebook technology groups we can advertise on to get the people we need?' Harry interjected.

I was slowly switching off. The morning meeting had run over and I was bored of listening to the other directors bitch at Harry. He still hadn't made a proper announcement about his intention to sell Middeon or where that left any of us.

When a third notification popped up, I assumed it was Chloe going out for a run but opened the app anyway. It showed her hurrying out of the door and down the driveway, not dressed in fitness gear or the clothes I'd left out for her. I frowned and replayed the image, the bag on her back had to be weighty, the straps pulled at her shoulders and she walked slightly hunched. What was in there? I didn't like the look of it and where was Chloe going? Something was off.

'I have to go I'm afraid, chaps, I have another meeting,' I said, closing my notebook.

'No worries, Tom, we were wrapping up anyway,' Harry replied as I stood from the table and made my way to the door.

After a quick pitstop at my office, I grabbed my keys, barking at Bella to 'clear my schedule' as I dashed past.

I drove way too fast down the country lanes. I swerved onto the driveway and was out of the car, letting myself into the cottage in seconds without bothering to announce my arrival. Chloe hadn't come back, I knew from the lack of camera notifications.

Upstairs, I found the bed still unmade, which was highly unusual, and when I checked, some of her items were missing – a few clothes, deodorant and make-up. I scoffed, feeling the vein in my neck pulse. The bitch was trying to leave me.

Racing downstairs, I jumped back into the car and headed for the village. It was quicker to walk via the stream, but when I found Chloe, I could hardly drag her back home by her wrist. I crawled deliberately slowly along the main street, ignoring the frustrated driver behind me. I made it past the post office and dry cleaners when up ahead I saw Chloe waiting at the bus stop. Thank goodness they only ran every half an hour.

When she saw my car, her mouth dropped open and she turned to walk away. I sped up, pulling in beside her, edging the car along the kerb as I rolled down the passenger window.

'Get in,' I said, through gritted teeth.

'No,' she replied, still walking, not looking at me, her arms swinging.

'Do you remember those photos, Chloe, the Polaroids from when we first got together...'

She stopped, mid stride as though playing musical statues.

'I've still got them. I wonder what would happen if they found their way to the internet, or to your parents' address?' I was enjoying every second of watching Chloe's turmoil, her shoulders sagging in defeat.

'You wouldn't,' she said, turning to me now, a hint of defiance in her voice.

'Wouldn't I?' I replied with a chuckle. 'Call it insurance.'

Chloe bent over and vomited on the pavement, her backpack slipping off her shoulder.

I got out and made my way around the car to open the passenger door, catching sight of Ben across the road.

'Running away with your fancy man, were you?' I growled, shoving her in the car before waving at Ben, awarding him my smarmiest smile.

He narrowed his eyes at me, obviously having witnessed our exchange. *Come over, I dare you.*

'Tom, please,' Chloe begged, wiping the drool from her mouth before I slammed the door shut and got back in the car.

Ben was still watching as I pulled away and I had to resist the urge to give him the finger.

Chloe had her face in her hands. She was such a mess.

'You. Don't. Get. To. Leave,' I shouted as I drove back to the cottage.

'You're not happy, Tom, that much is obvious, why can't we separate, it can be amicable. You can keep everything,' Chloe cried.

'I will keep everything, that's right, because I *own* everything, including you,' I snapped back.

Rage swirled in my belly at her audacity. Trying to run whilst I was at work. Did I have to lock her in? Thank God for those photos I'd taken, despite her initial protestation, close-up shots of us having sex – although my face was in none of them. Hers was though, a record of her sluttiness for me to keep forever, just for moments like this. I'd promised I'd burnt them, and I did – some of them, show of good intentions – but my favourite ones I'd kept. The same place where I kept everything: her passport, our marriage certificate, the documentation of the purchase of the cottage, her old banking account, even her birth certificate. Nothing was where she could find it.

I'd told her before, but without me Chloe was nothing. It was clear she needed reminding.

46

CHLOE

We'd barely got through the door, my bag skittering along the wood floor as Tom lobbed it. I turned to face him, expecting a barrage of abuse, but he pulled back his fist and punched me hard in the gut. Dropping to my knees, I gasped for air. One hand holding me up, the other clutching my stomach. Mouth open, I tried to suck in air, but everything had closed, there was no oxygen to be found.

'Get up,' Tom said, nudging me with his foot.

Beneath my knees was a letter, a postmark from London, my mum's handwriting. I tried to conceal it, but Tom snatched it up.

'What's this?' he said, looking at the postmark. 'Your mother I presume?' He slipped the envelope into his back pocket.

Finally, I took in a huge breath, coughing and spluttering but managing to get to my feet, still hunched over.

'Don't look so shocked. What exactly did you expect? Do you really think I'd let you run off with another man, or was it your mother you were running to?'

'I... I wasn't,' I stammered.

'Do you take me for a fool?' Tom screamed into my face.

'No,' I whimpered, stepping back from him. Unsure if he was about to launch another attack. He'd crossed a line. We'd been married for three years, yet he'd never hit me before, not until now. What came next?

Tom swiped the bag up from the floor and pushed me into the kitchen, upending it so the contents spilt out onto the table. The roll of cash I'd buried deep plopping on top last. Without a word, he picked it up and put it in his inside blazer pocket, my mobile too.

'Go and put this shit away.'

I gathered my clothes and toiletries in my arms and took them upstairs, trying not to let the tears fall. It would make him angrier if I cried. My stomach was swollen and bruised and it hurt to straighten my spine.

A knock at the door sounded from below as I put my toiletries back in our shared bathroom. I prayed it wasn't Anita but heard unfamiliar voices floating up from downstairs.

'Chloe, can you come down?' Tom's voice was as soft as silk as he called up the stairs, betraying the violence that had come before. Was he expecting someone? He hadn't said.

I quickly checked my reflection in the mirror, the timing was far from great. I was red-faced but otherwise looked all right. Smoothing down my hair, I tried to walk naturally down the stairs, freezing on the bottom step when I saw two police officers standing in the kitchen.

'Darling, the police have been called, perhaps our tiff was a little loud.' Tom acted bashful, but I could tell the female officer wasn't buying it.

'Could you come this way please, Mrs Beswick,' she said, leading me into the dining room, away from Tom.

It was my chance. I could beg them to take me away, tell them he wouldn't let me leave. This was my escape route. I could tell them everything.

'Are you okay, Mrs Beswick? We've had reports of a disturbance and stopped by to do a health check.'

I opened my mouth to speak, to let the words rush out an over-whelming wave of relief washing over me.

Tom's voice carried from the kitchen. 'It's silly really, we were arguing about some missing photographs, from our wedding day. Chloe got ever so upset as I think I threw them out by mistake.'

Tom's emphasis on the word photographs made my breath catch in my throat. His message was clear: keep quiet or those intimate pictures would find their way to my parents. I couldn't bear the thought of my father seeing those photos. It would be humiliating for us both. Not only that but my parents prided themselves on being upstanding citizens of their local community, volunteering at charity events and members of the council committee. If those photos got out, it wouldn't only be my reputation ruined, the family name would be tainted. It would break their hearts.

My chest in a vice, I couldn't speak as the reality of the situation came crashing in, barely noticing when the female officer placed a hand on my arm.

'Mrs Beswick? Were you arguing over photos?' she whispered.

Eventually, I nodded, unable to stop the tears falling.

'Did the argument become physical?'

I stared at her, imploring her silently to help, but how could she? I was trapped and Tom had leverage.

I shook my head. 'No,' I managed.

'Mrs Beswick, do you feel you are in any danger?' she pressed.

'No,' I repeated.

She grimaced as though she could see straight through me, waiting to see if I was going to change my mind.

I pressed my lips together.

'Okay, well, you can call us any time if you feel under threat. Just dial 999 and we'll be here in minutes.' The officer finally released my arm and reluctantly joined her partner in the kitchen.

I loitered in the doorway, trying not to meet Tom's eye.

'Just a spat, eh, darling? We'll get those pictures back, the photographer is bound to have them stored in the cloud or something,' Tom soothed as my throat closed up. 'Well, thank you for your time.' Tom showed the officers out and I moved to put the kettle on, almost on autopilot.

A minute later, he appeared behind me, his fingers wrapping around the back of my neck in a vice-like grip.

'Did you call them?' he hissed.

'No! How could I, you had my phone,' I said, reaching for a teaspoon out of the drawer.

Tom changed position, pressing his body against the drawer to close it and crushing my hand. I winced as he leaned against it, gulping in air as the pain ran up my arm.

'Tom, please,' I begged until he moved and I wrenched my hand out, pressing it against my chest, fingers numb.

He turned towards the sink, chucking in the envelope and blasting it with hot water until the ink smudged and the paper disintegrated. I'd never know what my mum had replied.

'I'm going back to work. You aren't to leave, understand?' He turned around and left, taking my keys with him.

Once I heard the turning of the lock on the front door, I slumped to the floor and sobbed.

47

SAVANNAH

I'd heard nothing from Tom all day yesterday. I'd expected a text at least after he'd turned up unannounced on Wednesday night, but he hadn't been in touch. I'd spent this morning at university, sitting in on two lectures and working on my research proposal on anti-discrimination. My phone hadn't made a sound, yet I was more irritated than disappointed.

I wasn't the sort of girl who waited for my phone to ring, but Tom hadn't booked in any more appointments. I'd been focusing on the end game when I'd suggested we were past that, trying to convey we were more than just client and escort, but I hadn't considered the revenue I'd be losing seeing Tom for free.

Chloe hadn't reached out either and I felt out of the loop. Had I pushed too far with Tom the last time I saw him? Maybe he felt backed into a corner and had run back to his wife with his tail between his legs?

I didn't have time to dwell on it as I had an early-afternoon appointment entertaining Ralph, the retired police detective. He was a gentle man in his mid-sixties who was sharply intelligent and softly spoken. Sadly, he'd lost his wife to cancer over ten years ago and I believed he came to me more for the company than the sex.

Once he was gone, I returned to my books, deciding to hang around and make the most of the peace. My neighbours back at my flat in Crawley had a raucous toddler who was prone to tantrums at least once an hour which normally involved launching his toys at the wall.

At around three, desperate to stretch my legs, I grabbed my handbag and headed out of the door. Jubilee Library – a massive modern building with three floors and a business centre – was just down the road and I wanted to search for some information for an upcoming case study on discrimination in education.

Yohan, my lecturer, had pulled me aside this morning to compliment me on the quality of the paper I'd submitted on the impact of European Union Law on UK equality law. He admitted he had high hopes for me achieving a first-class honours degree and it really gave me a boost. With the end in sight, I couldn't wait for the day to come where I'd be able to walk away from this life and start on the next chapter. One where I'd be measured by my professional capabilities and not just by my bra size.

48

TOM

I'd slept in the second bedroom last night, unable to bring myself to even look at Chloe. I'd worked late, going back into the office after the police left to catch up on what I'd missed, debating whether to drop in on Savannah, but she was another headache I couldn't contend with. Perhaps it would have been easier to maintain boundaries with her, but we'd crossed a line and couldn't go back. Right now I needed some space to work out how to move things forward.

Instead I'd driven my car home and left it on the drive without bothering to go inside or unlock the door for Chloe, and walked to the Rose & Crown. She could wait and think about what she'd done. I had to get a handle on things.

I'd propped up the grimy bar and ordered a Jack on the rocks, which became the first of many. Getting more drunk as the hours passed, hoping I'd bump into Ben and give him a good thrashing. He was younger than me, but given the chance, I'd give him a beating he wouldn't forget. Maybe then he wouldn't be so interested in my wife.

Fortunately for him, he didn't stop by and I'd stumbled home after the landlord called time, zigzagging down the path by the stream, nearly falling in at one point.

The alarm was like a siren this morning to my thumping head, but it was nothing a cold shower couldn't fix. Chloe hadn't emerged from the bedroom, still sulking. I couldn't see why when she was the one who'd caused the whole thing, thinking she could just run away. At least the police officer last night seemed to grasp it was just a squabble which had been blown out of proportion. They weren't interested in domestics and had far more important things to be doing which worked in my favour.

Clearly unrepentant, Chloe was not motivated to fix me breakfast so I grabbed a croissant and headed off to work, leaving her a long list of indoor tasks that would keep her idle hands busy. I'd locked the door anyway and with the cameras front and back, Chloe wouldn't be going anywhere without me knowing about it.

On a Friday, the office was quiet, a lot of people worked from home. However, I had some accounts to set up for invoicing and was happy to keep my door shut and get on with it. Harry stopped by after lunch, out of breath and sweating in the heat, his shirt glued to his back.

'I've just got wind Clearwater are coming in, Tom, so we need to make sure the accounts are watertight.'

Inwardly, I groaned at the amount of time it would take me to go through everything with a fine-tooth comb.

'Everything is sorted in terms of what you asked me to redistribute, but is there anything else I need to know about?' I asked, trying to keep the sarcasm from my tone. If Harry had holes in the company finances, I had to plug them, otherwise we were a sinking ship. Any potential buyer would run a mile.

'Hmmm, there might be. I need to check a few things and I'll get back to you on Monday.'

I struggled not to roll my eyes. Harry was a liability and it wouldn't surprise me if he was up to something behind the scenes, maybe not so much as tax fraud, but if he was overpaying his salary or putting money through the company, we were screwed. I could only hide so much. It was a problem I didn't need on top of everything else.

'I fancy a drink, how about you, Tom?' Harry said when I didn't reply.

'I'm up to my eyes in this,' I replied, pointing at my monitor, although I was considering dropping in on Savannah on my way home. I wouldn't be able to see her at the weekend and with the fertility appointment, laughable as it was, on Monday, I had to abstain from tomorrow.

'Don't work too hard, mate,' Harry said, wiping his brow with a handkerchief and heading out of the door.

I didn't want to dwell on what else Harry needed me to hide. What if I'd been employed as the fall guy? It did happen and I wasn't sure how much I could trust my new boss.

I stretched my back, cricking my neck from side to side. I'd been staring at the screen too long.

After a five-minute walk around my office, I sat back down and finished the last of the account set-ups, emailing all parties involved to let them know we were good to go. Then I logged off and headed for the door, so I could drive down to Brighton.

* * *

A tall blond man was leaving the building as I approached the entrance to Savannah's and I managed to catch the door before it clicked shut. I hadn't had a chance to take a good look at him – was he one of her clients? My stomach clenched at the thought of another man's hands on her, but I had to get over it. I'd decided to re-establish the boundaries. I was a paying customer, and despite the wobble with Chloe, I couldn't let myself see our relationship for anything more than it was, even if Savannah wanted it to be.

I tapped gently on the door, and a minute later, when there was no answer, I knocked louder, pressing my ear to the wood but hearing nothing through it. Savannah had to be out. I took out my phone to call her, but as I was about to dial, I heard the front entrance open behind me and there she was, her face crumpled into a frown as soon as she saw me waiting.

'I don't think you have an appointment,' she said coolly.

'I was hoping you'd be able to squeeze me in,' I said, giving her my most disarming smile and pulling a white envelope out of my blazer pocket.

She raised an eyebrow, her expression stern. Had I upset her? Did she feel like I'd rebuffed her advances?

'You better come in then,' she said, taking the envelope from me and putting it in her bag.

49

CHLOE

My stomach had felt tender as soon as I'd got out of bed, waiting until I was sure Tom had left.

I put on my running gear, determined not to let the events of yesterday spill over into today, and went downstairs. In the kitchen, I saw Tom had left me a list of things to do, with no apology for the day before despite him punching me in the stomach and crushing my hand in a drawer. There was no good morning, or message of any kind, just a list of random tasks: checking the expiration dates on all of the food in the cupboards and washing all the curtains. I gritted my teeth, I bet he'd had a good laugh to himself thinking things up to keep me occupied.

My thoughts strayed back to watching Mum's letter disintegrate in the sink and how it had crushed me. I desperately wanted to know what she'd written, but for now I had to be content with the fact she had replied. Maybe she'd turn up and rescue me because I couldn't see any way of escape now, even after the police had turned up so unexpectedly.

It had to have been one of our neighbours who'd called the police on us, but the cottages were detached and not at all on top of each other. Were we that loud? At least the address would be logged on the police system as having responded to a domestic callout. The female officer promised me they could be back in minutes if I needed them to. I clung to that thought.

My initial plan was to spend the day tearing the house apart, looking for Tom's hiding places. If I could find those Polaroids, he wouldn't have anything to hold over me. Although when I saw the chores he had conjured up for me, I feared I wouldn't have much time before he got home. Half of me wanted to ignore it, he could go to hell, but I was afraid of the consequences. I had a new fear for Tom and his cruelty. He'd never been violent before yesterday. Was it a slippery slope? More acceptable for him to do it again now?

When I tried the handle of the front door, wanting to get a run in first to clear my head, it didn't budge. Tom had locked it, which meant I wasn't allowed out. He'd forgotten I had the back door keys and could always go via the garden gate, but both entrances were covered by security cameras and Tom would see. It wasn't a risk I was willing to take. So now I was a prisoner in my own home?

I chewed on the inside of my cheek, blood boiling. I could always turn the cameras off, it was as easy as switching off the plug. I could say we'd lost power or the internet had gone down, but Tom would know I was lying and the thought of enraging him terrified me.

As I went back upstairs to have a shower, another idea struck me. Our bedroom window was at the side of the house, right by a trellis of climbing roses I'd planted when we'd first moved in. I leaned out of the window, tugging at the wooden lattice, would it take my weight? There was only one way to find out. Opening the window as wide as it would go, I swung a leg over the windowsill, attempting to stick my foot in one of the gaps and find a good hold. The rubber sole of my trainers helped, but I made the mistake of looking down. Damn it was high, and even if I got down, would I be able to climb back up and through the window again?

It was the only way out of the house without being caught by the cameras as once down on the ground I could squeeze through the gap in the hedge right onto the path that led to the stream. Defiance bubbling inside of me, I swung my other leg out and gingerly shimmied down the trellis, getting caught by a couple of thorns before I jumped the last few feet. A smile spread over my face, an up yours to Tom. I'd done it and quickly sprinted through the hedge and carried on down the stream.

It occurred to me a couple of miles in how freeing it was to not have my mobile. Tom must have locked it away or taken it to work. It was a good thing because he couldn't track me, unless he called the landline and found out I wasn't there. It made my muscles pump harder to run the five-kilo-metre route I usually took, and when I'd done the loop, being sure to approach the cottage from the side again and not the front, I stared up at the open bedroom window. It seemed so high from the ground, I wasn't sure I'd have the nerve to climb back in, but if I didn't, Tom would know I'd been out and that wasn't an option.

Steeling myself, I tried to scramble up the trellis quickly, catching my already sore hand on a rusted nail which had worked its way loose. In less than a minute, I'd reached the window ledge and hauled myself in, plopping to the carpet. Exhilarated, I remained where I was, catching my breath. I'd found an escape route and the next time I had any gardening chores on Tom's list, I'd make sure to prune the roses back as much as I could get away with. Reinforcing the fixings would be a good idea too. I was light, but the trellis was too and not meant to be climbed by anything other than plants.

It took an age to work through Tom's list, but by three o'clock I'd managed it. Dinner was a quick pasta dish that needed little prep, so I began my search, starting in Tom's office which was adjacent to the lounge. He wasn't particularly tidy and there were papers everywhere, but I knew my documents or the Polaroids wouldn't be anywhere obvious. The drawers to his desk were unlocked, but I found nothing of interest inside. I checked beneath his desk in case there was a key to a lockbox or something sellotaped, but the wood was bare.

I ran through his bookshelf, pulling out the collection of mostly non-fiction, trade journals and finance guides, flipping through their pages before replacing them. Nothing was hidden inside. I even looked under-neath the rug and behind the curtains. Perhaps they weren't in his office at all, although it seemed the most obvious choice. It was his space not mine and I rarely came inside other than to clean.

Leaning back in his chair, I stared around the room, the framed print on the wall catching my eye. I hated it. Tom had told me it was by a Swiss artist Henry Fuseli and was called 'The Nightmare'. A sleeping woman with a devil-like creature sat on her chest. He'd bought the large print after seeing it exhibited whilst travelling across America in his twenties. It didn't go with the room, but it was his space so I'd made no comment when he put it up. The image made me shudder, but curiosity got the better of me and I grabbed a corner of the frame, easing it back from the wall, gasping to discover a built-in safe.

It hadn't been there when we'd viewed the cottage so it was something Tom had to have had installed. He'd wanted to unpack in here and now I knew why. It was something I was never supposed to know about. Which meant whatever was inside it could be valuable to me.

50

SAVANNAH

Finding Tom outside the door of the Airbnb on my return from the library was a surprise, although it irritated me that he thought he could just turn up when he felt like it. I was about to lean in and give him a kiss when he waved a white envelope in my face. I got the hint, he was a paying customer, for today at least. It was one step forward and two steps back. Maintaining my smile, I unlocked the door and invited him inside.

Tom wanted his usual and I went through the motions, all the time my stomach churning with annoyance at my misstep the last time I'd seen him. I was right, I'd pushed him too far, too soon, but I didn't want to raise the subject if Tom didn't.

'You seem like you're elsewhere,' Tom said, stroking my back as I laid naked on my front.

He wasn't wrong – Chloe's other half of the money seemed unobtainable now. I'd had my chance and I'd blown it – the fact he'd turned up with money to pay for my time told me that. It was a professional arrangement, not a personal one, but I couldn't deny I'd become invested in Chloe's predicament.

'I'm fine,' I lied. 'How's things with you?' I wasn't interested in making conversation. I wanted Tom to leave, so I could drive home and wallow in self-pity, maybe have a glass or two of wine and watch Netflix but I had to keep up appearances and play nice.

'I don't know, my head's all over the place. Chloe is being a bitch. I can't stand to be around her.'

'Oh dear,' I said. Perhaps I still had a shot?

'She seems intent on wanting to leave, says she doesn't want anything, but as soon as she's gone, I bet she'll be demanding her half and I don't see why I have to give it to her.' Tom flexed his jaw, his tone venomous.

'Is she insured? Perhaps you need to find an alternative way out of your marriage,' I joked, chuckling darkly, but something sparked in Tom's eyes. His expression made a cold unease creep into my chest. 'I was kidding,' I added quickly, plastering on a smile as I propped myself up on my elbows.

'I know, but hey, it's not a bad idea.' He laughed, checking his watch. 'I better get going.'

Tom rolled off the bed and started getting dressed, leaving me with no idea as to what he was thinking. Had I just suggested he murder his wife? More worryingly, was he considering it?

51

TOM

I drove home without the radio on. Savannah had given me a lot to think about with her off-the-cuff comment. Could I kill Chloe and get away with it? Claim on the insurance, pay off the mortgage and be free to have Savannah all to myself? It would solve all my problems.

In reality, the idea was preposterous, but despite my intentions to stay a client, the pull to be with Savannah romantically remained. I fantasised about poisoning my wife, using something that wouldn't be discovered. How do you fake a natural cause of death, a heart attack for instance? She was young, fit and healthy, so any sudden death would be an anomaly automatically investigated. It couldn't be done, not without risking my liberty and I wasn't about to do that. The idea of the rest of my life inside a prison cell was abhorrent and not something I cared to ever experience.

I pulled into the cobblestone driveway of the picturesque cottage I loved. If she left me, I'd have to sell it, even though her name wasn't on the deeds, and I wasn't going to let that happen. Lawyers could work miracles nowadays. If footballers' wives could claim future earnings of their husbands in their divorces, Chloe wouldn't walk away with nothing. Plus, if Chloe wasn't with me, she wouldn't be with anyone. She was mine, until the bitter end, till death do us part. Her death at least.

Inside, dinner was already on the table. Chloe sat waiting patiently for me to arrive before she started eating.

'How was your day?' she asked, her voice light, friendly. Not what I was expecting.

'Fine, yours?'

'Busy... but good.'

I eyed the pasta dish, alarm bells ringing. Chloe was being too nice. Gone was the surly woman from yesterday. Had my thoughts on the drive home manifested themselves to her, was she thinking the only way out was to bump me off?

I started with the garlic bread, chewing slowly. The wine had already been opened and Chloe sipped from her glass.

'Let's put yesterday behind us,' she said before taking a mouthful of pasta.

Perhaps I'd overreacted – she was eating it, so it had to be fine.

Hunger broke my resolve and I joined her.

'I think that's a good idea,' I agreed, until I figured out another solution anyway.

I guessed she was just trying to be nice to avoid another day locked in, but either way we had a pleasant evening in front of the television. Her nose was stuck in a book and I watched a dramatisation of the Vietnam War.

'What are we doing this weekend?' Chloe asked as we headed upstairs to bed, knowing I had our weekends mapped out.

'Well, Mum has invited us around for a barbecue on Sunday as the weather is nice. Perhaps you could make a pavlova or something to bring and I'll pick up some meat tomorrow.' Plus I wanted to sort out the shares my parents had invested; they might have some more to put down and I'd be only too happy to take care of that. 'I'll probably have some work to do as well,' I added. The mammoth task of getting the accounts straight before Clearwater visited loomed large. Something in my gut told me Harry was hiding more than he was letting on. If Ian, my predecessor, had refused to do something he wasn't comfortable with, perhaps Harry thought he'd have more success with me. I stewed on the notion of what that meant for my future and what I'd have to do to stay employed at Middeon.

52

CHLOE

After multiple attempts to decipher the code to get into the safe yesterday, putting together random combinations after ticking off Tom's birthday, my birthday, our wedding anniversary and other memorable dates, I still hadn't managed to crack it. The only way forward was to play nice until I could work it out, sure I'd find what I was looking for inside.

I'd wait until next week when Tom was at work and go through his papers carefully, see if he had it written down anywhere. Another option was that it was stored on his phone, but he rarely let that out of his sight. Even though I couldn't get into the safe yet, it symbolised hope of my escape which was more than I'd had Thursday night.

As we enjoyed a late breakfast of toasted crumpets and fruit from Anita's basket on the patio in the sunshine, Tom received a call from Jim, who invited us over for lunch. I wasn't surprised at the abrupt invitation as Tom had given me my phone back when he'd got up. When I looked, on it were texts I'd missed from a worried Anita. Luckily, the messages, which he'd already opened, didn't give anything away. They were just enquiring if I was feeling better and asking me to get in touch. I guessed he knew now that Anita was like a dog with a bone; if he held on to my phone any longer, she'd soon come knocking if she couldn't get hold of me. As soon as Jim's name flashed up on Tom's screen, it was obvious Anita had engineered his call, desperate to make sure I was okay.

Tom picked one of my favourite dresses to wear – a white cotton broderie smock – and on the way there, we bought some flowers and a bottle of wine. I took in the splendour of their oak-beamed house with its manicured lawn and curved driveway, where a fountain stood in the middle. It was huge in comparison to our cottage. All that space for only two people seemed ludicrous, but Anita had confided when we'd had coffee that she'd never been able to have children, despite them trying for years in their youth.

Anita was out of the door to greet us before Tom had even turned the engine off, enveloping me into a hug as soon as I was out of the car.

'Are you okay?' she whispered into my ear before pulling away.

I nodded, my smile stretched thinly over my lips, squeezing her hand in a 'we'll talk later' gesture.

Turning to Tom who was shaking Jim's hand, she said, 'I've made a quiche and we have cold meats, cheese, bread and the Pimm's is already in the fridge.'

After a short tour of the downstairs, where Jim and Tom spoke about the house's history, I offered to help Anita bring the food out of the kitchen onto a large decking area in the garden where we were to eat.

'What happened?' Anita hissed as soon as we were alone.

'He found me. I didn't even make it onto the bus. The cameras,' I explained when Anita looked dumbfounded.

Her shoulders sagged and she blew the air out of her cheeks.

'He hit me – the first time ever – and then he locked me in,' I confided, to which her eyes bulged. 'I've found a way out, but he has a safe and I need to get into it. I'm sure he's hidden all my stuff in there – my passport, documents.' I didn't mention the Polaroids, embarrassed at the thought of Anita knowing about the pictures I'd let Tom take of me.

Anita's face had turned a pale grey and she opened her mouth to speak.

'Beer, Tom?' Jim called over his shoulder as he entered the kitchen, stopping to give his wife a kiss on the head.

I glanced at Anita and gathered up the salad and cutlery, taking it outside.

'It's beautiful, isn't it?' Tom said, already seated at the table, admiring the cultivated garden. His little green monster raising its head above the parapet.

'It is,' I agreed, not wanting to add it was way out of our league. Instead, I returned to the kitchen to bring more food through.

'He took my phone, but I got it back this morning,' I said in a hurried whisper once we were alone again.

Anita gasped. 'We've got to come up with a plan to get you out of there. I can't believe he hit you! I'm so sorry, darling.' She grimaced before handing me a basket of sliced baguettes and a butter dish. The men were calling to us from the garden.

With no more excuses to be alone, we headed outside to eat, chatting about Middeon, which seemed impossible for Tom and Jim not to bring up in each other's company. While they were deep in office politics, Anita leaned over to tell me about the grievance Marcus had received for sexual harassment and how Jill, his wife, wasn't coping well.

'He was suspended this week, while they investigated a claim that he allegedly touched the behind of one of his sales managers,' Anita whispered.

My eyes widened. 'Did he do it?'

'Probably,' Anita scoffed. 'Jill's in bits, but no one witnessed it, so it'll be business as usual come Monday, no doubt.'

Halfway through relaying her call from Jill, Anita was gently scolded by Jim for discussing such a sensitive topic but carried on regardless. It fascinated me how Anita and Jim were with each other, they seemed as solid as a rock and he let her rule the roost, happy to go along for the ride. Such a stark contrast to mine and Tom's relationship.

It was why I was so surprised when Anita confided in me later as we were loading the dishwasher that she believed Jim was sleeping with someone else.

'Who?' I asked, open-mouthed. The idea was ridiculous. Not Jim, he adored Anita, it was obvious beyond the way he looked at her. It was in his gentle touches and the way he let her rib him senseless even in company.

'I don't know... but I do know he's paying for it.'

53

SAVANNAH

On Saturday, feeling frustrated at what little progress I'd made with Tom, I ended up doing what I always did when I felt low, I went shopping. I pulled out my flexible friend after my only client for the weekend had left and hit the lanes in Brighton. My reasoning was that I was buying work clothes as I perused the rails of Ann Summers to see if anything jumped out at me. At least I could put it through as a business expense.

I treated myself to a frappé from the coffee shop and popped in a nail salon to see if they could fit me in for infills on my acrylics. A lady called Susie was free and she chatted openly about her mundane life of school runs, day trips and toddler parties as if we'd known each other for years. It sounded vile and despite me believing my proclivity to children would change with age, it hadn't yet. I was far too selfish. Plus, right now, my body was my income. No one would pay to have sex with me if I was the size of an elephant and bore the scars of childbirth – no one normal at least.

Although perhaps, the idea struck me as Susie wittered on, I could pretend I was pregnant. What if Tom thought I was having his baby? Too drastic? Probably, but it was something to ponder. As long as he wasn't considering murdering his wife to be with me. Despite Tom's weirdness when I joked about it, I was sure he didn't have it in him.

Chloe hadn't been in touch either – so much for her absolute necessity to be kept updated. Maybe she was buried under the patio already.

'What's so funny?' Susie asked as I let slip a morbid giggle, the thought ridiculous.

'Oh nothing, sorry. What were you saying?'

'I was just saying my husband never does the night feeds, yet I work as hard as he does,' Susie moaned.

'It's not fair, is it?' I offered, my mind already drifting back to last night.

After Tom had left and with no plans, I'd decided a Friday night would be the perfect opportunity to hit the bars in London, try to find some investment bankers to lure my way. I'd driven back to Crawley to get ready and jumped on the train. It had been a successful evening and I'd handed my card to two men who'd bought me drinks, whispering in my ear how much they'd like to 'get to know' me. That was how it normally worked, I'd leave them wanting more, flirting just enough to get their attention. Once I had them reeled in, I'd say I had to go and hand them my card. It clearly stated escort and it was up to them if they wanted to get in touch. Nine out of ten times, I'd receive a call within a week.

Tim was promising, an investment banker and not bad-looking, married of course, but weren't they all. Lewis owned a gallery in Covent Garden, slipping me his card within five minutes of introducing himself. He had to be raking it in to even afford the business space there. One guy, Eric, hit on me, but he gave me the creeps from the outset, something wasn't quite right about him and my intuition after years of being in the game was usually spot on. He did not get a business card.

'So what are your plans for the rest of the day?' Susie asked, jolting me back to the present me as she carefully painted on a seductive pink called 'Chase Me'.

'I've got an essay to write, so I'm going to stock up on some snacks and hit the books.'

'Oh, sounds fun.' Susie sniggered and I had to resist the urge to roll my eyes at her flippancy. It wasn't fun, but getting that degree was going to change my life, and as my mother had always told me, hard work paid off.

54

TOM

We stayed at Jim's until the late afternoon and ended up getting a taxi home because one beer turned into five and I was over the legal limit. Jim would not stop talking about his boat, *Nikita*, named after the Elton John song Anita loved. Sailing didn't interest me, although it wasn't as dull as golf. Jim offered to take us out for a sweep around Chichester harbour one weekend and I couldn't stop the thoughts popping into my head of Chloe accidentally falling overboard. I knew she couldn't swim, although Jim said they had life jackets onboard.

I'd watched Chloe and Anita with their heads together, gossiping like schoolgirls, but was unable to hear what they were saying. Jim had pulled his phone out and was showing me photos of *Nikita* moored at Chichester. To be fair, she was a beauty and I couldn't believe how much she had cost – almost fifty-five grand! By the time we left, I was green with envy at Jim's lifestyle, a house like theirs, a boat and holidays three times a year. What sort of salary was Harry paying him?

The sum of money that would be paid out for Chloe's life insurance was looking more attractive by the day.

'I've had a lovely day,' Chloe said, slipping her hand into mine, her palm damp.

'Yes, it's been very pleasant,' was all I could manage.

'It's a shame we can't, you know,' she gave me a coquettish smile and it took me a second to cotton on to what she was referring to. 'The fertility appointment,' she explained.

'Hmmm,' I agreed, although I still couldn't get my head around why Chloe was being so nice. Had the shock to the system from me losing my temper shaken her that much? While she seemed to be full of affection for me, I couldn't bring myself to reciprocate. I no longer trusted her motives. 'What were you and Anita talking about?' I asked.

'She thinks he might be sleeping with someone else.' Chloe studied my expression, but I couldn't hide my surprise at the statement.

'Jim? No,' I scoffed, stomach tightening.

'Not only that, she thinks he's paying for it!' Chloe couldn't keep the incredulity from her face.

I swallowed hard, Jim wasn't sleeping with Savannah too, was he?

'I can't imagine he would be, he's so devoted,' she added.

Which, of course, meant I wasn't. I peeled my hand away from Chloe's, the warmth from her palm churning my stomach. Either that or the idea of Jim and Savannah going at it.

'You'd never cheat on me, would you, Tom?' Chloe asked, her cheeks-tinged pink from the jug of Pimm's her and Anita had polished off.

'Of course not, don't be so ridiculous,' I scolded.

Was it cheating? Not all the time I was paying for it surely, I was merely procuring a service. Anyway, having sex with Chloe was like shagging an ironing board and half the time she was never present anyway. No doubt thinking about fucking the gardener instead of the man who provided for her.

I stared out the window, maybe drowning wouldn't be such a bad way to go.

55

CHLOE

I had to drag myself out of bed on Sunday. Faced with another day of acting like the good wife while in the midst of a hangover didn't spur me on. Added to that was a barbecue at the in-laws where I knew the conversation would revolve around conceiving an heir to the Beswick empire – it was going to be a slog of a day. Still, I got up and made eggs Benedict, Tom's favourite, while he enjoyed a lie-in with the coffee I delivered to his bedside, even though it galled me to do so.

Yesterday Anita had confided her fears about Jim to me, making me promise it wouldn't go any further, but I'd delighted in seeing Tom's reaction to the news. I knew he wouldn't mention it to anybody. Savannah was a secret it seemed nobody talked about but everybody shared. Had he, like me, put two and two together? Anita said she'd seen cash withdrawals of five hundred pounds on Jim's bank statement coincide with the days he was home late. Not just late but freshly washed and smelling of some woody scent. I knew instantly he was another of Savannah's clients. My heart broke for Anita, who, unlike me, had a happy marriage. The rug had been pulled out from under her feet but for me it was added ammo for my arsenal.

I imagined it drove Tom mad knowing half of the team were sleeping with his mistress-come-escort. Perhaps it would propel him forward to try to convince her out of the game. Either way, I was leaving, whether the plan with Savannah worked or not, but I had to get the Polaroids back first. Which was why I was being sweetness and light, as much as it made my stomach roll. I'd had to force myself to take Tom's hand in the car yesterday, thinking only of the end game.

I hadn't seen Savannah all week, with Tom locking me in. Although I was desperate to speak to her and find out what he'd been saying, if she was any closer to sealing the deal. Perhaps I'd ask her outright about Jim. I doubt she'd lie.

On top of that, the tests at the fertility clinic were looming and my period had not arrived early like I'd prayed it might. It was lovely having a couple of days' reprieve of Tom's pawing, although I knew his interest in me was waning. But if I didn't come up with a plan, my contraception would be exposed. It was like having a tower of cards precariously balanced, the tiniest movement would set them all tumbling. The doctor couldn't fit me in for a coil removal for two weeks, despite me begging over the phone yesterday while Tom took a shower, there were no available slots the receptionist had told me.

'I've ordered a taxi to take me to collect the car and I'm going to stop off at the supermarket and pick up some of those kebabs Mum likes. Can you whip up your lemon pavlova?' Tom instructed once he'd cleared his plate.

'Sure,' I replied, grateful he didn't ask me to go with him. My muscles yearned for a run, but any time alone had to be spent trying to get into the safe. Every spare second I'd had I'd tried to come up with combinations that would mean something to Tom, but with little success.

Putting the oven on to warm up, I ran to his office the moment the front door clicked shut. This time, I tried his mum's birthday, then his dad's. Neither worked. I tried the date we met in the bookshop and the date he started at Middeon, still the handle wouldn't budge. I punched at the metal door in frustration, wincing as my hand was still bruised from when Tom had trapped it in the drawer.

'Bastard,' I hissed.

I was running out of time, Tom would be back soon and I needed to start making the meringue.

* * *

When he returned, he narrowed his eyes at me as he entered the kitchen. 'I thought you'd be showered by now.'

'I had to go to the toilet, my stomach is a bit funny from yesterday,' I lied, smiling sweetly as I put the whisked meringue in the oven.

'Well, chop, chop,' he said without a hint of a smile.

The barbecue was as expected, although the sun refused to break through the clouds and it wasn't warm enough to sit in their garden. Stoically British, Tom's parents pressed on with the event anyway and I nibbled at a kebab, always nervous to put a foot out of place in front of Gwen and Charles.

'Eat something, darling, you're skin and bone,' Gwen reprimanded before adding a sausage to my plate.

Tom shot me a look and I ate it without complaint, despite the grease turning my stomach.

'So, Tom, your mum says you've looked at what we can do with our investments now our financial advisor has retired.' Charles bit into his beefburger, ketchup spurting out onto his shirt.

'There's a couple of good opportunities I've seen,' Tom said, clearing his throat. 'Obviously there's no guarantees, but they've proven to have good returns.'

I frowned at Tom. As far as I was aware, he knew nothing about stocks and shares or investing. What was he up to?

'Sounds positive. Charles and I were thinking about buying a place in Spain maybe, in a couple of years,' Gwen said.

'I'll have to set up an account obviously, but you'll get regular statements.' Tom rubbed his palms on his thighs and the penny dropped. Was he going to steal money from his parents? If so, what was it for? We were doing okay for money – he told me I didn't have to work, despite wanting to. It had to be for Savannah. Did she have a pimp or something who needed paying if she was going to be released from escorting? My mind whirred with questions as I listened to Tom spin off some big numbers I knew he'd pulled out of the sky.

I lowered my eyes to my plate and kept out of it, my attention snapping back when Gwen stood to collect the plates.

'Mum, sit down, Chloe will clean up, won't you, darling?' Tom patted my knee and I glared at him before getting to my feet, taking the plates out of Gwen's hands as fire blazed in my belly. What was I, the hired help?

'Oh, that's kind of you.' Gwen smiled at me, as though I'd been the one to offer.

I retreated to the kitchen. Gritting my teeth, I pulled on Gwen's rubber gloves and got started. At least it would get me away from them before the conversation turned to babies.

56

SAVANNAH

Tom must have been feeling amorous on Sunday night, a late-night text exchange turned into a video call where he asked to watch me pleasure myself. He told me he was only torturing himself because he was having tests today to check the ability of his swimmers. He assured me he wasn't the problem, it had to be Chloe. Typical of a man to assume he wasn't the problem, but I went along with it, even going so far as to joke I had perfect childbearing hips, should he wish to plant his seed.

However, video calls didn't equal payments and I was hoping one of the men I'd handed my card to on Friday night might call this week. Today was going to be a full day, I mused as I checked my calendar whilst lying in bed. I had to get to Brighton to see the councillor at eleven, already stocked up on baby powder for his visit, and then I had a lecture to attend at two. Tuesday would be quieter, Tom was the only client I had booked in, so at least I had time to prepare for a mock trial Yohan was putting on later in the week.

Stretching, I rolled onto my side, glad to see the morning sunshine peeking through the curtains. Yesterday was cloudy and dull and the weather always affected my mood.

As I got up to get into the shower, a call came through from an unknown number.

'Hello?'

'It's me,' Chloe said breathlessly. She had to be calling from the phone box as before.

'I was wondering when you'd call. Where have you been?'

'Can you meet me in Copthorne village in half an hour?' Chloe asked, ignoring my question.

I checked the time. 'It's not even half past eight,' I complained, padding to the bathroom.

'I don't have a lot of time.'

'Neither do I, I have a client at eleven.'

The line went quiet for a couple of seconds until Chloe spoke again.

'Is it Jim?' she asked.

'No,' I replied, 'it's not.' How did she know about Jim? Did Tom know too?

'I tried to leave him, he found me. He went crazy.'

'Are you okay?' I asked, hearing Chloe's voice waver as my chest tightened.

'Yes... can you come?'

'I'll be there,' I assured her, hanging up and returning to my wardrobe to get dressed. I'd have to forego my shower and squeeze one in before the councillor arrived.

57

CHLOE

When Tom went off to work on Monday, instructing me to be ready for collection at two, I decided not to waste my time alone on the safe. I was all out of ideas for codes and until inspiration struck I had to revert to my other plan, namely Savannah. Tom had relented and given me my keys back when I begged to be allowed out for a run, promising I wouldn't be long and he could track my location on my phone.

Jogging into the village, I used the payphone to call Savannah. I needed an update and it had been over a week since we'd spoken. I had to know whether she'd managed to reel Tom in. Although if he was still pushing for fertility tests, I guessed not.

The looming appointment had my stomach sinking with dread. I couldn't get out of it, my period hadn't materialised and even if I feigned sickness, Tom would make me go.

I paced the pavement, waiting for Savannah to arrive, when someone tapped me on the shoulder.

'Morning,' Ben said as I spun around, 'you're out early, off for a run?'

'Yes,' I said, momentarily flustered. 'Well, no, I'm meeting a friend.' Ben's tight white T-shirt and tanned neck made my insides somersault. He hadn't shaved, which made him look rugged and a little more mature. It suited him. 'Are you off to work?' I asked as the silence stretched out between us.

'Yep, just grabbing some water,' he pointed towards the newsagents I was loitering outside. 'It's going to be a warm one today.'

'Better than the rain.' I cringed at my attempt at conversation.

'Was everything okay the other day, you know, when I saw you?' Ben asked, no doubt referring to Tom pushing me into his car.

'Um, yes, we're fine. Tom had a bad day, that's all,' I said, annoyed at myself for making excuses for him.

'Does he have a lot of them?' Ben's eyes narrowed, only making him more attractive.

I squirmed, cheeks flushing. 'A few,' I admitted, surprised at my honesty, but something about Ben made me want to tell the truth.

'Have you ever thought about leaving?'

'It's not as easy as that,' I replied stiffly, twisting my wedding ring around my finger.

Ben looked away into the distance. Was he disappointed? Had he been the one to call the police that day? Would I have called them having witnessed a domestic in the street? Maybe not. How many of us would have turned a blind eye?

Ben held my gaze. Was he blushing?

'Well, you know where I am. Just call me, whenever.' He smiled and I fought the urge to grab his face and plant a kiss on his lips. Instead, I nodded, a little piece of myself dying inside. What I wouldn't give to dive into his arms and ask him to take me away from it all.

He gave a little wave and disappeared inside the shop, giving me the opportunity to make tracks.

'Are we getting coffee?' Savannah said, strolling towards me ten minutes later after I'd walked the length of the village, looking in all the shop windows.

'No, let's walk.' I directed her towards the stream, and we fell into step side by side. She'd arrived in leggings and a T-shirt, fresh-faced with her locks clipped up. Thankfully, she was wearing Converse trainers and not heels, so we looked like a pair out for their morning exercise.

'Do you run everywhere?' she asked, the corner of her mouth turned skywards.

'Run or walk. I can't drive, Tom won't let me,' I replied, noting Savannah's incredulous stare. 'Do you have a client called Jim?' I asked as the question popped into my head, 'Another director at Middeon?'

'I don't discuss details of my clients, Chloe.' Savannah pursed her lips.

That was a yes. How could Jim do that to Anita? How could Tom do it to me?

'I thought you called me here to talk about Tom? Tell me what's been going on,' she said, her tone clipped, already looking at her watch. I knew she was pushed for time.

'I tried to leave while he was at work, but he caught me in the village and locked me in the cottage.' I dodged a woman with a buggy and jogged to keep pace with Savannah, her long legs meant large strides.

'He locked you in!' she exclaimed, her brows furrowed. 'What happened?'

I rubbed at my hand although the pain had subsided.

'He punched me in the stomach and crushed my hand in a drawer.'

Savannah took a sharp intake of breath. She opened her mouth to speak, but I jumped in.

'Are you getting anywhere with him?' The desperation in my voice made me cringe.

'He's keen, but there's a couple of stumbling blocks.' Savannah tucked a stray hair behind her ear.

'What stumbling blocks?' I asked.

'He's worried you're going to take half of everything,' she began.

'That's rubbish,' I interrupted. 'I've told him he can keep it all!'

'He thinks you'll go, then you'll stake your claim. Also, I think having a family is holding him back too.'

I closed my eyes, frustration coursing through my veins.

'These things take time,' Savannah soothed.

'I don't have time,' I snapped, folding my arms across my chest. The plan had been stupid from the outset. What was I thinking? It was never going to work. Tom was only too happy to have his cake and eat it too. I was over two grand down, with the last of my escape fund taken by Tom, and for what? I was still no closer to getting away.

'How do you think he'd react if I fell pregnant?'

My eyes widened, but Savannah held out a hand to silence me before I spoke.

'I mean, not actually, but what if I pretended I had. Which way would it push him?' Savannah bit her lip as I considered the question.

There was no knowing what he'd do. Tom was unpredictable. But I doubted he saw Savannah as mother material, someone who sold her body for sex. It would hardly fit in with the Beswick ideal.

'I'm not sure. I know he's getting pressure from his parents to have a child, but you getting pregnant doesn't solve his problem, does it?' I scratched my arm, even talking about Tom made my flesh crawl.

'No, I guess not.'

'When are you seeing him next?'

'Tomorrow.'

What would happen once Tom found out I had a coil fitted? He might chuck me out then and there, but there was also the possibility he would hurt me again. The hair on the back of my neck stood on end, despite the warmth of the morning.

I stopped in front of Savannah, blocking her path along the narrow walkway. 'I really need this, Savannah,' I pleaded.

'I'm doing the best I can,' she replied, her voice softer. She rubbed at my arm and I melted into her, letting the tears fall. Tenderly, she placed her hands on my shoulders, easing me away from her. 'Come on, you've got to keep it together. We can do this, I know we can.'

I sniffed, wiping my nose on the back of my hand, the release of pent-up stress and anxiety leaving me wrung out. Was she being kind or just after the other half of her money? It made no difference, there was no way I'd be able to pay her the final amount. It was pie in the sky.

'And if anything like that happens again call the police.'

Savannah made it sound so easy; she had no idea of what it was like living with Tom, his impulsiveness, his mood swings. I was constantly on edge, waiting for him to lash out.

'I will,' I said, there was no point explaining to her how difficult a call to the police could be. The last time they'd come, I hadn't been brave enough to speak out, but how I wished I had.

58

TOM

Harry called an emergency meeting at ten o'clock, just me and him, spending hours going over the accounts.

'Look at them as though you were doing an audit, Tom – what do you see?'

But it was a mess, to say the least. All Harry was interested in was plugging the holes, and after a couple of hours, I saw there were many.

'I'll do my best, Harry, but I'm not a miracle worker.' I sighed, eyes going square as my stomach rumbled. I had to pick Chloe up at two if we were to get to Chichester for three, but I hadn't reminded Harry I had to leave early.

The man was dripping in sweat, his handkerchief saturated, barking at his assistant, Faye, to turn the air conditioning up. It was a warm day, but it was more likely Harry was sweating as he feared his erratic spending would be uncovered. If Clearwater understood the accounts as I did, they'd easily see how much Harry had spent on everything but technology. For transparency, any potential owners would have access to it all, so they could see what they were buying, and no one wanted a sinking ship.

'We have to do something. Clearwater are coming in and it's your job, Tom, to make sure the books are bulletproof. You're the finance director,' he snapped.

'I inherited this mess,' I shot back, unable to hold my tongue. It wasn't my fault he couldn't control himself. Surely Ian must have warned him he couldn't keep spending like he had.

Harry smacked his hand on the table in frustration. 'Dammit, Tom, I'll make it worth your while.'

With what, I wanted to ask. There were barely any spare funds left beyond salary payments.

As if reading my mind, he added, 'I have shares, I can transfer them to you.'

Although I wasn't sure how shares in a company close to going under was supposed to be an incentive.

'We need a project that didn't work, something we can say the funds were leaked into. A non-starter. Technology we can say we invested in that didn't get off the ground,' I said, the idea coming to me in a moment of clarity.

'That's it,' Harry declared, picking up the phone and instructing Faye to call Graham into the boardroom. 'Graham must have something we can use.'

Graham, the technology director, arrived five minutes later and we got to work. There was a non-volatile memory chip Middeon had been going to invest in, which saved data even after a device was turned off. However, after testing, it was deemed too slow to read and write data to warrant throwing money at it. We spent an hour creating a false accounting trail which would show thousands had been spent on the creation and branding of the chip before the technology was judged to be unsuccessful in later trials.

'You may well have saved my bacon, Tom,' Harry admitted once Graham was dismissed. He was red-faced but no longer sweating, although his shirt was stained with perspiration. I wrinkled my nose. Harry was disgusting and the thought of him being with Savannah made me want to vomit.

'I think,' I said cautiously, 'you may need to tighten the purse strings, Harry – at least for a while.'

'Yes, yes, you're right. Expensive tastes. Speaking of which, are you still seeing the lovely Savannah?'

I pursed my lips and Harry roared with laughter.

'I'll take that as a yes. Proceed with caution, my dear boy.' He slapped my back again, knocking the air out of my lungs, before declaring he was going for a late lunch.

As soon as he left, I shut down my laptop and hurried to my car.

* * *

Chloe was waiting on the driveway, clutching her bag and gnawing at her nails when I pulled in. I leaned over and opened the door for her.

'Nervous already?' I chuckled.

'Terrified,' she admitted with a weak smile.

'It'll be fine,' I said, patting her knee. I loved the purple sundress I'd chosen for her to wear, it always made her look radiant, although she still couldn't hold a candle to Savannah.

'Tom, what if we can't have children?' Chloe asked as I headed for the A27.

'Well, I'll have to find someone who can.' I laughed, only half joking.

59

CHLOE

The room was supposed to be warm and inviting, a pale shade of apple green, but the examination table in the centre with its large round overhead light made me break out in a sweat. Tom had been led away from the waiting room and given a cup for his sample. He was likely sitting in a windowless room with lots of dirty magazines living his best life whilst I'd been deposited in a torture chamber.

'Hi, Mrs Beswick, I'm Laura. I'm going to be looking after you today.' Laura entered ready with a warm smile designed to make me relax, but I could feel my blood pressure rising by the second. 'We're just going to take a little blood, then I'll pop you up on the table for a pelvic ultrasound.'

I swallowed hard, sweat pooling at the base of my spine.

'You've gone a little pale, Mrs Beswick. Would you like some water?'

'I'm frightened of needles,' I admitted, unable to control the tremor in my voice.

'I understand, it's fine, you don't have to look. Focus on the posters on the wall, over my shoulder,' Laura said as she gently laid my arm flat.

Saliva flooded my mouth and I closed my eyes, a veil between me and the 'sharp scratch' Laura said was going to come.

It was quick and relatively painless, although my head swam.

Laura pushed a plastic cup of water into my hand, urging me to sip.

'Take your time, I'll get everything ready.'

Laura moved around the room, prepping the machine, connecting the probe and opening a drawer to retrieve the gel used to make insertion easier.

My legs would not stop trembling and when Laura pulled the curtain around us, asking me to remove my underwear and lay on the table with my dress bunched around my hips, I fought the urge to be sick. I wanted to say no, to race from the room. I couldn't let her examine me, to see the contraception I'd had fitted, but as if on autopilot, I did as I was told, acutely aware Tom was only a few rooms away.

I had no excuses, my mind blank as I laid on the table. Laura likely thought I was rude, or extremely nervous, as her attempts at making polite conversation were ignored. I stared at the ceiling, tears rolling down the side of my face and into my hair.

'I promise I won't hurt you, Mrs Beswick, we're just going to have quick look at your uterus and ovaries, to check everything is functioning as normal. Now, if you can relax.'

I squeezed my eyes shut as the probe was inserted, cold and alien. Dragging in air as though I was about to dive underwater.

'Right, okay,' Laura seemed to say more to herself, 'we've got a good picture, off to a great start.'

I opened one eye and watched as Laura frowned at the monitor, clicking at the keyboard to enlarge the blurry grey image I didn't understand.

'Umm, Mrs Beswick...' she said, her voice coated in trepidation.

I pursed my lips together and focused on the ceiling, waiting for what I knew was to come. Feeling as though I was on the edge of a cliff with the rocks tumbling beneath my feet, unable to keep my balance.

'...You appear to have an IUD fitted.'

60

SAVANNAH

The councillor left and I sat abandoned, covered in a film of baby powder. It would be his last visit, he'd said. His wife had become suspicious and, ironically, despite his profession, it turned out he wasn't a good liar. She'd told him if he wanted to stay married his visits to me had to cease. It saddened me that I'd lost a reliable source of income because of something beyond my control.

Harry hadn't called to book another appointment either, which was unlike him. As I was already undressed, I sent him a flirty text and a photo of my breasts, wiped clean of powder, in the hope it would lure him, but had no immediate reply. My client list was dwindling, but I didn't want to venture into the world of webcams, although I'd heard it was lucrative. Anyone could record my footage and they'd have it forever. Once I had my degree, I wanted to disappear without a trace and leave this world behind.

My brief walk with Chloe had unsettled me. I couldn't believe Tom had hit her. Unable to correlate that side of him with the one who visited me, but Dad had been the same: one face at home and another projected to the outside world. Not one person in our local community had associated sweet, mild-mannered Aidan Kerry with my mum's bruises. I had no idea Tom was aggressive, but Chloe was scared, that much was obvious, and it meant the pressure was on me to get results. If I were her, I would have left months ago, but I saw how she'd been conditioned, just like Mum. It boiled my blood. As much as the money would come in handy, the real pull for me now was making sure Tom got what he deserved.

How had Chloe known about Jim too? I prided myself on being discreet and I couldn't imagine he'd let the cat out of the bag, even to Harry or Tom. Did his wife suspect, like the councillor's had? If so, maybe she'd confided in Chloe. Perhaps Jim had been careless covering his tracks, but without speaking to him, I could only speculate.

I had a hot shower and packed up my things, needing to make sure I got to my lecture on time. Pushing away thoughts of Tom, Chloe and Jim, aware my brain had to be ready to soak up all that Yohan was teaching me. I was going to get that first-class degree if it killed me. Now more than ever I wanted to leave this life behind and start again.

61

TOM

I didn't need any of the smutty reading material they provided, I only needed the photos of Savannah I'd saved to my phone – password-protected of course. Looking at those had me swiftly standing to attention – that and the thought of seeing her tomorrow. Remembering to get the sample in the cup was the tricky part. Half the thrill was the possibility of being walked in on, even though I'd locked the door.

Afterwards, I waited back in reception for Chloe, leaving my sample behind. I hadn't expected her to appear so quickly. She looked wretched, her entire neck mottled with red blotches covering her face. Had she been crying?

'Are you all right?' I asked.

'Can we leave?' she whispered, already heading for the door.

The receptionist had explained when we'd arrived that our tests results would be sent to us and discussed at our next appointment, two weeks away.

'What happened?' I asked as I opened the door for Chloe.

'It wasn't pleasant, that's all,' she said, her lips pressed so tightly together they were white.

We drove home in silence. I tried to initiate conversation, ask what she was cooking for dinner, but all I got were one-word answers. What had gone on in that examination room?

'I'm going to have a shower,' Chloe said as soon as we got in the door, ditching her handbag on the table.

My stomach rumbled in protest. It had been a long day and I hadn't eaten.

'After dinner,' I replied, but she shook her head and ran up the stairs, leaving me speechless.

Rage boiled in the pit of my stomach. She was my wife, how dare she disobey me. Taking the stairs two at a time, I reached the bathroom and turned the knob, but the door was locked, the shower already running.

Little bitch! If she was so desperate for a shower she could stay in there all night.

In the spare bedroom, I dragged the chair from the dressing table across the landing and propped it underneath the doorknob, leaving it in place as I went downstairs to cook some pasta. I had work to be getting on with anyway and I revelled in the fact Chloe was going to have a long and uncomfortable night on the tiled floor.

While the water boiled, I rooted through Chloe's handbag she'd left on the table, but there was nothing of interest inside, other than her phone. The app I used to keep tabs on what she searched for and who she messaged hadn't revealed anything. In fact, all that fuss over her not having one and she barely used the thing, other than her pointless chatter with Anita.

I dug into my simple pasta with pesto ten minutes later, chuckling to myself. Was Chloe hungry? She would be, come tomorrow. That would teach her. I left the saucepan and dirty bowl in the sink for her to wash up in the morning and retreated to my office. My task for tonight was to create an account at Hargreaves Lansdown to show my parents how I had invested the funds they were going to transfer over.

I had no idea what I'd do with it and would need to research, but at least the money would be in my account and not theirs. It didn't necessarily mean I was going to use it, but my future inheritance was safer with me than with them. What did they need a house in Spain for anyway? Dad was in his early seventies, Mum not so far behind, they could lose their marbles at any time. In fact, it might be a good idea to suggest getting a power of attorney in place.

Later as I downed a whisky, ignoring Chloe's hammering on the door which drifted from upstairs, I scrolled through the channels for something interesting to watch, turning the volume up to drown her out. *The Sixth Sense* was on, a classic, and it was at the bit the boy discovers the little girl was poisoned by her mother. Could I watch my wife fade away, become so ill she couldn't get out of bed? What if she was already pregnant – there was always a chance.

Chloe was quiet when I eventually made my way to bed. She didn't even make a sound as I moved past the door. I managed seven blissful hours sleep without her tossing and turning or stealing the covers. Refreshed when the alarm went off, I got up and removed the blockade from the bathroom door, twisting the handle, amused as to what state I would find Chloe inside.

She was sat on the toilet, her hand between her legs, wads of toilet paper in her palm.

'I'm bleeding,' she said, dark circles perpetuating her eyes as though she'd not slept a wink.

'Oh, you're not pregnant then,' I said as she stood and waddled past me towards our bedroom, returning a minute later with a tampon in hand.

She glared at me as she squeezed past, giving away what she was thinking despite her not uttering a word.

I rubbed my hands together, remembering last night's film and the bottle of antifreeze I had in the garage. 'How about I make you breakfast?'

62

CHLOE

The bastard locked me in the bathroom all night. My body ached from the hard tiles and I only had a hand towel for which to choose between a pillow or a blanket. I'd begun to bleed in the early hours, a few days early – likely, the probing yesterday had brought it on.

When Laura had pointed to the screen to show me the IUD device I already knew was there, I'd burst into tears.

'I can't have his baby, I'm leaving him,' I'd said, my nose streaming.

Laura's mouth had opened to speak and I'd gripped her arm, pressing my fingers into her flesh.

'He hurts me.'

'Is there someone I can call for you?' Laura's face had drained of colour, terrified of the crazy woman manhandling her.

'You can't tell him I have a coil fitted,' I'd begged, but Laura was already shaking her head, rising from her stool and backing away from me.

'I can't—'

'Please,' I'd begged, imploring her to understand.

She'd stared at the door, as if wishing someone would come in and take over, escort this mad woman from her examination room.

I'd sobbed, lifting my hands to my face.

A second later, Laura had straightened up and looked right at me.

'Okay, I can make the results appear inconclusive, but you'll have to come back to be tested again, so you need to get the IUD removed before you do.'

'Thank you, thank you.' My words had come out in a gush of air and I'd pushed myself off the bed, adjusted my dress and hurried to the door, desperate to escape, yet scared to look back in case Laura changed her mind.

I'd felt so dirty afterwards, I longed for a shower, but Tom had wanted his dinner first. For once, I'd ignored him, but, of course, he'd had the last laugh. I'd hammered on the door for around an hour on and off, exhausting myself once I'd learnt I was locked in. I knew Tom's punishments were never swift and eventually made my peace with being there all night.

My growling stomach and blazing anger had kept me awake, so when Tom presented me with a fry-up – I assumed his way of an apology – I loaded my fork up for each of my ten bites. Too hungry to sulk and too tired to argue.

'I'm off to work, so if you can clear up,' Tom said as he picked up his satchel. It wasn't a question.

The kitchen sink was a mess of pans from last night as well as this morning, but as soon as the front door clicked shut and the lock was turned, I crawled upstairs to bed.

63

CHLOE

I'd managed a few hours' sleep after Tom left for work, but stomach cramps woke me up and I spent an hour glued to the toilet. Had the eggs been past their best? Nausea swept over me in waves and when the doorbell rang mid-afternoon, I was tempted to ignore it. The idea it might be Ben or Anita propelled me downstairs, where I found I couldn't open the door at all. Tom had locked me in.

Hurrying out of the back door, the one Tom had forgotten I had a key for, I opened the side gate to find Anita on my doorstep with a takeaway coffee cup in each hand.

'Hi,' I whispered, waving her over and pressing a finger to my lips.

'Oh, hello,' she mouthed, coming towards me and looking me up and down. My dressing gown was grubby and in desperate need of a wash. I was sure my hair was sticking up in all directions too and after realising the state I was in, I was grateful Ben hadn't been my mystery visitor.

'This way,' I said quietly, hoping Tom wouldn't check the camera and see Anita had come around the side of the house. The one at the back was available to stream all the time, but there was no motion sensor. It was a shame the only way out of the back garden, fenced in with six-foot panels, was through the side gate onto the driveway, otherwise I would have escaped long ago.

'Are you okay?' Anita asked.

'I'm not feeling well,' I admitted, gesturing for Anita to go inside.

'I'm not going to lie, you look terrible,' Anita said once we were in the kitchen. She held a coffee out to me and I took it, the smell swirling up my nostrils making me feel instantly sick. I set it down on the table and lowered myself onto a seat. 'Is something wrong with the front door?'

'Tom locked it,' I said. There was no point in covering for him. Anita knew what was going on.

She raised her hands to the heavens. 'We need to get you out of here, Chloe. Have you managed to get into the safe?'

'Not yet and there's stuff in there I need before I go anywhere. I just need to work out the code.'

'Really?' Anita admonished. 'Is any of it worth hanging around for? What if he hurts you – I mean *really* hurts you?'

The thought had crossed my mind, but I'd dismissed it. As long as I played nice, did what I was told, it would be okay.

Yet you spent last night on the bathroom floor, my brain reminded me.

'He won't,' I assured her.

My only way out now was a midnight flit with the clothes on my back – that and the contents of the safe. Those Polaroids were the only thing stopping me from leaving with Anita. When I thought about the porn-like poses Tom had coerced me into and the possibility of my parents seeing them, not to mention the rest of the world, all of the air left my lungs. He'd lied about destroying them and I had to get them back.

'Have you found anything more out about Jim, who he's seeing?'

Anita shook her head, eyes glassy.

Indecision weighed heavily upon me. Should I tell Anita, my only friend in the world, that I knew who her husband was sleeping with? Savannah hadn't confirmed it but deep down I knew. She was probably on the Middeon payroll, which was why she was at the dinner. The quarterly raffle prize.

I had nothing to lose. I wasn't going to be paying Savannah the rest of the money, I had none to give. She didn't seem to be getting far with Tom; he was too invested in me falling pregnant. 'I think I know who it is. I think you know her too,' I said, watching confusion spread across Anita's features.

'Who?'

'Savannah, the redhead,' I said, waiting for the penny to drop.

Anita narrowed her eyes, her jaw clenching. 'Harry's woman?' she spat.

'Tom's sleeping with her too. I think they all are. She's an escort,' I said, my voice devoid of emotion.

'Oh my God,' Anita exclaimed, a sob bursting from her lips. 'That bitch! She's a prostitute?'

'There's a lot I need to tell you,' I said, before throwing caution to the wind and filling Anita in on everything.

64

SAVANNAH

'I want to ravish you,' Tom said as he planted his lips on mine the second he was through the door on Tuesday afternoon, tugging at the lace slip I'd put on. Biting down on my shoulder, he gripped my behind so hard, he had to have left marks.

'Easy tiger,' I said, trying to regain control, but Tom was het up. He'd tossed the white envelope onto the side, already pulling me to the bedroom for me to get down on my knees.

Foregoing the shower, Tom helped himself to the red cord, hastily tying my hands. He couldn't undo his flies fast enough, pushing himself into my mouth, head lolling back and groaning in delight. Grabbing at my hair, he thrust himself deeper and deeper until I gagged, coming quickly before I had a chance to complain. Although, women who were paid for sex were never allowed to complain. It didn't matter if we were treated rough or abused, we were made to believe it was all part of the service, to accept the unacceptable. It was why I always chose my clients so carefully – or I had, up until now. It seemed the more time I spent with Tom, the more his true colours shined through. I should have taken Chloe more seriously from the outset.

'Mind if I have a shower?' he asked when he'd finished, no inclination to pleasure me today.

'Mind untying me first?' I countered.

He frowned as though that wasn't the original plan but untied me anyway, kissing the top of my head in a belated show of affection. 'I won't be long.'

I opened one of the beers I'd bought, swilling the liquid around my mouth as though it was disinfectant. Tom seemed charged, energised, making me jump when he bounded out of the bathroom and leapt onto the bed.

'Come here,' he said, his hair slick from the shower, patting the duvet next to him. 'I'm going to do it.'

'Do what?' I asked, lying on my side facing him.

'I'm going to take you away from this. I've found a way. It'll take time, but it'll work and we'll be loaded and together.' Tom's eyes gleamed like diamonds catching in the sun.

'How?' I asked, fearing I already knew the answer to my question. After all, I'd unwittingly put the idea in his head.

'Don't worry about that, but in a few weeks I'll be free.'

Before I could respond, Tom grabbed my head, pulling me towards me, lips connecting, mashing his teeth against mine. It was the first time the hairs on the back of my neck stood up around him. The first time I'd felt a rush of fear with a client in years.

After a quick roll between the sheets, I wanted Tom to leave so I could go home, but he seemed in no hurry to get back to his wife. We had a cigarette and a beer on the terrace and I was relieved to be away from the bedroom. All the time, Tom grinned to himself, sat back in his chair with his legs propped up, his good mood radiating from him. It was unnerving and I drank the rest of my already opened beer quickly, remarking on how tired I was in the hope he'd get the hint and leave.

I'd got in too deep and wondered how I could extricate myself from the situation. I liked the money but not enough to get caught up in whatever Tom was scheming. Chloe had been right, Tom was dangerous and unpredictable and I needed to warn her because she wasn't safe with him in that house any longer.

65

TOM

Savannah hadn't been as receptive to my news as I'd hoped, but I was sure she'd get used to the idea. It was, after all, going to be a big change for her. I'd expected her to be pleased she'd only have to meet my needs and not those of countless others she entertained. I didn't dwell on that thought, imagining Savannah being plundered by anyone other than myself made me seethe.

When I got home, Chloe was still in her dressing gown, complaining she didn't feel well and she'd only got up to make my dinner. She sipped at a glass of water while I ate a sloppy meal of pie and mash. Food from the freezer, shoved in the oven at the last minute. I wanted to throw it back at her, but she looked pale and listless. A step in the right direction.

'Go back to bed, I'll bring you up a cup of tea in a bit,' I said, trying to sound concerned.

She pushed her chair back and clutched at her barren stomach as she moved gingerly towards the stairs, looking more like a geriatric than a woman in the prime of her life. Yes, it was time to move on. Savannah would become the second Mrs Beswick. We'd move away, selling the house I loved to go somewhere no one knew us. I'd get another job if I needed to, of course. Although once Chloe's life insurance came through neither of us would need to work. We'd be living the high life, footloose and fancy-free, until I knocked her up.

I had my doubts as to whether Savannah would be as pliable as Chloe had been. She'd take some work whipping into shape, that much was obvious, but if I was honest, I wasn't sure I wanted the fire which lurked beneath her cool exterior to be extinguished. Perhaps it was where I'd gone wrong with Chloe. She'd become robotic with no backbone.

When she was tucked into bed, my mother called, wanting an update on our fertility appointment. I told her we wouldn't know the results for at least a week, but whatever the problem was, I had no doubt we'd be able to overcome it. She seemed satisfied and there was no point worrying her with my marital problems. When Chloe passed away, she would be as shocked as everyone that our so-called happy existence had been shattered. It was doubtful she'd ever accept Savannah into the family no matter how long I left it before introducing them.

I boiled the kettle, making sure the tea was overly sweet, and delivered it to Chloe with two digestives.

'Make sure you drink it, you need to keep your fluid levels up,' I said to the unmoving lump under the duvet.

Chloe grunted an indistinguishable response and I left the musty room. She clearly hadn't showered all day, but she had managed to put last night's and this morning's cooking apparatus in the dishwasher at least. I'd leave it for her to unload in the morning.

Later, I retired to the second bedroom, which had a much more pleasant odour, slipping between clean sheets and staring up at the ceiling, a smile spreading across my face. Everything was going to work out, just as I'd planned.

66

SAVANNAH

'Finally,' I squealed on Wednesday morning, fresh out of the shower as I checked my phone. Harry had responded to my saucy photo – better late than never. He advised was having his last Middeon dinner this Saturday.

I screwed my face up at the message. Why was it the last one and why so soon? Normally they were quarterly, but it had only been a few weeks since he'd held court at Glenthorne Manor. It didn't make sense, but on the plus side next week I'd be sitting pretty on five grand for an evening's work.

Laying down on my bed wrapped in a soft chenille bathrobe, I called my mum, knowing she'd be back from her early-morning cleaning job at the local primary school. She never wanted to talk about herself, only ever wanting to hear how I was and how the studying was going. I could practically hear her beaming down the phone when I told her Yohan's comment about getting a first. She was forever telling me how proud she was of me, the first of the Kerry clan to go to university.

I found the distance between us had made us closer; living on top of each other in that tiny house had made our relationship strained. I sent her money every week, not so much as to raise suspicion, she thought I worked in an office part-time around lectures. It was nice to send her a bit of extra cash so she could treat herself or put it by in case Dad failed to pay the rent. She rarely mentioned him and I didn't ask, although she did tell me my brother Craig had a new job down at the harbour in Waterford and had got engaged to his long-time girlfriend Siobhan. By the time I got off the phone, I was feeling homesick, more for one of Mum's hugs than Ireland.

Getting up so as not to dwell, I stifled a yawn, perusing the rail of clothes in my wardrobe to take to the Airbnb. Jim was coming later on in the afternoon and I needed to pack a bag and bring some groceries with me. I'd not slept well, Tom's admission had weighed heavily on my conscience all night. He hadn't spelt it out, but I feared Chloe was in danger. I had to forewarn her, although I'd see her on Saturday at the dinner. Was there a way to contact her sooner? I didn't know where Tom lived and I had no phone number for her. Little I could do until she got in touch again.

There was the rest of her money at stake, the second part of our bargain, but I was more concerned for her safety. He was going to leave her for me, he'd said as much, but how he planned to do so wasn't as transparent. What if he harmed Chloe and I could have prevented it?

67

CHLOE

I dragged myself out of bed on Wednesday morning, stomach still tender and a raging headache flaring at my temples. My mouth was dry, tongue resembling sandpaper as though I'd been partying all night. Tom hadn't bothered to wake me, he hadn't even slept in our bed, yet he must have come in to get dressed and select my clothes for the day as they were hanging up on the wardrobe as normal. I'd woken up after he'd left for work, feeling the after-effects of a celebration I'd never attended.

After spilling everything to Anita yesterday, she'd listened patiently, horrified at what I'd got myself into with Savannah.

'There must be a better way,' she'd said, perplexed, despite my desperation.

I'd told her about the Polaroids, waited for her to judge me, but she hadn't. Anita had been kind, placing her leathery hand on mind as I'd bowed my head in shame.

'The photos don't matter, it'll all blow over, whether he leaks them or not,' Anita had tried to calm my mounting panic.

'He'll make it his mission to humiliate me if he still has them when I leave. I know him, he'll say he found them, that it's me with someone else, that he had nothing to do with it. His face isn't in any of the shots.'

'Isn't there something the police can do, aren't there laws on revenge porn now?'

I didn't know, but I wasn't going to leave it to chance.

Before Anita had left, I'd hastily written another letter to my mum, for her to post on my behalf. Giving her Anita's address to respond, as was her idea. That way, Anita could keep the response safe and it wouldn't end up in Tom's hands. In my second letter, I'd been honest, writing how unhappy we were and I was considering leaving, hoping Mum might extend help or at least offer a safe haven for me to shelter. Although it meant it could be a race against time to get the Polaroids as leaving without them didn't bear thinking about.

I showered away the grime which clung to my skin, washed my hair and dutifully put on the outfit Tom had laid out for me. Cut-off jeans and a sleeveless blouse – a hurried choice in my opinion, he hated women in denim. I couldn't stomach breakfast and headed straight for the office to attempt to crack Tom's code, having woken with a renewed purpose to get inside the safe.

Within an hour, I'd given up. Nothing I came up with worked and in the end I was making up random combinations out of sheer desperation. There was a slot for an override key, but Tom kept the key well hidden. Either that or he had it on him all the time. Yesterday, Anita had suggested drilling into it, but I wasn't a safe cracker and had no idea what I was doing. I needed someone good with their hands, a knowledge of power tools. Someone like Ben.

Ignoring the persistent stomach cramps, I took a slow walk along the stream into the village, glad to be out in the fresh air and grateful Tom hadn't locked me in. I longed to run, to feel the wind in my hair, but my energy was sapped. I could have called Ben, I had stashed his card in the bedpost, but wasn't going to risk using my mobile. It was as useful as a brick now I suspected Tom could see everything I did on it.

At the village pharmacy, I bought something to settle my stomach and stopped by the store to get some groceries to make Tom an easy stir-fry for dinner. I had little inclination to cook, but his obvious disdain for my offering last night meant I had to try. Whatever bug I'd picked up had left me listless.

My only motivation was to get into the safe. As a last resort, I tried the Rose and Crown after wandering the village high street, in case Ben could be found enjoying a beer in the sunshine, but he wasn't amongst the lunchtime rush.

With legs like lead, I made my way back home, thoughts straying to Anita and her devastation at learning Jim was sleeping with Savannah. How many marriages had that woman destroyed? Anger coursed through me. Anita wasn't just upset, she was furious – although she'd calmed down by the time she'd left. She hadn't said whether she was going to confront Jim, that was her business. Despite the bombshell I'd dropped, she was mainly concerned with my well-being, urging me to get out of my marriage as soon as possible.

But it was easier said than done.

68

TOM

'Another dinner, Harry. Really?' I said incredulously when Harry popped into my office. Clearwater had arrived yesterday and were dutifully doing their rounds. Finance had been the second department they'd visited and I'd spent the morning poring over the accounts with them, relieved to find they seemed satisfied with how the sheets had been balanced. Little did they realise just how much balancing had taken place!

It was in the afternoon when Harry, celebrating already, announced he was going to put on one last Middeon dinner this Saturday.

'Harry, we can't afford it!' I sighed.

'Sure we can, one last one will be fine.'

'Clearwater aren't even out the door yet?' Plus any potential buyer could access the books.

'Tom my boy, you worry too much,' he said, patting my shoulder as my brow furrowed. My lip curled in irritation, Harry was a patronising bastard.

'We've been lucky so far, but if anyone digs too deeply—'

'They won't,' he cut me off.

Harry shook off my concerns, clearly back to his old self. His only concern was to find a buyer for Middeon now. Mine was making sure I wasn't going to be anyone's scapegoat and I couldn't trust Harry as far as I could throw him, and given his sizeable bulk, it wouldn't be far. I knew nothing about the man other than his love for golf, booze and women.

'Fancy a round of golf on Friday, Tom, get some more practice in?' Harry said, as if reading my thoughts.

'Sure,' I agreed, trying to muster a smile. The stress of Clearwater's visit had culminated in a throbbing headache and I rubbed at my temples. I'd say anything to get him to leave.

'Excellent. Don't forget, bonuses are announced early July. Keep doing what you're doing and yours will be pretty much guaranteed.' Harry smirked, white spittle pooling at the corners of his mouth. I looked away in disgust.

Harry left the room, leaving a musky scent of stale sweat behind. I needed some air.

'Bella, I'm heading out for half an hour, hold any calls for me,' I said as I strode past.

'No problem, Tom,' she chimed back before resuming the incessant tapping on her keyboard.

Outside, the fresh breeze wrapped itself around me and my shoulders relaxed. So Harry was throwing one last dinner. How could he be so stupid. Not after I'd shown him on multiple occasions how in the shit Middeon would be if he didn't put the brakes on his lavish spending. The entertainment budget was down to zero. Perhaps a big deal had been signed I didn't know about, or another investment from Asia had him buoyant. Clearwater were in for the week and everyone at Middeon would be on edge until they left on Friday, including me.

69

SAVANNAH

'I think this will be the last time,' Jim said stiffly as he tied his Windsor knot. I lay on the bed, the sheet barely covering me. He looked ludicrous in his striped shirt, red tie and matching braces. Socks pulled high up to his calves and no trousers.

'You always say that,' I replied, smiling sweetly and watching him frown down at me, tiny grey hairs poking out from flared nostrils.

It was true, Jim had what shoppers call buyer's remorse. We had almost the same conversation every time he visited. Unlike my other clients, Jim felt the betrayal of his wife with every fibre of his being.

'I mean it this time.' His tone indicating it wasn't up for discussion.

Perhaps I was right and Anita was onto him – why else would Chloe have asked if Jim was one of my clients?

'Okay,' I said, sitting up and holding out my palms, placating him. Did he think I was going to beg him not to go? Despite my clients dropping like flies, there were always plenty more to be found.

Jim picked up his trousers, about to put them on until I spoke.

'How is Anita? I must remember to say hello on Saturday.'

The colour drained from his face.

I widened my eyes dramatically. It was churlish of me, but I couldn't help myself. 'Didn't Harry tell you, there's another dinner on Saturday. I'm so looking forward to seeing everyone,' I continued.

'You don't talk to my wife, you don't even speak her name.' Jim's eyes darkened and he took a step towards me, pointing his finger. I'd never seen even a hint of temper from Jim. He was always so placid.

'Why not?' I asked innocently. 'I'm sure we could be friends, she seems nice.' I pouted.

He glared at me, his face glowing crimson, thrusting on his trousers and shoving his shirt roughly into the waistband.

'This was a mistake. *You* are a mistake,' he snapped.

I swallowed the irritation down – who did he think he was. I drew my legs up until my knees pressed against my breasts.

'What's wrong with you? Does Anita know about us?'

Jim launched himself at me, his fingers wrapping around my throat before I had time to react. For a guy in his late fifties, he moved like the wind. Sweat glistened on his balding head and he gritted his teeth as he shook me back and forth. My head rolled like it was on a stick. I clawed at his fingers, terror replacing the air in my lungs.

'There is no us and you don't fucking talk to my wife, understand,' he spat before releasing me, shoving me backwards onto the mattress.

I coughed into the pillow, drawing in breath so fast, I saw stars.

Jim stalked out of the room and a few seconds later the front door slammed.

Too stunned to speak, I rubbed at my neck, pain radiating from the base down my spine. I'd underestimated Jim and his temper. The mere mention of Anita had infuriated him, driven him to a point I wasn't sure he was going to return from. I used to be so good at reading people, but the past week, first with Tom, now with Jim, had left me doubting myself.

There was no time to dwell on what Jim had done. How he'd crossed the line like others before him. I got dressed, a fire burning in the pit of my stomach. I had to get to the bank before it closed and make a deposit, not wanting to have large amounts of cash sitting around. Then I'd go home and spend my evening working out how I'd take them all down. I was going to blow up Middeon. It would be my last hurrah. Harry was no longer at my beck and call, Tom was a psycho and it was over with Jim. Screw them all. I wasn't something they could discard like a piece of rubbish. No one would be able to stop me opening my mouth and spilling their secrets. Telling all the wives what their husbands won besides the money in the raffle. I'd make sure I gave them a show they wouldn't forget.

70

CHLOE

Tom hardly spoke to me when he got home, mumbling something about auditors being in and having a stressful day at work. On the plus side, he didn't complain when I presented him with chicken stir-fry and noodles. A quick meal thrown together, I didn't have the energy for much else, consumed by disappointment I hadn't made any progress with the safe.

I ate little, my stomach still tender, although I was feeling better. Ten small mouthfuls under Tom's watchful gaze, but thankfully he didn't insist I clear my plate. His mood darkened still when I refused his offer to join him for a glass of wine as he watched television. I couldn't face the acidity of it. When he suggested a cup of tea instead, I declined that too, concerned the milk would curdle in my stomach. He never usually offered, perhaps he was feeling guilty for being so awful recently, although the damage was done. I was leaving, no matter how nice he pretended to be. It never lasted anyway.

On Thursday morning, I woke early and prepared breakfast for him, taking the opportunity whilst he was in the shower to raid his wallet and check the keys to see if any might fit the safe, but they were all too big. Tom was sullen, giving me one-word answers as I tried to make conversation. Eventually, I gave up. Perhaps he was close to leaving me for Savannah? I clung onto the hope I was right.

When he left, leaving me a list of half-arsed chores he'd come up with on the fly, I breathed a sigh of relief. I was alone again. The atmosphere in the house was oppressive when he was around. I flew through his list of tasks in record time, dusting, hoovering, cleaning the fridge and windows before lacing up my trainers and jogging to the village.

Anita had messaged mid-morning and we'd agreed to meet for lunch at the small brasserie. I'd checked with Tom if I could go and surprisingly, he'd said it was fine. I know he wanted me to get in with the wives, it was a social circle he approved of, as long as I maintained the façade of our happy marriage. Anita was already there when I arrived and I apologised for my gym wear.

'Oh, don't be silly, sit down. Are you feeling better?'

'I am,' I said, and I did, my stomach had settled overnight and I'd woken hungry to replenish the calories I'd missed. 'I'll have the tuna niçoise salad please,' I said to the waitress when she came to take our order.

'I'll have the same,' Anita said. 'Jim came home last night in the most awful mood,' she confided once we were alone.

'Tom too. He said something about auditors being in, so perhaps it's stressing them out. His outbursts are so unpredictable, I never know when he's going to lose it.'

'I'm so worried about you staying there, are you sure you won't leave?'

I shook my head. 'Not until I have the Polaroids.'

I told Anita how I'd had another unsuccessful attempt at getting into the safe and was considering asking Ben for help. If he managed to drill into it, I could leave immediately, no hanging around for Tom to discover what I'd done.

'The problem is the cameras. If Tom sees him come to the house, there'll be hell to pay.'

'Can't he jump over the back fence and through a window?'

'They are six foot! And anyway, how am I going to explain that to Ben?' I snorted, imagining the conversation. Ben would run a mile if he was in his right mind.

'Maybe he'll think his luck has changed.' Anita laughed, lightening the mood.

The waitress delivered our salads and we tucked in, washing them down with sparkling mineral water.

'I haven't let on I know about *her*.' Anita wrinkled her nose as though her words left a bad taste in her mouth.

'Are you going to?' I asked.

'I don't know, I'm still mulling over whether to confront him or not. I can't deny I'm devastated, but more than that, I'm so angry he could do that to me. My first husband was a cheating control freak, I never thought Jim would be the same.'

'Perhaps they are all cheating control freaks.'

'The thing is, I don't want her to ruin my marriage. We've been happy.' Anita sighed.

'I'm going to see if I can meet her this afternoon, I need to know what is going on with Tom,' I said, the decision coming to me spontaneously.

'It's funny isn't it, I want her out of the picture, whereas you want her very much in the picture. One woman, sleeping with both our husbands,' Anita mused as the waitress collected our plates.

'And countless others I'm guessing,' I replied.

Anita shuddered, shaking her head. 'The thought makes my skin crawl.'

Before I left the brasserie, I took a selfie with Anita and I sent it to Tom, showing I was where I'd said I'd be. If he thought I was spending the day with Anita, he wouldn't be concerned my phone was off. I'd say I ran out of battery if I needed to, my last location showing as being in the village.

'I need to call Savannah,' I said once we were outside, marching towards the phone box. Anita trailed a few paces behind, her bracelets jangling as she wrestled a Chap Stick out of her handbag.

'Why don't you just use your mobile?' she called after me.

'He'll check who I've called,' I shouted back over my shoulder.

Savannah answered the phone, sounding harassed. She was in the car, the noise from the traffic outside a backdrop to our call. 'I'm on my way to Brighton I've got a client meeting me there later, I can't get to you right now.'

Would I be able to get to Brighton and back without Tom knowing? If my phone was switched off and he thought I was with Anita, he wouldn't question my whereabouts, would he? It was about half an hour away, although I had no idea what time the trains ran. I spied Anita through the glass looking in the charity shop window and an idea struck me.

'What's the address? I'll meet you there.'

Savannah grumbled at first but reluctantly reeled off the address and I hung up, stepping out of the phone box and looking expectantly at Anita.

'Fancy going for a drive?'

71

SAVANNAH

'It's open,' I said to Chloe through the intercom as I pressed the buzzer.

I'd only arrived at the apartment fifteen minutes before, having spent the morning at university in an imitation courtroom trial. It was much more interesting than a lecture and really gave the students an opportunity to step into a real-world scenario. I'd planned to write up some notes when I got here as Ricardo was my only client this afternoon, but he wasn't coming until four. But then Chloe had called.

I pulled open the door, revealing Chloe dressed in running pants and a T-shirt. Her hair was clipped back from her face and her cheeks tinged pink.

'If you ran here, I would be impressed,' I said, stepping back to let her in.

'It's a bit far, even for me,' she said, hinting at a smile.

'Want a tea or coffee?' I offered.

'No thanks. This is nice,' she said, looking around the apartment.

'Thanks. I wish it was mine, but sadly not,' I replied, adding, 'How are you?'

'Okay, I guess. I won't stay long. I just wanted an update.' She chewed at her lip.

'Yeah, I was hoping you'd get in touch,' I said, feeling my pulse quicken.

Chloe's eyes lit up. 'Is he leaving?'

I sat down on the sofa, gesturing for her to join me. Perhaps what I had to say she'd need to be sitting down for. But she remained standing.

'Is he?' she asked again, already agitated and starting to pace.

'He is.'

'When?' Her tone was urgent.

'I don't know.'

'Well I'm not paying you until he's gone.' Chloe crossed her arms, narrowing her eyes at me. Attitude I'd never seen from her before – perhaps like me, she'd had enough of the bullshit.

Despite Chloe's abrupt visit and defiance, I was relieved to see she was all right. Perhaps Tom's cryptic words were nothing more than a fantasy and I'd blown the whole thing out of proportion, concocting murder plots and cover ups.

'Has he made plans?' Chloe was becoming increasingly frustrated by my silence, but what could I tell her. It wasn't as if he'd given me much to go on.

'No, he just said in a couple of weeks he'll be free to move on.' I debated how to tell her what I feared, even if it was outlandish. Forewarned was forearmed and she should know that Tom could be thinking of a way out of their marriage that didn't involve divorce – or that's what he'd implied. But now, in the cold light of day and with Chloe standing in front of me, I faltered. Surely I must have been mistaken; he couldn't really be considering the alternative. Internally, I argued with myself. I wanted to warn her, but what if Tom was talking rubbish and the whole thing blew up in my face?

'Why is it taking so long?' Chloe glared at me, frustration streaming from every pore.

'Because I'm not a fucking magician that's why!' I hissed back.

We scowled at each other, both of us jumping when a knock came from the door.

'Jesus, great timing!' I quipped, raising my eyes to the ceiling, but when the knock came again, followed by a voice we both recognised, Chloe's mouth hung open in a silent scream.

'Savannah, it's me, let me in.'

I gasped, locking eyes with Chloe, whose face had turned deathly pale.

Tom was outside in the communal hallway, a door standing between his mistress and his wife.

'Fuck,' I whispered, gesturing towards the patio doors. 'You'll have to climb over the glass into the car park, you can get around the front from there.'

I smoothed down my hair and placed my hand on the doorknob, but Chloe was rooted to the spot.

'Move. Now,' I hissed, and finally she did.

I waited until the door slid closed and Chloe was out of sight before plastering on a smile and opening the door.

'Surprise visit?'

Tom looked dishevelled, his top button undone, tie pulled away from his neck. His hair looked as though he'd been raking his fingers through it. Wrapping an arm around my waist, he pulled me in for a lingering kiss. 'I had to get out of the office, Harry is doing my head in. Sorry, do you have anyone here?' Tom looked over my shoulder into the apartment before adding, 'I thought I heard voices.'

'I was on the phone.' I tried to still the tremble in my hand, reaching for the nearest bottle on the worktop to pour us a drink. Vodka was what I'd grabbed, but Tom drank it anyway. I did too, needing to quiet the panic rising in my chest. If Tom discovered his wife here, he would be livid.

I glanced through the blinds onto the terrace outside. The door was ajar, but it looked like Chloe had gone.

'I brought money,' Tom said, handing me an envelope. 'I wanted to see you, if you're free. Work has been difficult. Sorry, I should have called first, but I just jumped in the car.'

I was the cure for a stressful day for many of my clients.

I wanted to hand Tom the money back, tell him I was no longer available and I didn't want to get any more involved in his marriage than I already was, but we were way past that. The attraction had dissipated, he was nothing more to me now than a cash machine.

'I have a short gap,' I said, draining my glass of the vodka while Tom took his blazer off.

72

TOM

I took her on the sofa, tearing off her clothes, too impatient to get to the bedroom. The release with my final thrust had me groaning in pleasure. She'd been quiet, a little more reserved than usual, but I'd been quick and maybe a little heavy-handed, going straight in without any warm-up, not even getting fully undressed. Usually, her show of enjoyment, fake or otherwise, made it all the more erotic. Going through the motions, as Chloe did, wasn't a crowd pleaser, but I was satisfied and the stress of the day had floated away in minutes.

I'd drawn out the rest of the bonus – all of Harry's money now gone. I didn't care whether Chloe asked where it had disappeared to. If she did, I might even tell her the truth. Tell her I'd blown it all on a high-class hooker I was intending to make my second wife.

When Savannah was mine, I'd leave her tied to the bed all day, knowing her mouth would be waiting to receive me when I was home from a hard day's work. The idea made my cock pulse, but I wasn't ready to perform again, not straight away.

'You're amazing,' I said, passing Savannah her underwear to put on.

'You get what you pay for,' she replied, her sarcasm not lost on me.

'You're right about that, but not for long.' I grinned.

'Oh, it will cost you,' she drawled, pulling her top back over her head.

'I'll have more money than you'll ever want, trust me.'

'And when are we embarking on this new life?' Savannah asked, reaching for a cigarette and lighting it.

'Soon. I need to take care of a few things first. It has to look like an accident.'

Her eyes narrowed. Had I said too much? Surely we were on the same page. Savannah had to know Chloe was the only obstacle and it wasn't as easy as divorcing her. She wouldn't be interested if I was a penniless divorcee.

Savannah looked away, blowing smoke out in a long plume. Her body language changed. Shoulders tensing, she bit her lip.

Eventually, she looked back at me. 'Jesus, Tom, I didn't think you were serious.'

'She'll take half of everything. I can't afford to buy her out. I'll have to sell the house. If I can collect her life insurance, we'll be set for life. You won't have to whore yourself.'

'Whore myself?' Savannah snapped, fire sparking in her eyes.

'Well, that's what you do, isn't it?' I raised my voice to match hers. 'And don't pretend you're not interested in the money,' I spat, wrenching up the zip of my trousers.

She threw me a hateful glare, shaking her head. 'You better leave, before I say something I'll regret.' Her whole body trembled with rage, neck mottled. Despite that, she looked stunning, red hair brushed over one shoulder. She took my breath away.

'You don't mean that,' I said, my voice softer.

'I absolutely do.' Her face was pinched.

'Fine, you'll come crawling back. Once you realise what's in it for you.'

I waited for her to answer, but she didn't, her gaze conveying a hatred I was sure she didn't wholeheartedly feel. What had I said? Was it the whoring herself comment? She could hardly defend that.

I snatched up my blazer, a ball of frustration growing in my stomach as I slammed the door on my way out. Women were hard work, too emotional. Savannah couldn't see sense – all I was doing was providing her with a solution to our problems. It wasn't like I was asking her to help me; she wasn't going to be complicit in any crime. There would be no offence committed, just a tragic accident but I needed to give it a little more thought.

I'd been a fool spiking Chloe's drinks with the antifreeze in the garage, heavily sugaring everything in the hope she wouldn't notice, but any death of a young, seemingly healthy woman would be investigated. It was the first thing I'd thought of after watching that film – a poison ready to hand. Most people owned antifreeze, but on reflection it had been stupid. A toxicology report would be requested in the event of an unusual death and those closest were always suspected.

No, it had to be an accident, one I couldn't be held accountable for. I'd have to go back to the drawing board. I'd hoped Savannah might have been a team player, offered a suggestion maybe, but I'd been let down again.

I jumped in the car, slamming the door harder than intended. Instead of going back to the office sated like I'd expected, I was wound like a tightly coiled spring. More stressed now than when I'd left. Once Clearwater were out of the way and the bloody last Middeon dinner, I'd focus my attention on getting Chloe out of the picture. Perhaps then Savannah would see sense, she might even have cause to be grateful. I was doing it for her after all.

73

CHLOE

I clamped my hand over my mouth to stop my whimpering. Unable to comprehend what I'd just heard.

In a panic, I hadn't made it over the glass panel of the terrace before Savannah let Tom inside. Cornered, and terrified I'd been spotted, I'd shrunk down behind a rattan chair closest to the door, limbs shaking. I hadn't been able to draw the heavy patio door closed in time, leaving a two-inch gap, and I could just about hear the voices inside. I held my breath, praying I couldn't be seen from my hiding place, my pulse smashing in my throat.

Sandwiched with my back against the glass and my knees touching the side of the chair, I bore my weight on one leg, ready to vault over the partition as soon as it was safe to do so. Breath ragged, I'd concentrated on what was happening inside, watching Tom take his blazer off before wrestling Savannah onto the sofa. Vomit had crawled up my throat as, unable to tear my eyes away, I'd watched as my husband had sex with another woman.

Whenever we were intimate, I sent my mind elsewhere. Any physical affection I'd had for Tom had disappeared once he'd shown his true self, mere months after we'd moved into the cottage. He mistook my lack of libido for indifference, but it was more than that. His touch now repulsed me.

I'd felt nothing but disgust as he thrust into Savannah again and again. It was over quickly.

They were sitting up now and the smell of cigarette smoke wafted through the crack. I blinked back tears unable to believe my ears as Tom mentioned my life insurance, knowing neither him nor Savannah had any idea I was listening. He wouldn't divorce me, no matter what terms I offered. My husband, the man I'd fallen head over heels for and come to hate, the one who'd controlled me for the past three years, intended to end my life.

The callous way he talked about it shook me to the core. Savannah looked appalled, although Tom insinuated she knew something. How could she sit across from me and look me in the face knowing what Tom was planning? What kind of monster was she? I thought she was on my side, that she was trying to help, but she was only after the money. Trying to rinse us both for her own financial gain. They deserved each other.

Anita was right, I had to leave. The Polaroids didn't matter. I'd never been properly afraid of Tom before, despite his recent violent outbursts. He could be cruel, but up until now I had no idea of the lengths he'd be willing to go, the lines he'd cross. I should never have got Savannah involved. She'd done what I'd asked, Tom was bewitched by her, but I'd set in motion a chain of events that had spiralled out of control. Once he'd made up his mind, he was a runaway train, nothing would get in his way.

When the front door slammed, Savannah put her head in her hands. At first I thought she was crying, but a minute later she stalked out of the room muttering to herself. Without waiting, I jumped over the glass and into the small flowerbed below. I wanted to confront Savannah and give her a piece of my mind, but I knew Anita was waiting and if Tom saw her, there would be questions. She'd parked around the corner and I'd promised I wouldn't be long.

Looking over my shoulder for Tom's car, I sprinted towards the residential street and found Anita waiting.

'Drive,' I said as I jumped in the passenger seat, startling Anita into action. I sank low into the leather, tears streaming down my face.

'What happened?' Anita asked, her face as white as a sheet as we pulled onto the main drag out of Brighton, but I couldn't answer her through my sobs.

Were the events of the past few minutes real? Had I just witnessed my husband admit intent to end my life? My insides were like ice, blood chilled to the bone. I'd leave tomorrow. There wasn't enough time today. I wouldn't be able to get home and pack, plan where I'd go or my route before Tom came home from work – if he went back there at all. I willed Anita to put her foot down. I had to get home before he did.

74

SAVANNAH

That piece of shit. Who the hell did Tom Beswick think he was? I was so close to blurting it out then and there. Enlighten him about the deal I'd made with Chloe to lure him away. All so she could escape her terrible marriage because she claimed he wouldn't let her go. It turned out she was right. He wouldn't, not alive anyway.

I'd had to bite my tongue, the urge to wipe the smug grin off his face prevalent, to tell him I'd been stringing him along all this time. I'd met men like Tom before, ones who thought they'd never lose. The way he spoke about Chloe, the way he'd just spoken about me, it was obvious he believed he was superior. Positioned high up on a pedestal he'd built for himself, and I was going to enjoy watching it crumble.

Tom's appearance minutes after Chloe's had freaked me out. It was too close for comfort and on reflection I should have turned Tom away at the door. What if he'd discovered his wife? Would he have hurt us both?

I hadn't had a chance to warn Chloe, and now I knew the threat was real I couldn't let him get away with harming her, especially if he was using me as some kind of motivation. I was going to cut my ties with the pair of them.

As I showered, scrubbing every inch Tom had touched, it occurred to me that Chloe could have been on the terrace the whole time? What if she'd seen or heard what Tom had said? I'd been so incensed by his comment, I'd forgotten to check if she was still there.

Wrapping myself in a towel, I ran back to the patio door, water dripping onto the floor, wrenching it open, but the terrace was empty. I pressed my acrylic nails into my palm, half-moon crescents left in the flesh, ruing the day I ever met Tom, or Harry – any of them.

I just had to get through my appointment with Ricardo and then I'd be catching a train out of Brighton for the dazzling lights of London. Lewis, the gallery owner I'd handed my card to last week, had called just after Chloe had, inviting me for dinner. He'd said he had a couple of events to attend and would love to have me on his arm. Terms could be discussed over our meal, but, if it wasn't too short notice, he wanted me to come to the gallery in Covent Garden before it closed so he could show me around. I wasn't sure whether he wanted a hostess or an escort, but either way it didn't matter. He was loaded and not bad-looking, it would be easy money.

Tonight would be a new direction for me and I intended to grasp it with both hands. I was done with Brighton and Crawley. It was time to move on. Who knew the people Lewis might introduce me to. The gallery or his social circle might be streaming with powerful high earners, maybe even someone who owned a legal practice. I never stopped hustling, it was ingrained in me. However, it was time to clean the slate and rebuild. Middeon was old news, I was going bigger.

75

TOM

I bypassed the office and headed straight home, sending Bella a text to let her know I'd log on from there. Work was chaotic with Clearwater on site, everyone was highly strung and Harry had barely been seen out of his office, he had to be laying low as whispers about why he was selling Middeon were doing the rounds.

Savannah had pissed me off, getting her knickers in a twist over an offhand comment about her whoring. Perhaps I could have used more appropriate terminology, but it wasn't as if I was lying. She sold her body for sex; you could sugar-coat it all you liked, but fact was fact. She'd come around. As soon as Chloe was out of the picture, she'd come crawling back. How could she not with what I was offering. A new life no longer at the mercy of men's perverted sexual whims. I was saving her from that, but she was too damn independent, something I was sure I'd be able to squash in time.

I pulled up on the driveway and let myself in, calling out Chloe's name, but the house was silent. It was clean, the chores I'd asked her to do had been dutifully completed, but my wife was nowhere to be seen. Frowning, I pulled up her location on my phone: last seen in the village over two hours ago. Where the hell was she? Then I remembered the selfie she'd sent, lunch with Anita. Those two were probably still gossiping in the brasserie, a couple of bottles of wine in. Although it irked me whenever Chloe wasn't around when I got home. A good wife would be there, waiting to take my jacket, a cup of tea or a glass of wine at the ready. I wasn't asking for much. I'd get to work training Savannah straight away, although I feared it would take longer given her wilfulness.

I logged on to my computer and checked my emails, placing a call to Chloe while I waited for them to download. It went straight to voicemail. She knew she was supposed to have the damn phone on all the time in case I needed her. My wife clearly needed reminding.

When my inbox refreshed, there was nothing which needed urgent attention, so I snatched up my keys ready to find Chloe, but before I reached the door, knocking came from the other side.

'Chloe?' a voice called from beyond the wood, a streak of blonde hair flashing past the diamond-shaped window.

I opened the door, expecting Anita, eyes widening at the sight of Shirley, Chloe's mother, on the doorstep.

'Oh, Tom, hello, I was hoping to see Chloe,' she said, a tightly stretched smile on her lips.

I hadn't seen her for a long time, perhaps over a year. Had she come because Chloe hadn't answered the letter she'd sent? The stupid woman had never liked me and had tried to stop us getting married. Shirley had said it was too soon, Chloe barely knew me, but I'd whisked her away and managed to convince her a whirlwind wedding was romantic. Putting her on the spot in the gorgeous Seychelles with everything all arranged, she agreed despite her mother's reservations.

'Chloe's not here, I'm afraid, she's at a spa day with her friend Anita, been raving about it for weeks.' I stepped out of the door and closed it behind me. I had no intention of inviting her inside. 'Sorry, Shirley, I'd invite you in, but I've got to rush back to work, there's a crisis with the auditors.' I awarded her my most disarming smile, but Shirley crossed her arms, frowning at me. She was one woman my charm wouldn't work on.

'Is everything all right between you two?' Shirley asked, unable to help sticking her nose into our business.

'Of course it is, everything's fine,' I replied, trying to hide my irritation. I carried on, unlocking my car and climbing in. 'I'm sorry for the wasted journey. She won't be back until late, but I'll get her to call you.' I started the engine, revving loudly.

'Tell her I'll come back tomorrow,' she shouted over the noise.

'Will do,' I said, reversing off the driveway and watching her disappear in my rear-view mirror.

What had Chloe told her mother that caused her to turn up unannounced? I gripped the steering wheel, the vein in my neck pulsating. Things were getting out of control and I didn't like it. Chloe wasn't where she was supposed to be and Shirley looked suspiciously like she didn't believe everything was rosy between me and her daughter. What lies had Chloe been feeding her? I believed entering Shirley's number with an incorrect digit into Chloe's phone would be enough to phase out their contact. Chloe had a different telephone number and Shirley didn't have it. I hadn't expected her to turn up. Unless Chloe asked her to come?

I had to tighten the reins, Chloe needed reminding who was in charge and what was expected of her. I eased my foot down on the accelerator and sped down the country lane towards the village.

76

CHLOE

The bar was sticky to touch and I wrinkled my nose, pushing my glass towards the bartender, signalling for another gin and tonic. It would be my fourth, but it had worked to numb the overwhelming feeling of despair which had washed over me on the drive back.

Anita hadn't wanted to let me out of the car at the village. When I'd finally calmed down, I'd told her what happened, how Tom had turned up unexpectedly and almost caught me at Savannah's. I'd described what I'd witnessed from the terrace but left out what Tom had said. I still couldn't process it and I knew she'd panic and refuse to take me home. I had to work it out in my own head, but I did tell her I was leaving for certain, regardless of the Polaroids, and she was relieved.

The Rose and Crown had been almost empty when I'd arrived. Although now it was filling up with workers finishing for the day. No one gave me a second glance, sat alone, propping up the bar and staring glassy-eyed at the line of spirits that adorned the wall.

I had no idea if Tom was at home or if he'd gone back to the office. I hadn't dared switch my phone on. I was still reeling from what had happened at Savannah's apartment. The adrenaline of potentially being discovered in my hiding place and having to listen to Tom talk about getting rid of me as though I meant nothing to him. My brain was fried, an overload of information and emotions I couldn't begin to process. When Anita drove away believing I was headed home, I'd slipped into the pub, necking my first drink in minutes and ordering another immediately after, using cash I'd taken from Tom's wallet this morning.

It was all I could do to block everything out. I didn't want to think or feel and gin made me blissfully indifferent. I didn't even care about Tom's wrath when I got home late.

'Chloe?' Ben appeared at my side. 'I thought that was you?'

'Hi!' I said, a little too excitedly, nearly falling off the stool.

Ben's hand reached out to steady me, catching my upper arm, his calloused hand rough on my skin. 'Woah, careful. How come you're sitting here drinking alone?'

'I've had a terrible day,' I said, 'but the gin helps.' I raised my glass in a toast and took a large sip.

'Okay.' Ben's eyes danced, unable to hide his amusement.

Without needing to order, the barman slid a pint over to him and he took up the stool beside me.

'For both of these,' he said, pushing a twenty-pound note across the bar and signalling to my drink too.

'Thank you. Have you just finished for the day?' I slurred.

'Yep, it's been a tough one, had to ground out tree roots and the machine stopped working. Needs a new part.'

I nodded, trying to focus on Ben's handsome face, although it was slightly blurred.

'Tell me about your terrible day.'

'My husband is sleeping with an escort and I found out he's going to try to kill me,' I giggled, the words sounding preposterous in my mouth.

Ben choked on his pint, coughing and eventually joining my laughter. 'Well, that doesn't sound like the best.'

I knew he thought I was joking, but I didn't care, I enjoyed looking at him. He even smelled great, a heady mix of sweat and cedar. I licked my lips as Ben watched my eyes wander down to the v of his neckline, clearly tickled by my drunkenness.

'I hate to be a party pooper, but perhaps you'd better make that your last drink. Your husband may well kill you if you return home in this state.'

Ben gulped his pint, a foamy moustache lingering on the top of his stubbly lip. I fought the urge to wipe it away with my thumb.

'Maybe,' I giggled, draining the rest of my glass in two mouthfuls.

I attempted to get off the stool, my trainer catching on the rung almost causing me to fall into Ben's lap, but I righted myself just in time.

'Do you want me to get you a coffee? Help you sober up a bit?'

'At yours?' I asked, a hand on my hip. I was terrible at flirting, plus I was in gym wear with barely any make-up on and what was left was likely smudged from crying.

'Well, I guess, we could. If you're sure?' Ben said, although he didn't look confident. Shouldn't I be the one to be cautious about going back to a strange man's place? Although Ben wasn't strange, I knew him, a little.

'Let's go,' I said, before I changed my mind.

77

TOM

I crawled along the village high street, which stretched only a hundred metres, searching for my wife. Unable to find her, I parked in a side street on a double yellow line and made my way to The Brook Brasserie, where I knew she'd met Anita. Through the window, most of the tables were filled, but I couldn't see Chloe's blonde bob anywhere. Maybe they'd gone back to Anita's house? Chloe would have checked with me first though, wouldn't she?

I looked up her location again, but it hadn't updated. Her phone had to be off. Was she with that gardener Ben? Was Anita covering for her? My temples throbbed as I locked and unlocked my jaw rhythmically, irritation mounting. Where was she?

I dialled her number, but the call went straight to voicemail as I'd suspected it would.

'Chloe. Where are you? Call me. Now,' I snapped. She was in big trouble. How dare she switch her phone off.

A loud cheer came from the beer garden of the Rose and Crown, all the tables outside full as punters enjoyed their post-work tipples in the glorious sunshine.

Looking left and right, I stalked across the road, sweat gathering at my brow. If she was in there, God help her. I'd drag the stupid bitch out by her hair if I had to.

Pulling open the door, I surveyed the bar. Inside the pub was almost empty. An old man in a flat cap with a sleeping collie beside him perused the newspaper, a half-drunk pint of bitter in his hand.

'You seen a woman in here, petite, blonde bob?' I said to the woman behind the bar.

'No, my lovely, but I've just come on shift. Can I get you something to drink?' She smiled, lipstick stained her teeth.

'No thanks,' I replied, trying to hide the sneer. The last time I'd been in here, I'd felt as though I needed a tetanus shot, but it was the only drinking establishment in this backward village.

As I turned to go, I bumped into a burly man in a dirty vest who practically shoulder-barged me out of the way despite the bar being empty.

'Watch it,' I growled, turning to leave.

'Hurry up, Wall Street is waiting.' He laughed, putting his empty pint glass on the bar, turning his back on me.

He was referring to my pinstriped suit and tie. I glowered at him, dirty cargo trousers, desert boots and stained vest. A builder, no doubt, obviously jealous of those in higher places. He wasn't worth ruining my suit over.

I stormed out of the pub vowing never to go back inside the dank excuse for a drinking venue.

Rage built inside me as I stalked up and down the row of shops, determined Chloe had to be here somewhere, but eventually I returned to the car only to find a parking ticket stuck on my windscreen.

'You'll pay for this,' I muttered, tearing it off and tossing it on the back seat.

78

CHLOE

Ben steered me into his small, terraced house overlooking the pub. The front door opened into the lounge and he directed me to the sofa in front of the television. It was reasonably tidy, bar a few cycling magazines and an empty crisp packet on the coffee table.

'How do you take your coffee?' he asked, cheeks reddening as he picked up the crisp packet and slipped it in his pocket.

'Milk, one sugar please,' I replied, a little disappointed we hadn't headed straight for the bedroom. The gin had made me brave and amplified the attraction to Ben tenfold. He was gorgeous, his sandy hair brushed back from his forehead, tiny woodchips sprinkled on top like confetti. Freckles dotted his nose and cheeks from hours spent in the sunshine and I briefly imagined where his tan ended. 'Actually, can I use your bathroom?' I asked, my bladder straining under all the gin I'd consumed.

'Sure. Top of the stairs,' he called through the door as the kettle boiled.

The cabinet above the sink was sparse – shower gel, shaving foam and a small bottle of cologne I couldn't resist the urge to spritz into the air. I flushed and washed my hands before staggering down the steep staircase, clinging to the handrail.

Ben was still in the kitchen and I joined him, leaning against the opposite counter whilst he finished the coffee.

'I'm sorry if I've cut short your evening.'

'I only ever stop in for one, that's the weekday rule,' he chuckled, turning to face me.

I stared at his dirty blue T-shirt, the wrinkles where it bunched together on his shoulders. He was too young for me, plus I was married, but both of those things seemed suddenly irrelevant.

'All the rules have gone out of the window today,' I mused, closing the gap between us with one step and pressing my lips against his.

For a second, Ben froze, his hands reaching up to my arms to guide me away, but my fingers found the back of his neck and pulled him in close, guiding his body into mine.

His kiss was soft, like I was made of glass, fragile and easy to break. I wanted to drink him in, consume him. My hands trailed down his back, slipping beneath his T-shirt reaching bare skin.

'Stop,' he said, easing me away from him.

'What? Is it me?'

'You're wasted,' he said gently, a half-formed smile on his lips.

'I'm not,' I protested indignantly.

'You are and if you weren't, you wouldn't have kissed me. You're married.'

'To a man who is paying another woman to have sex with him,' I retorted, stung at Ben's rejection.

He sighed, shaking his head. 'Well, he's a dickhead if he's doing that and you need to kick him out.'

I laughed at the suggestion. Ben had no idea what sort of man Tom was. He had all the power, he held all the cards.

'Was it you who called the police that day?' I asked.

'I didn't like the way he manhandled you into the car.' Ben looked sheepish, but I wanted to tell him how grateful I was. Tom might have done more than punch me in the stomach if the police hadn't shown up.

It was hopeless and Ben was right, I was drunk and I'd regret coming onto him when I'd sobered up. The humiliation of rejection would be enough, plus I couldn't drag him into mine and Tom's imploding marriage.

'I'm a hot mess.' My eyes were brimming with an onset of unexpected tears.

'You're hot, for sure.' He laughed, trying to lighten the mood. 'Sober, yes, definitely yes, but not today. Drink the bloody coffee before my I change my mind.' He pushed the cup into my hand. 'It'll be okay, you know,' he said as I took a sip, wiping away my tears with the back of my hand.

If only I could believe him.

79

SAVANNAH

Lewis's gallery in Covent Garden was stunning. A contemporary venue with whitewash walls that I was expecting to house a load of boring paintings with muted colours. However, I was pleasantly surprised. Nestled between a jewellers and a women's boutique, Lewis owned a turquoise blue premises that attracted the eye due to its bright colour. On display in the window were various canvases with a jungle theme. The centrepiece, a head of a tiger painted in yellow and orange, drew me in.

I rarely felt nervous in any setting, but butterflies flittered inside my chest as I pushed open the door, a loud clang of the bell overhead making me jump. There was one couple near the back who Lewis was talking animatedly to about an expressionist piece they were admiring. Looking over his shoulder, as if sensing my presence, he smiled before carrying on his conversation.

I spent a while moving around the space staring at the modern art adorning the walls until a dark forest cascaded in moonlight captivated me.

'I see you've found my favourite.'

I started, not realising Lewis had crept up behind me. He smelt so good, his aftershave reminiscent of crashing waves onto the shore.

'It's very dark, isn't it, I love it.'

'Me too. If it doesn't sell, I'm going to buy it.'

'How much is it?'

'Three grand.'

I blew air out of my cheeks, eyebrows almost reaching my hairline. 'Wow.'

'Yep, worth every penny though.' He pointed at the canvas. 'This guy was homeless once, kicked out by his parents because he refused to study medicine like his father. Amazing talent.'

I found Lewis's quirkiness endearing. He wore navy chinos with a white linen shirt, a pastel pink scarf wrapped around his neck. A feminine look, although he pulled it off. Not classically handsome, he did have piercing blue eyes and a curly brown mop of wild hair which he often ran his fingers through.

'Right.' Lewis clapped his hands. 'Let's shut up shop and go for something to eat. I'm ravenous.'

He locked up and we walked a few doors down to a tapas restaurant where he knew the owners and we were swiftly seated at a table in the back.

'I must say, Miss Savannah, you do look ravishing.'

'Why, thank you,' I replied, appreciating his manners although I knew better than anyone the masks people wore in company.

When the waitress appeared a minute later, Lewis ordered a bottle of Cabernet and multiple dishes for us to pick at and we made small talk until our food arrived. He told me how he'd acquired the gallery and been running it successfully for two years, then asked how I'd got into escorting and some of the places I'd accompanied clients to.

It had been a while since I'd had a high-flying client who wanted someone to attend functions with and I sensed he was scoping out my suitability.

Our food arrived and Lewis waited until we were alone, laying his napkin across his lap and helping himself to some tortilla. I followed his lead, selecting some squid, cutting it into small pieces. It was delicious.

'Right, shall we get down to business?'

'Of course,' I replied.

'I'm looking for someone I can call on to attend events, functions, occasionally assist with hosting exhibitions at the gallery. Basically I need a wife.'

I raised my glass to my lips, stifling my smile. 'And you haven't managed to find one?'

'Not one that holds my interest, no,' he said conspiratorially.

'Understood.'

'Let me speak plainly. You're stunning, Savannah, you speak eloquently and, from what I've seen, you have good table manners. I'm sure you'd be able to entertain even the dullest connoisseur.'

'I have an abundance of experience on that front.' I smiled, glowing at the compliment.

'How would a thousand an event suit you to start with? Expenses paid, of course.'

'And does that include...' I lifted my chin, waiting for Lewis to fill in the gap.

'Sex? No, my darling, I don't pay for sex.' He dabbed at his mouth with his napkin. 'I find it much more enjoyable if both parties are willing.'

'So you don't want to have sex with me?' I asked, for clarification, a little surprised.

'I didn't say that,' he winked, 'I said I don't pay for it.'

'I see.' I relaxed into my seat, amused at the turn of direction. Lewis was only interested in my being on his arm and he was going to pay me handsomely for it. 'How regular would these events be?'

'Weekly, sometimes more. I'd cover hotel expenses, clothing – I'm quite picky on outfits, so we'd have to go shopping – not that you don't look flawless,' Lewis said, gesturing to the emerald-green dress I'd put on before leaving Brighton. 'What do you say – we could have a trial run next week. I've been invited to an auction; I doubt I'll bid, but it would be good to show my face and do a little networking.'

'I'll book you in,' I said, smiling so hard my cheeks hurt.

80

TOM

I'd been home an hour when Chloe rolled in looking a mess. Her eyes were puffy, black mascara sat beneath her lashes, and from her gait, it was obvious she'd been drinking.

'Where have you been?'

'With Anita,' she said, barely even looking at me. No apology, no rush to get dinner started, no question of how my day had been. She'd forgotten her place.

I gripped her upper arm, digging my fingers into the tendons. 'Really? All this time?'

'Ow, you're hurting me.' She tried to free herself, but I held on tighter, burying my nose in her hair before shoving her away.

'You smell of cologne. Have you been with *him*?' I shouted, feeling the red mist descend.

'No!'

'Get upstairs, you disgusting little whore. Go and wash him off you.'

Without protest, she began climbing the stairs. I followed behind.

'Perhaps I should post some of those Polaroids through his door, or has he already seen your wares?' I spat, yanking her hair and watching her head snap back, her knuckles white on the banister, trying to maintain her balance.

Silently she climbed, not rising to the bait. One thing I couldn't stand was being ignored.

I pushed open the bathroom door and shoved her in. She moved towards the shower, sliding the door open.

'Oh no, you need a bath.' I grinned, reaching inside the cupboard beneath the sink and pulling out a bottle of bleach.

Her eyes widened as I put the plug in and ran both taps, water pooling at the base of the tub. I relished the look on her face as I unscrewed the safety cap and poured the contents of the quarter bottle into the running water – a shame it wasn't full. I wrinkled my nose, the strength singed the hairs in my nose.

'I'm not getting in there,' she said, crossing her arms, although her shaky tone didn't match her stance.

'Oh you are, my love. You need to be punished.'

'For what?' Chloe cried, tears welling in her eyes. 'I haven't done anything.'

'You haven't done anything? What about switching your phone off, not answering my calls. For rolling in late, drunk and smelling like a cheap tart.'

'You'd know all about that, wouldn't you,' she hissed, venom in her voice.

I pulled my hand back and slapped her across the face.

She clutched her cheek, eyes out on stalks.

My palm stung with a delicious pain I knew she was feeling too.

'Now take your clothes off.'

The water was still running – lukewarm, I guessed. I turned the cold tap off.

'The longer you take, the hotter the bath will be.'

Immediately, she removed her Lycra top and leggings, a sports bra and shorts beneath. The opposite of sexy. The opposite of Savannah. Did Chloe know about her? Realisation hit that I didn't care either way.

She stood in front of me naked, broken.

'Turn around.' I wanted to see if she had any trace of infidelity on her bare skin. The gardener had turned her head, it had been obvious the way she'd fawned all over him when he'd visited to prune the blossom tree. He couldn't have her. No one could, even if I didn't want her any more.

When Chloe finished her slow twirl, she faced me, cheek crimson.

I looked her up and down. 'You're revolting. No man would want to shag you.' I turned the hot tap off and leant in the doorway. 'Get in the fucking bath,' I instructed, watching as she obediently lowered herself into the tub. Bleach permeated the air, scratching at my throat. 'Now stay there until I tell you to get out.'

I left her and went downstairs to find the menu for the curry house. Chloe would be soaking away her sins for quite a while.

81

CHLOE

The bath was too hot and my skin felt on fire for the first few minutes until I acclimatised. Thankfully, the bleach had been diluted enough not to cause any serious damage, but the smell made me wretch. Too much gin and no food, I heaved into the water and considered standing so only my feet and ankles would in the bath but he'd be listening out for any movement. If he heard water sloshing he'd be up those stairs quicker than I could react.

My eyes burned with furious tears. Why was I so fucking weak? Why didn't I pack a bag and go?

Because you're scared. You're terrified of what he'll do.

Tom wouldn't let me leave. He'd changed since he'd met Savannah, he'd always been cruel, but lately he'd become prone to violence, like he could no longer control himself. Maybe I was finally seeing the real him. If Tom thought he was losing his hold on me, he wouldn't stand for it, and now I knew he wanted to kill me, I was petrified to do anything to push him over the edge.

I'd leave tomorrow as soon as he was out the door and on his way to work. I should have called Anita when I was at Ben's and got her to pick me up. It was stupid of me to come home. I resisted the urge to sink beneath the surface, to end it all before he could. But I wasn't about to let him win; he'd taken everything else from me, I wouldn't let him take my life as well.

My thoughts drifted to the future, how difficult it would be to recover myself again, to rebuild. Wherever I went I knew I'd have to hide. He'd come looking. Tom would never stop searching for me, that was something he'd promised. Yet again I berated myself for falling for him in the first place but I wouldn't let him tarnish all men for me.

Ben was kind and he'd been dragged into my mess. No wonder he'd rejected me. I'd been stupid to spray his aftershave in the bathroom, I should have known Tom would sniff it out. He never missed anything.

After a while, the water grew tepid and I shivered, my stomach growling at the smell of tikka masala wafting up from downstairs. I was hungry, but it was unlikely I'd get to eat anything.

I prayed Tom wouldn't leave me here all night like last time. It was ridiculous, I wasn't even locked in, the bathroom door left wide open, but I couldn't bring myself to move. If I put a foot out of the bath, it might send him over the edge. Wives were killed by their husbands every day, that was the harsh reality, and I didn't want to become another statistic.

I flinched when, eventually, footsteps climbed the stairs and Tom appeared in the doorway, his blue eyes cold and hollow.

'Get out and put on the red.'

* * *

'Your mother came by yesterday,' Tom said in a throwaway comment over breakfast, in between mouthfuls of porridge I'd dutifully made him. I'd have spat in it if he hadn't watched me like a hawk as I'd stirred the saucepan.

'She did?' My tone was all wrong, too hopeful, too desperate, and Tom sneered, enjoying my turmoil.

'Yes, well, you were out with *Anita*,' he said, quoting with his fingers, 'and I didn't want to disturb you.' Had he tried to call to let me know? I doubted it.

I bowed my head, wishing I'd not switched my phone off.

My heart soared. Mum had come to see me; she must have received my letter. Would she come back? I knew I couldn't ask, I didn't want Tom to see how desperate I was. She would help me escape, though.

'You better go and get dressed, we'll be leaving shortly,' Tom said, putting his plate in the sink. He couldn't even be bothered to put it in the dishwasher.

'We?' I asked, my chest suddenly tight.

'Yes, didn't I tell you? I'm dropping you off at my mother's on the way. She's dying to spend the day with you.'

82

SAVANNAH

I woke on Friday still elated at my meeting with Lewis. It was strange, as soon as sex was off the table, I'd relaxed and enjoyed his company. We'd moved on from the tapas restaurant to a cocktail bar, where he'd told me about the characters I'd be entertaining, from all sorts of backgrounds but with one thing in common: money.

He even went so far as to suggest my relocation to London if things went well, something I dismissed immediately. House prices were far too expensive, but he'd said there was the possibility of renting from him, heavily subsidised he'd added. It was as though I'd won the lottery. Lewis was my golden ticket. Working solely for him, if the income was enough, would mean I'd be able to move out of Crawley and I'd have no need for the rental in Brighton.

Handing him my card was the best decision I'd made in a long time. Just one last Middeon dinner to get through and then I'd be free. I still intended to go out with a bang of course. Harry and Jim would get what was coming to them when I outed the raffle secret, but what Tom had said yesterday had iced my veins. There was no time to waste, I had to find a way of tracking Chloe down. She needed to know what he was planning so she could protect herself. I'd tell her to run as far away from her husband as she could.

Tom had to live in or near Copthorne, where Chloe had asked me to meet her for coffee, so perhaps that was the best place to start. Maybe the locals would know where exactly they lived. It wasn't far to drive, maybe fifteen minutes or so. I had considered calling Ralph, the retired detective, but I knew he would turn me down if I asked him to get me an address, despite having the right connections. So it was up to me to find her.

How was I supposed to warn her without Tom knowing? What if he was at the house when I found it? Pulling on some clothes, determination to find Chloe spurred me on. She had to find out the truth.

83

TOM

I should have known, the moment I got the email. As soon as the meeting cancellation hit my inbox, Harry postponing our golf afternoon. Apparently something had come up. It didn't hit me what until a rapt knock came at the office door and Bella passed on a summons to meet with the Clearwater team.

It was nothing short of an interrogation, surrounded by three number crunchers, and having to explain a discrepancy discovered between the income and profits recorded. Money had gone missing and they wanted it accounted for. Plus I had to explain the exorbitant spending on the entertainments budget. I did the best I could, rattling off client dinners and the failed project, but they claimed the numbers didn't add up. Perhaps I hadn't been as thorough as I'd thought.

'I'm afraid these figures are most irregular. If it's not cleared up, we'll have to report our findings to the Financial Authority for them to investigate. We cannot possibly oversee a sale in good conscience until the missing money is accounted for.'

I tried to talk may way out of it, but my charm offensive was dismissed, so eventually I played dumb. I wasn't about to blow the whistle on Harry, who it seemed had been pocketing company money whenever he felt like it.

Our meeting ended and they left with nearly as many questions as they'd arrived with. Knowing we were likely to be flagged for potential fraudulent behaviour and I was powerless to stop it made my stomach churn.

Harry obviously hadn't come into the office because he was concerned he'd have too many questions to answer. Would we be reported for fraud? Nothing ever happened that fast, but as far as a potential sale went, we were a sinking ship. No buyer would pay the sort of price Harry was expecting when our books didn't balance and Clearwater wouldn't touch us if it looked like we were dodgy. Tomorrow I would see Harry – assuming the dinner was going ahead – and hand my notice in. If he thought I was going to be a scapegoat for his reckless decisions, he could think again. I had a contingency plan, one that involved my parents' money they wanted me to invest. I didn't want to use it unless I had to but it was good to know it was there.

After Clearwater left with tight lips and firm handshakes, I milled around the office, trying to resist the urge to pack my desk up. I messaged Savannah but had no reply. Chloe was in the good hands of my mother, who was taking her shopping, so if Shirley reappeared at the cottage, she wouldn't find her daughter there.

I told Bella I was heading out for a last-minute meeting around two and jumped in the car to Brighton. Savannah couldn't still be upset with me over that throwaway comment, could she? When I got there, I rapped on her door for ten minutes with no reply. Frustration at what was turning into a terrible day threatened to boil over and I almost got into a physical altercation at a red light as I was leaving to go back home.

Heading towards Copthorne where the gaps between the houses lengthened and the green spaces bloomed, I turned the radio on in the hope of finding a calming track. Not one woman in my life made it easy. All of them were a complete pain in the arse. I considered telling my mother to drop Chloe home early, but a few more hours would be punishment enough for her.

I'd suggested shopping for a new dress for the last Middeon dinner. Chloe was now as thin as a rake and I couldn't have her showing me up in an outfit that hung off her frail shoulders. Knowing how much my mother loved shopping, she'd be dragging Chloe around all day looking for the 'perfect' gown. Something that hopefully made her look demure and hid her sluttiness. Had she been whoring herself with that gardener yesterday? How else could she explain the aftershave she stank of? It was time for her to go. She was fast becoming uncontrollable and the stupid bitch couldn't even give me a child.

The only issue I could foresee in getting rid of Chloe was that if she was already sleeping with the gardener, it gave me a motive.

84

CHLOE

'Try the pink?' Gwen purred through the curtain.

I closed my eyes, pressing my palms flat against the plywood dressing room wall to ground myself. The pink monstrosity was similar to the one Gwyneth Paltrow had worn when she'd collected her Oscar and dissolved into a puddle of tears. It looked fabulous on her, but pale pink was not my colour. However, I had no energy to argue. It was the eighth dress I'd tried on – all of them had made my irritated skin prickle.

The bleach Tom had made me sit in hadn't burnt me, but it had left my skin red raw, dry and flaking in places. Gwen had suggested some eczema cream when she'd seen the state of my arms, choosing to ignore the pale green fingerprint-shaped indents Tom had left on my shoulders last night. He was rougher than he'd ever been. As soon as I got away from him, I'd never wear the colour red again.

'That's the one, so delicate. The spaghetti straps make it look like it's floating on you.' Gwen clapped her hands together in triumph when I came out of the cubicle. There was nothing she loved more than shopping and had driven us to Guildford, talking the entire time. Her voice razor sharp as she moaned about Charles's lack of enthusiasm to do anything since his retirement. I'd been spared her hypercritical eye although I did receive the Spanish inquisition on our fertility appointment.

I stared at my reflection. To be fair, the dress did look better on and it didn't highlight the circles under my eyes like the darker colours had.

'I think we have time for a facial, perhaps a body scrub would be advisable too – you want to glow in that dress, do you not, Chloe?'

I'd spent the whole day being spoken to like I was a child, but I didn't complain. It was easier to go along with it and swallow the bitterness flooding through me that I'd had to put off my escape for another day. I hadn't even known there was another Middeon dinner planned, but Tom buying me a dress for the occasion meant he had no design to get rid of me before the event. I had a reprieve, at least until Saturday night.

* * *

'Your skin a bit tender, honey?' the therapist said as she swathed my arms in the green tea-scented scrub, noting my wince.

'Too much sun.' I smiled through gritted teeth, her rubbing felt like a cheese grater to my skin. Another lie to add to the hundreds I'd made for Tom.

He'd taken my phone when I'd got up, the handset mysteriously disappearing from my bag. No doubt to root through it, but I hadn't been so stupid as to leave anything incriminating on it. I hadn't even messaged Anita back after she'd text to ask how I was. Tom had probably done it for me. It wouldn't be the first time he'd responded on my behalf, painting the picture we were blissfully happy together.

Eventually, the treatment moved on from the painful scrub and I was covered in a moisturising body butter so dense it felt like I was wearing an extra layer. The beautician must have brought out the most intense cream she had for my scaly skin. It did, however, calm my radiation-red glow to a soft sunset.

Gwen was waiting for me, make-up free and positively glowing, in the lounge area, sipping on a glass of chilled chardonnay. 'I've found this perfect shade of pink for your nails. I was passing the manicure table and there it was. Gabby will be along shortly to give you a quick manicure.'

'Gwen, I'm tired, you've worn me out,' I laughed, trying to inject saccharine into my tone, 'can we not head back now?'

'Goodness the youth of today, no stamina. If you are going to tempt Tom into making that baby, we need to ensure you look tip-top.'

I swallowed down the acid rising in my throat. Remembering last night and how he'd rolled over, his back to me once he was finished, like I was a discarded condom on an eighteen to thirties holiday. There had been no position he'd requested I sit in; my legs hadn't been elevated against the headboard. Of course he hadn't, there would be no conceiving of a child. He wasn't planning on making me a mother any more. He wasn't planning on me being around that long.

85

SAVANNAH

No one in any of the local shops recognised my description of Chloe and Tom – clearly they hadn't made many friends in the village. Likely because Chloe wasn't allowed out without her leash. Heaven forbid she made any friends that Tom didn't approve of. I thought I might be out of luck and it wasn't until I made my way to the pub that the lady at the bar gave me something.

'Is he tall, wears a suit?' She thought momentarily before continuing. 'Dark hair, bit on the grumpy side?'

I nodded, stifling a laugh. It was a perfect description.

'I heard the name Tom banded around yesterday, must be him. He almost got into a fight looking for his wife. It was around this time actually.' She peered at the clock behind her, a stringy cobweb led from the top of it to the ceiling light above her head.

'Any idea where they live?'

'I think they live along Chapel Lane, one of the cottages down there. One of my regulars did some work for them a while back. They usually keep themselves to themselves. Don't integrate, if you know what I mean.' The woman threw her head back and laughed. Her hair remained rigid despite her bouncing shoulders, I suspected due to the amount of hairspray she'd used.

I wasn't surprised by her comment: the pub was far too friendly and not chic enough for the likes of Tom Beswick, who would suit a Soho bar far better. I climbed back into the Audi, the petrol light flashing ominously as soon as I turned the key in the ignition. I'd have to fill the tank on the way home.

I set the satnav for Chapel Lane, which, when I got there, was a picturesque road that ran alongside a stream. It was idyllic, a lovely location to raise a family if you weren't a woman trying to escape a controlling marriage. Tom had isolated Chloe in the back end of nowhere.

When the bar lady told me the Beswicks lived in a cottage, I'd imagined a tiny home with a thatched roof and small dark windows, but the four along the lane were relatively modern. Grey slate and sash windows with cobblestone driveways.

Each had a car in the drive, except the third one. The absence of Tom's Range Rover paired with me not recognising any of the other cars made me believe I had the right one. I had a vague recollection I'd heard Chloe say she didn't drive.

I turned around and parked across the entrance to the driveway, scribbling a note to Chloe on an old receipt before coming to my senses. What was I going to do? Post it through the door for Tom to find. I stuffed it in the glove compartment and navigated the cobblestones in my wedges towards the front door. I rang the doorbell and waited, but no one answered.

Curiosity got the better of me. What sort of place did Tom have? Peeking through the windows, I saw a spotless front room, plumped cushions on a beige checked sofa and a large television sat on an antique-looking stand. I'd been expecting clean lines and chrome finishes and was surprised to find it looked homely. Chloe's feminine touch obvious.

There was a tall gate around the side, and after a quick look over my shoulder to see if anyone was watching, I unhooked the latch. The back garden was neatly trimmed with a bistro set for four on the patio, painted a duck egg blue. Pots adorned the rear entrance and I peered through the partly glazed back door. It was a farmhouse kitchen, in keeping with the cottage feel, again spotless, almost as though no one lived there.

My phone beeped and I pulled it out of my pocket, pulse quickening to find a message from Tom.

What the hell are you doing at my house?

A lump swelled in my throat and I retraced my steps back towards the gate, pushing through and hurrying back to my car.

Stay there, I'll be home in a minute.

The second message made my stomach sink.

Why hadn't I noticed the camera doorbell? They had motion sensors, didn't they? I hadn't even rung the bell.

I moved my car back, no longer blocking the driveway, pausing with the engine running. There was no point in leaving, Tom knew I'd been here. Was he returning early from work or was Chloe with him too? I had to think on my feet, come up with a reason as to why I'd arrived at his door. I stared out of the windscreen, drumming my fingers on the steering wheel as Tom's Range Rover turned into the lane and slowly approached.

86

TOM

'Why are you here?' I barked, after drawing level with Savannah's car and lowering my window.

'I had a call from Harry.' Savannah's eyes were wide, her usual porcelain skin glowing pink.

My brow creased. 'Told you, did he, how he's hung me out to dry?' I said bitterly.

'I was thinking, let's leave. Let's just go on Saturday, whilst the dinner is in full swing.'

My frown deepened. Was Savannah worried Harry was going to drag me down with him?

'I don't know, I need to think about it.'

'You own the house solely, right? You can sell it out from under her. It can all be done via solicitors, we don't have to be here.'

It made sense but what about the life insurance. There wasn't a lot of equity in the house. By the time I'd found somewhere else, the sales and legal fees would swallow up what profit I'd made.

As I was about to answer, my phone rang. I tapped at the screen on the dashboard, my mother's shrill tone flooding the speakers.

'Oh hello, darling, just to let you know we're on our way back. About ten minutes away. Are you at home? Be a love and put the kettle on, would you, I'm parched.'

'See you shortly,' I replied, ending the call. 'You have to go, Chloe will be back in a minute. I'll see you tomorrow.'

'What about—'

'I'll message you if I change my mind, but for now I'm not leaving,' I said firmly, annoyed I hadn't even had a chance to capitalise on Savannah's visit. I could have taken her inside for a fumble, but Chloe always managed to get in the way. At least Savannah was no longer angry with me. In fact, she seemed as keen as I did to start over.

True to her word, ten minutes later my mother arrived with Chloe in tow, laden with bags.

'We've bought a dress and shoes. Your wife will look spectacular,' she chimed, stepping past me into the hallway.

'Tea is in the kitchen,' I said, bearing my cheek for Chloe to brush her lips against as she followed behind. A show necessary for my mother.

Thankfully, she didn't stay long. Although all the while she did, she talked non-stop, wittering on about the shopping trip and spa treatments until my head pounded. When she eventually left, I breathed a sigh of relief.

'Go and put it on then.' I gestured to Chloe as she rubbed at her bare feet.

She obligingly headed upstairs with her bags and I headed into the office to boot up the computer. Had any emails come in about my meeting with Clearwater?

'What do you think?' Chloe said when she returned, as I was reading through the new emails, trying yet failing to inject some enthusiasm into her voice as she slowly twirled in the pink satin floor length gown.

'It's lovely,' I said, stiffly although I had absolutely no attraction for her any longer. 'You can get started on dinner.'

Her back was turned, her gaze locked onto the shelf of books.

'Chloe?' I said, irritation pouring from me. 'Did you hear me?'

'Sorry, yes. I'll get started.'

87

CHLOE

I couldn't believe I hadn't seen it before. All the time, the code for the safe had been sat right there, amongst his collection of books. What was worse I'd pulled it from the shelf, flicked through it to see if a slip of paper could be found inside. But the code wasn't on a slip of paper, the code had been in my hands, in the title of the book – *11/22/63* by Stephen King, the only fiction book I'd ever seen Tom read. Laying on the beach the day after our wedding in the Seychelles, he'd devoured it that week.

I itched to try the code, knowing in my gut I was right. But there would be no chance I'd get to the safe tonight, so instead I carefully stepped out of the dress and hung it up, putting my clothes back on before going back downstairs to cook dinner. At least if I was cooking, I knew Tom wouldn't be able to poison me. I wouldn't eat or drink anything he made me to be on the safe side. He could have been the reason I'd been so ill for a couple of days.

I'd half expected him to try to drown me in the bath last night. Although how would he explain the bleach to the police? Tom wasn't stupid, he'd make it look like an accident if he intended to claim on my life insurance and I had a feeling he'd be watching my every move like a hawk. I had to be on my guard and use the next opportunity to get away. There was the possibility I could leave in the middle of the night, but Tom was such a light sleeper and because we were quite remote, he always kept the doorbell camera alert on, so if anyone approached our door, it would chime. I could hardly climb out of the bedroom window without waking him either. I was trapped, for the next day or so at least.

'We've had a letter from the fertility clinic,' Tom said while I was at the stove, stirring the mushroom risotto.

My back stiffened as I heard him tear open the envelope.

'Oh really?' I replied, voice light as silk. I didn't dare turn around, knowing he'd see fear written across my features.

Tom cleared his throat and I heard paper rustle, imagined him flicking the page out with his wrist, then silence while he was reading.

'Bullshit,' he shouted a minute later, a crash making me jump.

I whipped my head around, heart in my mouth, the wooden spoon dripping in my hand. Tom had swept the table settings onto the floor in a fit of rage. My centrepiece, a gorgeous cream jug with the roses he'd sent, was smashed into pieces and lay in a puddle on the tiles. He paced the room, one hand on his hip, letter outstretched, reading it again.

'What is it?' I asked, although I was dreading the answer. Laura, the sonographer, must have come clean and recorded the actual results of my internal scan. He'd found out I had lied to him. I was sure Laura had taken pity on me, that she understood my plight. The spoon wobbled in my shaking hand as the blood drained from my face, making me momentarily light-headed.

'Fucking imbeciles,' he said, kicking out at a chair and sending it skidding across the kitchen.

Finally he looked at me, face thunderous.

'You,' he pointed, baring his teeth like a wild animal. 'Did you do any research for that place? Clearly they don't know what they are fucking talking about.' He tossed the letter onto the table and stormed out of the kitchen, muttering to himself.

I snatched up the letter, scanning it as fast as I could.

Mrs Beswick's blood test results showed normal hormone levels and ovarian function. However, results of Mrs Beswick's internal scan were inconclusive and we would suggest coming back for additional testing.

I blew air out through my cheeks, sending a silent prayer to Laura, and read on.

Mr Tom Beswick's results show only 9 million sperm per millilitre of semen, whereby the average is around 75 million sperm per millilitre. Therefore, we can conclude Mr Beswick as having a low sperm count which may contribute to his ability to conceive naturally.

A laugh bubbled up in my chest, making its way to my throat, but I clamped my lips together to keep it in. No wonder he was so outraged. He had never assumed *he* was the problem, it had to be me, which, of course, in part it was, due to my IUD. But perhaps we wouldn't have conceived anyway. Poor Tom, what a bruise to his fragile male ego and in writing too.

I giggled to myself, stirring the risotto. Perhaps I'd take it with me or frame it for him as a parting gift.

88

SAVANNAH

I drove away trying to calm my racing heartbeat, inhaling air in through my nose and out my mouth. I didn't know what possessed me to bring up Harry, I was clutching at straws, but Tom seemed to run with it and I was glad I didn't have to elaborate and get caught out in my lie.

There was no way I could get a message to Chloe, not before the Middeon dinner, which was why I'd suggested running away. At least Chloe would be safe, but Tom seemed rigid in his plan. He couldn't walk away from the money; greed had its claws in him. I'd tried, but I couldn't do any more now. I'd speak to Chloe tomorrow, warn her what he was planning, then I'd absolve myself from the whole damn situation with a clean conscience.

When I got home, a bouquet of flowers had been left outside my door, a spray of beautiful lilies. Inside, I tore the envelope from the cellophane and saw they were from Lewis. During our dinner he'd asked for my address to send some dress samples and I saw no reason not to give it.

Looking forward to having you onboard. L

I grinned, Lewis was a life raft in a stormy sea I was going to cling to. For once, my charm instead of my figure had been enough for him to see what I was worth. It was refreshing and not something I was used to. Men treated me like I was an object and it served me to let them. After tomorrow, there would be no more of that.

I looked around the flat, a space I rarely spent time in, but I no longer felt the love for. Now I saw it for what it was: a stepping stone to greater things. Within three months, I'd make myself so indispensable to Lewis he'd relocate me to London, where I'd start a new life in the city. Paving the way for opportunities locally at legal practices where I could apply for an entry-level role once I had my degree, positive I could fit in my dream job around the events Lewis wanted me to accompany him to. The world would be my oyster.

As I arranged the flowers in the only vase I owned, binning the wilting ones I'd had from Tom, a text came through from Harry, letting me know tomorrow was on and to be at Glenthorne Manor for six. There was no offer to send a car for me as he had done previously. Maybe the money had dried up. No matter, I'd drive and leave the car there, knowing I'd have a few glasses of champagne. Anything to get me through servicing the raffle winner.

Just one more time... well, twice including Harry, who always expected his first.

I perused my wardrobe, fingering the dresses, all of which I'd worn before. I had a royal-blue backless dress with a high neck in a gorgeous satin, one of my favourites. I'd wear it with a smoky eye and nude lip, hair up to expose the skin. I held it against my body and spun around, the fabric almost floating.

Tomorrow evening would be a spectacular event. The only decision I had to make was when I would tell the wives that Harry had included me in with the raffle, how many of their husbands I'd been paid to screw whilst they were getting drunk at the bar. I couldn't wait to blow the secret wide open and watch the Middeon empire crumble.

CHLOE

On Saturday morning, I slipped out of bed before Tom was awake. I'd had a terrible night's sleep, unable to relax in such close proximity. He'd been in a mood all evening, drinking glass after glass of whisky and eventually falling asleep in the armchair. I'd feared he'd want sex, in some tragic way to reclaim his masculinity, a show of his virile ability after what the letter from the clinic had disclosed. Thankfully, the whisky had worked its magic and he was snoring soundly.

I'd not wanted to risk getting caught in his office trying the safe, so had made my way to bed as quietly as I could. Tom had come up a couple of hours later and I'd lay rigid, fearing he was going to smother me with a pillow. I'd eventually fallen asleep once I was sure he'd passed out again. When I got up a few hours later, I was glad to escape the musty whisky stink of the room and hurried downstairs to Tom's office. A cup of tea could wait, I had to capitalise on my husband sleeping in.

Steadying myself, I lifted down the morbid framed print of 'The Nightmare' and pressed the digits, replicating the set of numbers that made up the title of the Stephen King book. Eleven, then twenty-two followed by sixty-three. When I pressed the final three, there was a small popping sound and the door sprang open. I gasped, unable to hide my delight, reaching inside for the stack of papers, which I spread out on the floor in front of the safe.

Craning my neck, I listened for the creak of floorboards above, any sign Tom was awake, but all I could hear were the birds' morning song outside in the trees. I riffled through document after document, stifling a squeal when I found my birth certificate and passport in between pension statements. I carried on. My next find was our wedding certificate and then finally a white A5 envelope that contained the Polaroids. I flicked through them, my teeth gritted at the pornographic pictures Tom had taken. Shoving them back in the envelope, my body instantly felt as light as a feather. Without those, Tom would have no way to blackmail me.

A squeak came from above and I dropped the envelope like it was on fire. The bedroom door whined as it was opened and heavy footsteps padded to the bathroom. I held my breath, listening to the sound of Tom's urine hitting the bowl before rushing to gather all the documents together and shoving them back into the safe. It didn't make sense to get them out now. If I stashed them somewhere and Tom found them, it would all have been for nothing. I had the code, I now had to bide my time and retrieve everything before I left.

Palms sweaty, I closed the door, cringing as the safe beeped, announcing it was locked just as I heard the flush of the toilet and Tom's steps descending the stairs. Repositioning the gruesome print I hated and checking it was straight, I dashed out of the room.

'Coffee?' I said, meeting him in the hallway.

'What were you doing in the office?' Tom had pillow lines creased into his face, hair sticking up on one side like he hadn't changed position all night. I could smell him as he reached me, alcohol seeping from his pores.

'I was just tidying.'

The look on his face told me it was a lame excuse as soon as the words left my mouth, but I had nothing else.

'Snooping more like. Stay out of there,' he snapped, pushing past me and into the kitchen.

I followed him in and he headed straight for the drawer where the paracetamol was, popping a couple out of the blister packet.

'Shall I make you a tea, or a coffee? A fry-up maybe?' I stood on tiptoes, hearing my voice rising in pitch. I was pathetic.

'Coffee and a bacon sandwich,' he grumbled, filling a glass with water and swallowing the tablets. There was no warmth in his tone, and the look he gave me was one of disdain.

I bit my lip and busied myself making his coffee and setting the bacon to fry. I was so close to being free and getting out of my marriage, I could hardly contain my excitement. Knowing Tom wouldn't have any hold over me without the photos was what would get me through the day, and the evening. The dreadful Middeon dinner loomed large, but at least I'd see Anita.

Tom had given my phone back to me and there was a flurry of messages from her yesterday, light in tone but checking in. Tom had responded for me, stating everything was fine and she'd see me at the dinner. In response, she'd sent another, saying she was looking forward to seeing me and if I had time, could I whip something up for the bake sale she was running on Sunday.

It meant she knew I hadn't managed to escape and I'm sure she had many questions, but I was grateful she knew our exchanges were being monitored. I responded obligingly, leaving my phone on the table so Tom could see. The last thing I wanted to do was anger him in any way, to force his hand, especially knowing what I now knew. I had to be smart, remain on his good side and play it safe if I wanted to get out alive.

90

TOM

Chloe was annoying, like a puppy I wanted to kick for getting under my feet. I hadn't shared with her what was going on at Middeon. The filthy slut had no right to know anything about my life any more. Soon she'd be six feet under and her dreams of running off with the gardener would be no more. She buzzed around, trying to act like the wife she'd once been, but I had little patience – in fact, I could barely be in the same room.

My thoughts were consumed by Harry's betrayal on top of her own. How could he do that to me? Leave me to deal with Clearwater when I had no answers for them. I'd left multiple messages on his phone yesterday afternoon, my temper getting the better of me. At least tonight he'd have to face the music. Perhaps Savannah's suggestion would be the right course of action, but I wasn't about to run away now. Not before giving Harry a piece of my mind and collecting my reward for being married to that frigid bitch. I'd earned it. Patience was a virtue, but unfortunately one I didn't possess.

As soon as I'd eaten breakfast, I got in the shower, still woozy from all the whisky I'd consumed last night. The thought of a three-course meal later turned my stomach, although it would be worth it to see Savannah. I may not agree with her idea of us leaving together so soon, but for her to turn up at the house meant she'd forgiven me for speaking out of turn the other day. She still wanted us to make a life together once Chloe was a thing of the past.

I could hear my wife downstairs, loading the dishwasher. The clanging of the plates set my teeth on edge. She could have been so good, she could have been the one, but I'd broken her too easily. Perhaps I needed a woman with a bit of spirit, maybe I should have sought out a Savannah all along.

The first time I saw Chloe was two weeks before I spoke to her. I'd seen her through the window of the bookshop as I was walking past. Two days in a row, she'd loitered, brow furrowed, reading the back of a book, then putting it back and selecting another from the shelf, catching my attention. I'd been running finance training for one of Middeon's clients in South London and liked to get out and explore during my lunch hour. Back then, Chloe had long blonde hair, neatly contained in a ponytail and she wore a pencil skirt and blouse with low heels. She looked demure, classy, the type of woman who appealed to me.

Later, when I went back to the bookshop and enquired after the lady with the blonde hair, the owner knew exactly who I was referring to. She told me she came in regularly and was an editor, buying around five books a week.

The following day, I went back and observed her from a distance, watching what she bought, intrigued at how she conducted herself. Chloe was quiet, timid even, apologising if she got in the way of other customers whilst browsing. Even when someone bumped into her on the pavement outside because he was staring at his phone, she was the first to say sorry, not quite making eye contact. I noticed she seemed to shrink into herself, especially with the opposite sex, and that's when I knew she was perfect. Gentle and submissive, I could mould her into a good wife.

It might have worked if she'd fallen pregnant, but that wasn't to be. Plus she'd changed, no longer was she keen to attend to my every whim, the impeccable husband pleaser she'd once been. Now she was a chain around my neck.

Tonight, once we were home from the dinner she'd have her *accident*, she'd be a little tipsy and a fall down the stairs in high heels should do it. The tiled floor would be disastrous if she hit her head hard enough – and even if she didn't, I could help nudge the plan along.

91

SAVANNAH

I arranged my hair in an elegant updo, a few tendrils loose at the front and nape of the neck. It had been a pampering afternoon, exfoliating, then shaving, buffing and moisturising. I'd taken time on my make-up, matching my smoky eye to my dress in shades of grey with a hint of blue. I wanted to look perfect for the last Middeon dinner, especially when I planned to deliver some home truths to Harry and his guests.

My stomach was tight with nerves I tried to ignore. They deserved it. I would be shedding my skin, dissolving myself of the secret I'd kept for Harry all this time before I started a new venture with Lewis. Harry had confided a lot to me in the beginning, when I saw him twice a week. I'd put in the effort to dazzle him in the hope he could one day be my sponsor, but it never materialised.

He'd told me the night Tom won the raffle that a fancy promotion to finance director was what Tom had been sold, but it wasn't a reality. Harry knew he needed someone to help balance the books as his previous finance director hadn't been particularly accommodating of Harry's redistribution of company money. Whoever was newly appointed had to be dispensable if they wouldn't help Harry make the expenditure disappear.

The dinners alone cost thousands and Harry was spending over a grand a week to see me, and for all I knew there could be other escorts too. Everything was put on expenses. He shoved cocaine up his nose like it was going out of fashion and drank his weight in expensive red wine. Half the time, he couldn't perform he was so under the influence, which made my job easier.

When it became more common and he realised he was paying a fortune for a companion as opposed to someone to satisfy his needs, his bookings slipped to once a week, then a couple of times a month. I kept him onside though – the Middeon dinners were lucrative for a night's work and Harry had friends in high places, those he played golf with. I was always trying to persuade him to make introductions.

I'd known it wouldn't last forever. Harry wouldn't be able to hide under the bottom line and Tom's card was marked. There had seemed little point in telling him, what good would it do. I'd lose not one but two clients if I gave Harry's secret away, although after tonight they'd both be long gone.

I painted my lips with my favourite Charlotte Tilbury and stepped into high heels. Packing my clutch with a few items, I put my make-up, baby wipes, tissues, deodorant, a set of underwear and perfume into a carrier bag I could leave in my room. Harry had me work out of one of the bedrooms in Glenthorne Manor which had an en suite so I could freshen up between Harry and the raffle winner.

My weekend bag which I usually took had a broken strap where the stitching had come loose and I hadn't had a chance to fix it. It wasn't an issue, I'd be there before all the guests so no one would see me all glammed up, ruining the mystique with a cheap bag from the local off-licence.

At half past five, I left the flat and got in my car ready to make the journey to Glenthorne Manor. My stomach fizzed and I looked forward to the first glass of champagne to calm my nerves. Tonight was going to be a night to remember.

92

CHLOE

Tom looked me up and down, casting his reproachful eye over my appearance before our taxi arrived. Gwen had been right, the dress was lovely, despite my reservations about the colour, and Tom could find no fault except to make me change my earrings. He hated ones that dangled, preferring small studs. Once he deemed I was suitable, we waited until the taxi pulled up outside.

Our driver tried to make conversation, but Tom wasn't in the mood, pulling at his collar as though it was choking him. No such luck. He seemed wound like a coiled spring and I kept quiet in case I said something wrong.

When we arrived, Anita and Jim were walking in, so we joined them at the entrance.

Anita clasped my hand in hers, a smile spreading across her face. 'It's so good to see you, I've been worried,' she said.

'No, no, I'm fine, we'll talk later,' I whispered into her ear as I hugged her hello. 'No bangles today?' I asked, noticing the lack of adornments on Anita's hands or wrists.

'I'm going understated for a change,' she said with a wink.

Tom stood behind us, shaking Jim's hand.

'How are you, good sir?' Jim asked.

'Not great if I'm honest, bloody shitshow with Clearwater,' Tom replied.

Jim clapped him mournfully on the back and followed us in.

Savannah and Harry were standing in the hallway welcoming guests like they were lord and lady of the manor. Anita visibly bristled and I sensed Jim stiffen behind me as they approached. He reluctantly took a glass of champagne for Anita along with his raffle ticket, smiling tightly before moving on. It was left to Tom and me to greet them. Savannah smiled sweetly, although there was something in her stare that unnerved me.

I blanched as Harry said, 'You remember Savannah from dinner last week, Chloe?'

'Of course,' I replied cordially.

Harry then declared loudly, 'I don't need to introduce *you* do I, Tom?' Winking as he pressed a ticket into Tom's palm.

I swallowed the mortification down with a gulp of the champagne I'd been handed and moved away.

At the bar, Tom ordered a whisky, pulling a stool up for Jim as they dived into conversation, inches apart as though they were sharing trade secrets.

Anita gave a wave of her hand. 'Leave them to it.' She led me away by the elbow until we were against the wall and out of earshot of anybody. 'I've sent loads of messages. I was panicking when I got one back that was so obviously Tom in tone that I feared he'd locked you up again.'

'He took my phone again and had his mother babysit me. I couldn't get away, but I'm leaving tomorrow. I've found the Polaroids, my passport, everything.'

'Fantastic! Listen, I've had a letter from your mum, but I didn't want to drop it in, in case Tom was there. I have it here in my purse.'

My stomach somersaulted and I bounced on my toes.

Anita delicately retrieved the envelope and I slid it into my clutch bag. I needn't have worried, Tom and Jim were deep in conversation, the former gesticulating wildly.

My plans to tell Anita the truth about what I'd heard Tom say at Savannah's was momentarily forgotten as I was itching to read my mum's words.

'Let's pop to the bathroom, shall we, before they seat us for dinner.' Anita led the way through the crowd, greeting everyone she knew as she passed. I kept my head down, bumping smack into Savannah as she stepped in front of me. Anita was still moving through the throng, not realising I'd been caught up.

'I need to talk to you,' Savannah whispered in my ear.

'Not now,' I snapped, surprised at the venom in my tone. Here she was, still pawing at me for her money, knowing Tom was planning to end my life – I hated her. Thankfully, I was saved by Harry's rudeness as he pulled her out of my way to introduce her to somebody and I managed to catch Anita up in the hallway.

She held the door to the bathroom open and we both nipped inside. I turned the lock so we would have some privacy and felt in my bag for the envelope.

Dear Chloe,

My heart breaks at your letter, your father will be devastated. I'll come and collect you. You'll always have a bed here whenever you need it. For goodness' sake call me, your number isn't working.

Pack a bag, I'll be there Thursday if I don't hear from you before then.

Mum x

She'd come, Tom wasn't lying. Knees weak with a flood of emotion, I steadied myself on the sink. 'She came for me on Thursday – oh God,' I whimpered.

'I'm so sorry, darling, if only I'd got that letter to you sooner. Do you have her number, we can call her from my phone now.'

'No I don't – they don't have a landline any more and Tom inputted Mum's number into my new phone incorrectly, most likely on purpose. I'm so stupid, I should have got her to put it in her letter, or at least put mine in.' I smacked my forehead, mascara beginning to smudge underneath my dampening eyes.

Anita put her hand on my arm, soothing gently. 'It's okay, you can just turn up on their doorstep, your mum said you'd be welcome.'

'I will. As soon as Tom leaves the house, I'm gone, especially now I know what he plans to do.'

Anita frowned, the lines of her lips stretching. 'What does he plan to do?' she asked slowly as if fearing the answer.

'He wants to kill me.'

93

TOM

Jim couldn't believe his ears, assuring he had no prior knowledge of me being used as a scapegoat for Harry's spending. I was already fuming and that was before Harry's smug welcome and comment about Savannah. It had taken all my restraint not to land one on the end of his nose right there in the hallway. Exploding in front my colleagues wasn't an option and I needed a double whisky to calm me down. As soon as dinner was over and we were in the drawing room, I'd pull Harry Poulter to one side and shove my promotion up his arse.

The ladies had disappeared and I looked around for them.

'Oh, they'll be powdering their noses, won't they?' Jim was on his second double, matching me drink for drink. Was he anxious about tonight or trying to dull the tedium of the whole event? I couldn't tell.

'Hey, chaps.' Graham Spectre appeared over Jim's shoulder, muscling in wherever he could. Graham was a permanent bachelor, by choice allegedly, although I could think of no woman desperate enough to sleep with him. He resembled a troll. 'So, tell me, how's the prospective sale going?' he sneered.

'Fuck off, Graham,' I snapped, slamming my empty glass down and jumping off my stool.

'Dinner is served, ladies and gentlemen.' Harry's booming voice came from the door and I led the crowd out, not bothering to wait for Chloe, she knew her way back to the ballroom anyway.

Thankfully, Graham was down the opposite end of the table from me, although it didn't stop me glaring at him as we sat. A waiter came with red wine and I held my glass out, watching as Chloe appeared sandwiched between Anita and Victoria. She didn't look happy, but she never bloody did, and I narrowed my eyes as she approached.

'Sit down, you're late,' I snapped.

'We were in the bathroom, we didn't hear them call,' she said, whipping into her seat like an F1 driver.

I scowled at Harry and Savannah, reigning over the centre of the table. She looked flushed, as though the glass of champagne in her hand was one of many. Either that or because he'd just had his fill of her. I clenched my hands into fists beneath the table. It would be the last time she would be so close to Harry, I'd guarantee that. He'd never get his grubby mitts on her again.

As if sensing my gaze, Savannah looked up, smiling at me passively. I winked, relishing Chloe's white-knuckled grip on her wine glass beside me.

I expected an opening speech from Harry, but he was deep in conversation with Anton on his left. Instead, the waiters began serving the starter – parsnip soup, my least favourite.

'Ten,' I hissed at Chloe, taking out my irritation on her.

She bowed her head and immediately spooned soup into her mouth.

'This is lovely,' a woman said to my right. She had dark frizzy hair and had overpainted the lines of her thin lips, resembling a clown.

'Is it?' I sneered, sluicing my spoon through the beige liquid.

'I'm Jill, Marcus's wife. I don't think we've met.'

'Tom,' I cleared my throat, 'and this is my wife Chloe.' I forced a grin, leaning back in my chair so the wives could say their hellos.

Jill proceeded to talk all through the starter and most of the way into the main course. Boasting how she'd opened up her own practice as a bereavement counsellor in Steyning with Marcus's help, dropping the question, 'Have you experienced loss?' into the conversation as soon as she could. It was like sitting next to a member of the God squad.

I barely ate, grinding my teeth together so hard to keep my derogatory comments to myself. Chloe tried to interject, easily able to read me, but the woman just kept going. I was surprised she'd managed to clear her plate of roast beef and talk at the same time. My knee jiggled under the table. I just wanted this façade over with.

'I'm going to the bathroom,' I said, standing up and discarding my napkin across my chair.

My vein in my forehead was throbbing and once I'd urinated, I ran my wrists under the cold water. Just dessert to go and I could confront Harry, the anticipation was like a rock in my stomach. Once tonight was over, I'd be done with Harry and Chloe, both of them lead weights around my neck.

94

SAVANNAH

I chewed the rubbery beef, trying to look engaged in Harry's banter with Anton. There was nothing worse than looking bored at the dinner table, but my patience for the three-course meal to be over was wearing thin. I had to speak to Chloe, make her talk to me and more importantly listen. What was her problem? Did she think I was after my money, payment on stealing Tom away? I was never going to get it now, that was for sure.

Making eye contact wasn't an option, she barely looked up from her plate, and whenever I did glance over, Tom was eyeing me like a hawk whilst the woman next to him chewed his ear off. I could tell he was enjoying the evening almost as much as I was.

Harry had my envelope of money tucked in the inside pocket of his green blazer and even after oral sex when I'd arrived, he wouldn't relent.

'After the raffle winner. Rules are rules, Savannah,' he'd berated whilst zipping up his flies. I wondered who it would be tonight.

'Are you selling Middeon?' I'd asked before he'd left the bedroom to go downstairs and wait for his guests.

'Yes, pastures new and all that. It's time to retire.'

I'd snorted as he'd closed the door. I was on to pastures new, he was doing a runner and leaving Tom to tidy up his mess.

Emptying out the carrier bag onto the bed, I'd rummaged for my toothbrush and lipstick. At least I didn't need to have a shower. Harry had been in a rush, which suited me fine. I'd swirled the water around my mouth, rinsing twice before applying the nude lipstick. Back to being perfect once more.

'Pass the water, Savannah,' Harry said, jolting me back to the present.

I handed him the jug and saw Tom get up and stride out of the room, Chloe's eyes following him. Managing to attract her attention, I gestured towards the exit, mouthing the word bathroom and gesturing we should go, but she gave a shake of the head and drank her wine, refusing to look in my direction again. I tapped my foot beneath the table, the bloody woman wouldn't help herself.

Dessert was a chocolate brownie with cream, but the sight of it turned my stomach. I'd had too much champagne and couldn't entertain anything sweet. Instead I played a little game, my eyes darting around the room, finding Anita. She would be the first wife I'd confront once my duties were finished. I was looking forward to seeing Jim's devastation when I told his wife I'd been sleeping with him for months.

Who would be next? Marcus maybe? That sexual harassment claim had to have been true, the man was a deviant when he'd won the raffle. He'd be like squashing a fly with my shoe. I wasn't not sure how his wife would react, she'd likely spill the beans on what a terrible childhood Marcus had to make him so misogynistic. I giggled to myself, as I perused my selection. They all thought they were so superior, but their lives were like a stack of cards I was about to tear down.

95

CHLOE

Tom returned, pushing his dessert away as he sat. I'd eaten half of mine.

'Ten?' he asked and I nodded, dabbing at my mouth with a napkin. 'Well, I didn't see, so it doesn't count, do it again.'

He nudged his plate towards me, but I didn't move.

'Do it,' he whispered through gritted teeth.

'No,' I replied, not missing a beat.

Outraged, he glowered at me as Jill launched into a commentary on her weekend plans as though Tom had solicited it.

Beneath the table, I winced, he'd kicked out at my ankle, and I reached down to rub it as what remained of my brownie and cream landed in my lap.

'Oh, darling, I'm so sorry, what a buffoon I am,' he said, waving his hands in the air.

My pink satin dress was a mess of brown and white swirls, cream dripping down to the hem and into my shoe.

'You bastard,' I whispered, my face crimson. Standing up, I let the plate drop to the floor and rushed out of the room, utterly humiliated.

When I heard footsteps approaching, I hoped it was Anita, but when I whirled around, Savannah stood before me.

'Here let me help,' she said, grabbing my wrist and pulling me into the bathroom, dampening towels to try to fix the mess while I silently sobbed at my reflection. Crouched at my feet, she looked up at me. 'You have to leave him.'

'I will.'

'No, now. Don't wait. You're not safe.' Her tawny eyes were like saucers, imploring me.

'I know. I heard everything.' The admission stuck in my throat mid sob.

'Oh my God,' Savannah said, bowing her head. She was right to be ashamed, she was as much his accomplice. 'I'll keep him busy.'

'I bet you will,' I snapped, and she looked back up at me, sighing.

'Okay, I deserved that. Go, now, I'll tell him you're upstairs putting on one of my dresses or something.'

I gawped at her, what a ridiculous idea. Anything that fit Savannah's curves would hang off me, he'd never believe it for a second. It was better to stick to the original plan. 'I'm leaving tomorrow. He'll go to the supermarket for croissants in the morning, or meat for a roast, and I'll run.'

'It might be too late by then!' Savannah stood and we were practically nose to nose, although I had to crank my neck to stare up at her. 'Okay, fine. You do you,' she said eventually, chucking the towel into the sink. 'You can't say I didn't try.'

I watched her open the door and sashay out as Harry's booming voice announced after-dinner drinks in the drawing room for the directors and cocktails in the library for the ladies.

It was followed by a rapture of chairs scraping against the parquet floor as I tried to stem my tears. Looking down at my dress, there was no disguising the brown stain, level with my crotch. I had no other clothes, what was I supposed to do other than carry on, have Tom declare to everyone I was clumsy, announce he couldn't take me anywhere or even that I needed lessons in fine dining as he laughed at my expense. His gloating in my humiliation sickened me.

I unzipped the designer dress and stepped out of it. The inside had a black heavy lining, the stitching was impeccably neat and minimal so I turned it inside out, zipped it back up and shimmied into it again. Other than the side zip and a tiny label at my hip, it looked okay, I'd get away with it, and it was better than the brownie stain. From a distance, no one would even notice it was on inside out.

Holding my head high, I exited the bathroom, glad the amount of make-up I'd put on was doing its job hiding the evidence I'd been crying once I'd dabbed at my face with a tissue.

Tom would be pissed, but I no longer cared. My plan had been to get through the evening and the night that followed in one piece. To be meek and follow Tom's every instruction, every whim to stay alive, but I couldn't do it any more. I'd reached my limit and if he was going to kill me, then he had to know I'd die fighting.

96

TOM

Jim's face when he looked at his winning ticket was a picture. I'd never seen a man so horrified. There was a hush around the room after the chosen number was revealed and everyone checked their stubs. Savannah returned seconds before Jim reluctantly waved his ticket, grimacing. It couldn't be more obvious he had no interest in his prize as Jim headed around the edge of the drawing room to hesitantly shake Harry's hand.

Savannah beamed, kissing Jim on the cheek before he turned away from her.

'Congratulations, Jim.' Harry started a round of applause before clearing his throat. 'Right, ladies and gentlemen, it pains me to announce this will be our last Middeon jaunt. As you know, Clearwater have been in, preparing the business for sale.'

A groan rose up from around the room, but Harry waved it away.

'Hopefully you'll have a new owner soon as it's time for me to retire, but I would like to take this opportunity to thank you all for your continued hard work and diligence which has made Middeon the success it is today.'

I scoffed, shaking my head as Harry's gaze crossed mine. He raised his whisky in a toast and everyone joined in. I looked around the room, watching the knowing glances and whispering.

As soon as Harry's announcement was over and conversation started, I made my way towards him, latching onto his arm and interrupting his conversation with Anton about the round of golf they'd played yesterday. So he hadn't been busy, just avoiding me. I quietly seethed.

'We need to talk, Harry.'

'Yes, yes, let me have a drink first, Tom my boy. Business straight after eating gives me indigestion.' He shook his arm out of my grip, turning back to Anton.

'Here, you have it,' Jim said, appearing behind me, shoving his raffle ticket into my hand. I looked at him, eyebrows raised. 'I'm not in the mood,' he continued before collecting a whisky and knocking it back in one.

I stared at the winning ticket stub. I had two choices: I could hit the bar, drink some more whisky and stew in my juices until I had the chance to give Harry both cannons or I could go and spend a little time with Savannah upstairs.

Immediately, my decision was made and I left the drawing room, catching a glimpse of Anita around the corner. Had she been listening at the door?

'Jim won the raffle?' she asked, her mouth twitching.

'Yep, he's in the money tonight, Anita,' I said, moving past her with little inclination for small talk.

Where was Chloe if she wasn't with Anita? I didn't see her amongst the gaggle of wives leaving the ballroom after Harry had declared dinner was over. She was probably in the toilet crying over her dress. Served her right. How dare she say no to me. The sooner she was dealt with, the better. I had little patience for her continued indiscretions, but I'd worry about that later. First, I'd surprise Savannah. She would be the perfect source of entertainment, the highlight of what was a terrible evening.

97

SAVANNAH

I perched on the edge of the bed and plastered a smile on my face when a knock came from the door.

'Come in,' I purred, trying to hide my revulsion as Tom peered around the door instead of Jim.

'Surprise,' he said, with a little wave, walking straight over to the decanter to pour himself a whisky.

'What are you doing here?' I faked a smile, crossing my legs.

'Turns out Jim isn't in the mood. Must be my lucky day.' He grinned, although it didn't reach his eyes. The lines in his forehead deepened as he swallowed his whisky in one gulp and poured another. He was worked up about something, I could tell. It had to be Harry. 'Drink?' he offered, holding his empty glass out to me before refilling it.

I shook my head; whisky and champagne wasn't a good mix. There was a big difference between having a little Dutch courage and still keeping my wits about me.

I hadn't been looking forward to seeing Jim again, not after he got physical last time, but Tom wasn't much better. I guessed Jim was telling the truth; he didn't want to see me again and he definitely didn't want me anywhere near his wife. But he wouldn't be able to avoid it later.

I didn't relish being alone with Tom, but I had to keep the act going.

'There was me thinking you'd changed your mind and were coming to rescue me.' I held my hand out, checking my French manicure, trying to look nonchalant.

'Soon, just not tonight. Anyway, *you* certainly don't need rescuing,' he sniggered.

'You're the boss,' I replied. How far was I going to go with this? What happened when Tom turned up with his bags packed and engine running? When was I going to come clean?

If he knew I'd been stringing him along all this time. He'd be furious and we were up here alone. There was no guarantee he wouldn't lose his shit and paste me all over the room. I wouldn't put it past him. If he was planning on murdering his wife for money, who knew what he'd do when he found out I'd betrayed him.

'So what does this second-hand ticket get me then?' Tom's eyes glistened, a real smile unfolding on his face. He put his glass down and took off his dinner jacket, laying it across the arm of the chair.

'That ticket?' I said seductively, uncrossing my legs and leaning back onto my elbows. 'Whatever you want.'

98

CHLOE

Anita was gripping the glass of her martini so tight I was worried it would shatter. There was nothing I could say to placate her. She'd told me Jim had won the raffle; she'd overhead it outside the drawing room and had it confirmed by Tom. I hadn't wanted to go back into the ballroom after what my husband had done. Dinner was over anyway and as far as I was concerned, Tom could drink himself to death with the rest of the directors.

I'd loitered outside the library, waiting for the gaggle of women to stream past on their way to the bar. Anita had come by a few minutes later and we'd queued for our cocktails.

'Does he know that you know?' I asked once we'd found a quiet corner.

'No. I still haven't said anything. He's been different, better. I thought it was over.' Anger had morphed the soft features of her face. Lines deepened and she seemed harder, more angular.

'Let's get another drink,' I said as Anita's was already empty, failing to come up with any words of condolence. What could I possibly say to make it better? Jim was upstairs collecting his prize, I couldn't imagine how awful Anita must feel knowing that's where her husband was.

We returned to the bar, the wives around us deep in conversation, gossiping about something.

'What happened to your dress?'

'Tom knocked his dessert into my lap,' I explained, watching as Anita's mouth twitched, her gaze looking past me towards the door.

'Chloe, hi, I'm sorry we didn't get a chance to talk much at dinner,' Jill said, appearing behind us and elbowing her way into the conversation. She had two women in tow: one was Sara and the other one's name I'd forgotten entirely.

'That's okay. I saw Tom was keeping you entertained,' I said tightly.

'He's quite the talker.'

I laughed at her comment. Tom hadn't been able to get a word in edgeways.

'Would you excuse me, I'm just going to the bathroom,' Anita said.

I went to follow, but Jill blocked my way, turning her attention to the lady whose name I'd forgotten.

'What are you bringing to the bake sale tomorrow, Hannah?'

'My signature coffee and walnut of course,' she giggled.

'What about you, Chloe?'

'Umm, lemon drizzle again maybe,' I replied half-heartedly, watching Anita leave the library.

'Oh I love lemon drizzle,' Sara gushed. 'What combination do you use? I love the all-in-one method, it's so easy and gives perfect results every time.'

I smiled politely, trying to feign interest. The absolute last thing on my mind was baking a cake for a charity sale I wouldn't be attending.

'You weren't at the last one, were you? Anita brought your cake, didn't she? Well, let me tell you, it was a hit, there wasn't a crumb left,' Jill said. 'You must come tomorrow and see for yourself.'

'Sure, what time is it?' I asked, draining the rest of my Aperol spritz.

'Eleven at St John's church. Oh do come, Chloe, it's such a good cause and it gives us time to have a coffee and a chat without the men around. We haven't seen you since the last dinner.'

I nodded, although I was going to be tied up fleeing my controlling husband before he murdered me for the insurance money. These women weren't interested in being friends. Someone like Jill was a collector of acquaintances, looking for shallow self-absorbed minions to boss around. I sensed she had appointed herself queen bee of the Middeon hive. I'd been lucky I'd found Anita – or rather, she'd found me, in amongst this group of women whom I had nothing in common with.

'Right, who's for another?' Sara said, eyeing my empty glass.

'Definitely,' I replied, desperate to escape the conversation, turning my back on the others and trying to signal the bartender.

'Want to know a secret?' Sara nudged my arm as we stood side by side, the ruffles of her dress rubbing my skin.

'What?'

'I bloody hate baking,' she giggled again, sounding like a naughty schoolgirl.

I couldn't help but laugh, searching over my shoulder to see if Anita had returned, but I'd sensed her need to get away. It was awful trying to pretend everything was fine when it clearly wasn't. I'd spent years doing it, I knew all about that.

99

TOM

'Whatever I'd like?' I raised a solitary eyebrow. If only she knew all the things I wanted to do to her. If Savannah could see inside my deviant mind, perhaps she wouldn't have offered. I'd been tame up until now, but when she was mine alone, she'd see a different side of me.

'The usual to start,' I said, unbuckling my belt as I watched Savannah slip slowly and seductively out of her dress, easing the straps off her shoulders and sliding it down her bare chest. I licked my lips as my eyes perused the curves of her hips, the thong pulled up high on her waist showing so much bare skin. She waxed and was always smooth and hair-free, unlike Chloe, who thought it was perverse to get turned on at a hairless vulva. Like I was some kind of paedophile.

My cock hardened as I imagined burying my face down there, hearing her moan in pleasure.

Savannah got down on her knees in front of the bed, which had an antique oak frame with swirls in the wood. It wasn't a four-poster like the one she had.

'I didn't bring any ties.'

'Here,' I said, pulling my belt out of the loops and wrapping it around both of her wrists. I managed to secure her to the left bedpost, utilising the slither of a gap between the wood and the mattress. It would do.

I stared down at the fullness of her breasts, which were pert despite their size, before I pushed my trousers down to my ankles and put a condom on.

'Open wide,' I said, stroking her face gently as she took me in her mouth, and for a second, all of my worries melted away with the warm wetness. 'I'm going to bend you over this bed and fuck you until you scream,' I murmured and the corners of her mouth turned upwards as she swirled her tongue around the tip, nearly pushing me over the edge.

A couple of minutes later, I came, grunting with satisfaction. Savannah grinned up at me, licking her lips. If she was pretending she was enjoying it, she was one hell of an actress. I could always tell when a woman faked it. Chloe didn't even bother trying any more.

I unbuttoned my shirt, which in haste I'd neglected to take off, sweat dampened the back, deepening the blue hue.

'Stay right there, don't move a muscle. I'm going to take a shower, then it's your turn,' I said, pulling my shirt off and laying it on the chair with my blazer.

'Tom,' Savannah's voice came out a little whiney as she tried to wriggle her hands out of the belt. Clearly not comfortable on her knees with her arms twisted to one side, but one look silenced her.

'I'll be quick. Stay, please, you look beautiful,' I said, kissing the top of her head, a coconut scent emanating from her hair. A cold shower would be perfect to revitalise me, ready for round two.

I turned on the shower and opened a travel-sized shower gel meant for guests, humming to myself. Harry and Chloe were now the farthest things from my mind. Both of them a problem for later. For now, I wanted to enjoy this delicious slice of the evening with Savannah. The whore who had dazzled me from the moment I'd laid eyes on her and, quite possibly, had made me fall in love with her.

100

SAVANNAH

My knees were sore from the coarse carpet and my shoulder itched with hair fallen out of the clip. I couldn't reach it and I couldn't undo the belt either. Black, stiff leather bound my wrists, I was stuck until Tom came back to release me. He'd closed the bathroom door, but I could hear the shower running. I slumped back on my knees, there was no point in struggling. The last thing I wanted was unsightly rings around my wrists when I was socialising with the wives and telling them my secrets.

First, I had to get my payment before I did any of that. I'd pack my stuff up and put it in the car along with my money so I could make a quick getaway once I'd dropped a few bombs. I'd had a few glasses of champagne, but I knew I could still drive. I just had to get through the next twenty minutes or so, finish Tom as quickly as possible. The thought of him touching me knowing what he planned to do made my skin crawl and I nearly blurted out everything as soon as he walked in the door. But he looked unhinged already and I wasn't going to push him over the edge, especially not when we were alone.

I tried to change my position and force my legs out in front of me, I could feel the beginnings of a cramp in my calf and I was attempting to rub it with my elbow. Concentrating on my muscles, I didn't hear the footsteps behind me or the rustle of the blue carrier bag that went over my head. My blue carrier bag. The one I'd brought my refresh kit in, the one that was now stretched so tight across my face I couldn't breathe.

Wrenching at the bedpost, I tried to free myself, craning my head towards my hands so I could claw at my open mouth, but my neck snapped back, held tight by someone. Thrashing backwards and forwards, my legs flew out in all directions, scrabbling around, heels digging into the carpet, trying to get purchase. Without it, I was helpless, I couldn't scream or release my hands, it was impossible to fight off my attacker despite how much I jerked. They held on tight, grunting with the exertion although it gave me no clue as to who it was. Surely it wasn't Chloe?

Head swimming, my eyes rolled as I gasped for breath that wasn't there. A plastic taste entered my mouth as I sucked the bag in, limbs weakening with every second. My lungs were being crushed inside my chest, trampled by an invisible force. The pain was excruciating until I couldn't take it any more. Time slowed and it ebbed away. Darkness seemed to pour inside the bag, filling it up like liquid. It was like drifting under water, the sound of my heartbeat in my ears growing faint.

My hearing was the last thing to go, a second before I caught the word 'Bitch' hissed at my ear. Slumping backwards as far as the belt would allow, my body became limp, and as though someone had blown out a match, the lights went out.

101

CHLOE

I'd misread Sara who, it turned out, was quite the rebel, making it perfectly clear as we waited for our drinks she was poking fun at the matriarchy Jill ran.

'It's easier to go along with it sometimes, better to be on the inside looking out than the outside looking in, if you catch my drift.'

'It just all seems a bit...' I let my words trail off.

'Fake? Oh it is, it's all about image.' Sara rolled her eyes.

'You two are taking ages!' Jill appeared at my back, but Sara whizzed around and handed her an espresso martini.

'Here you go, Jill.'

'Have you seen Victoria's dress? It's bursting at the seams! I mean, I keep inviting her to Pilates, but she's always got an excuse.'

I gritted my teeth, outraged on Victoria's behalf. So much for female empowerment and sisterhood.

'I think she looks fantastic,' I said a little too loudly, catching Sara's smirk.

'Well, of course, that's not what Jill is saying,' Hannah piped up.

'No, she absolutely does. I'm wondering if she's going in for child number three.' Jill tried to dig herself out of the hole she'd created.

'What happened to your dress?' Hannah asked, frowning at the label poking out at my side. 'Weren't you wearing pink before?'

A flush crept up my neck. 'Tom knocked my dessert into my lap, by accident. It was a mess that couldn't be fixed, so I turned it inside out.'

'Ingenious,' Sara said, clinking her glass against mine.

'Quite,' Hannah agreed, although her wrinkled nose told me she didn't agree at all.

'I'm just going to pop to the bathroom,' I said, already heading towards the door, hoping to find Anita. As if I didn't feel self-conscious enough, I knew Jill and Hannah would be ridiculing me. They were like vultures on a carcass, picking it apart. Sara seemed the only human amongst them.

I passed Victoria on the way out, tapping her on the shoulder.

'You look amazing, I love your dress,' I said. I wasn't lying, the black cocktail dress was snug, but it emphasised curves I could only dream of having.

'Thank you. I've got such bad IBS at the moment, I'm so bloated,' she whispered, patting her stomach.

I breezed out of the door, glad I'd said something, feeling like I'd counteracted Jill's bitchy comment with my compliment.

When I reached the bathroom, a woman I didn't recognise was exiting.

'I wouldn't bother, someone has locked themselves in there. I'm going to find another toilet.' She stalked away, shaking her head.

I pushed open the door. The area by the sink was empty, but the heavy burgundy toilet door was shut.

'Anita?' I called out.

A second later, the lock clicked and Anita came out. She looked pale and shaky.

'I was having a panic attack,' she said, eyes blurry with tears.

'Shall I go and get Jim?' I asked, but she shook her head.

'It's passing now.'

We stood at the sink and I watched as Anita held out her hand, blowing out her fingers one by one as though they were candles on a cake. A trick she must have learned to combat attacks.

'You've torn your strap.' I stepped behind her, trying to fasten it back on.

'I've got a safety pin in my bag,' she said, rummaging in the gold clutch.

She handed me a travel sewing kit and I retrieved the pin, fixing the strap, ensuring it didn't show.

'God, what are we like – two wardrobe malfunctions in one evening,' I said, trying to lighten the mood.

'Except yours wasn't a malfunction of the dress but a malfunction of your husband,' Anita replied wryly. She pulled out a compact and dabbed at her face with the flat sponge, covering her shiny skin with mattifying powder.

'You look perfect,' I said, rubbing her shoulders and she smiled at me weakly, tapping my hand.

'Thank you, Chloe. Let's get back out there, shall we. I could do with another drink.' Her empty glass was by the sink, lipstick staining the rim.

'I warn you, they're like a pack of wolves tonight.'

'I'm not in the mood for those bitches,' she sighed as we left the bathroom.

'It'll all be over soon.'

102

TOM

I'd come out of the bathroom wearing only a towel expecting to find Savannah kneeling in position and wasn't prepared for what awaited me. The scene was like something from a horror movie. Dropping to my knees, I clamped my hand over my mouth to stifle a scream. Savannah lay still on the floor, her bound hands purple, head lolling backwards. Her mouth gaped, drool running from the corner of her blue-tinged lips.

'Oh God no,' I cried into my hand before crawling towards her, losing my towel in the process. Panic rose in my chest like an unstoppable tsunami, but I couldn't tear my eyes away from her lifeless body. I pressed my fingers against her bare neck, feeling for a pulse, but nothing registered.

I'd only been gone five minutes. Had Savannah had a seizure? Choked on her own tongue? Her hair was a mess, the clip hanging on to a couple of strands while the rest of her wild red waves hung limply down her back. One of her fake eyelashes had slipped down to her cheek. Had she shaken herself that hard?

Pulling myself to my feet, I staggered backwards, naked and vulnerable, looking around the room for something, anything, that would explain what had happened, unable to believe my own eyes or comprehend how the world had changed in the minutes I'd been gone. Hurriedly, I retrieved my clothes, pulling them on, yet unable to stop gawping at the sight I knew would haunt me forever. Savannah was dead, when moments before she'd been alive. I couldn't undo it, I couldn't save her.

Wiping away tears so alien to me, I pushed my feet into my shoes, grabbed my phone and dashed out of the room with the intention of raising the alarm, but when I reached the top of the stairs, I paused. If I told anyone I'd been with Savannah, I'd be the number-one suspect. Should I go back? Dress her maybe and lay her on the bed? I couldn't risk being found with her body – what if they thought I'd done it?

I wouldn't have harmed a hair on her head. I loved her, we were running away together. Then the reality came crashing in. I'd never be with her again.

Pull yourself together! My head took over and I wiped leaking snot from my nose. *Get control of yourself. Put as much distance between you and her as you can.*

It made no sense to flee, only the guilty did that, but I couldn't control my legs, which seemed to have a mind of their own. I bounded down the stairs, searching the library for my wife. She was moving amongst the crowd, heading towards the bar, following Anita. I forged a path after them, catching her arm.

'We need to leave. Now.' I kept my voice low, not wanting to create a scene. We needed to slip out quietly.

Chloe frowned. 'It's only half past nine,' she said but saw something in my eyes that made her comply – desperation or fear maybe. She briefly hugged Anita as I was already making my way towards the front door and out onto the sweeping gravel driveway. It was then I remembered we didn't have cars or drivers this time, we'd arrived in a cab.

'Fuck!' I said, already tapping at my phone to order a taxi.

'What's happened?' Chloe was at my side, trying to keep up as I strode towards the large metal gates.

'Keep walking.'

'Tom, you're scaring me, what's happened?'

'Shut up, I need to think.'

103

CHLOE

Ten minutes after we'd left, as we tried to navigate our way down the pitch-black country lane, headlights came around the bend and blinded us. Tom flagged down the taxi, climbing in and confirming his name and destination. We drove home listening to the muted sound of the radio, its volume turned down low. Tom stared out of the window, hands rubbing at the fabric of his trousers as though he was trying to wipe off something I couldn't see.

Had he argued with Harry, or Savannah? Had something happened with Jim? Questions rocketed around my brain, but I dared not voice them.

When we arrived home, Tom paid the driver and rushed inside, heading straight for the lounge and his whisky decanter. I stood in the doorway watching as he knocked a large glass back and poured another immediately. His hands shook in a way I'd never seen before and now, in the dim light of our lamp, I saw his face was ashen.

'Tom, what's happened? Tell me?' I urged. Anxiety climbed my chest like growing vines, although I had no idea what I should be afraid of, other than my husband.

'I was with you all night if anyone asks. We went upstairs, found an empty room, had sex.'

'I was with Anita,' I interrupted, confused.

'God dammit,' Tom yelled, throwing his glass against the wall, the plaster crumbling as the tumbler shattered on the floor.

My breath caught in my throat, fear clung to every inch of me. Goosebumps covered my arms and I backed away, taking refuge in the kitchen and debating whether to run upstairs and lock myself in the bathroom. What had he done? Had he gone mad, lost his mind? His voice broke through my panicked thoughts.

'We need to leave, pack a bag. We can catch a flight out of Gatwick,' he called.

'Where to?'

'Anywhere.' He sounded flustered.

I didn't want to leave, not with him. How would I get away from him if we were in another country?

His mobile started to ring, the imperial march sounding more ominous than usual.

'Fuck,' I heard him shout before the beep of the safe being unlocked. Thank goodness I'd left everything where it was.

The mobile continued to ring, stopping then starting again. Someone was desperate to get hold of him. My stomach clenched, alcohol swilling. Threatening to rise, I pushed it down. Something was terribly wrong.

I left the kitchen and climbed the stairs, doing what Tom had requested. I was leaving one way or another and it gave me a chance to put distance between us while he was clearly so unstable. I didn't want the next thing he threw to be aimed at me.

Halfway through the third trip from wardrobe to the holdall on the bed, laden with clothes, I tripped over my dress and tore it off, breaking the zip in the process. Pulling on jeans and a T-shirt, I carried on packing clothes and toiletries, listening out for Tom downstairs. His rattled voice rose up from the floor below; he was on the phone to somebody, but who? Savannah?

'I can't calm down for fuck's sake, Lenny,' I heard him bark. Lenny was his parents' solicitor. What was he calling him for?

I sat on the edge of the bed and prayed for the night to be over. I'd never been so terrified, not when Tom had punched me, or when he'd locked me in the bathroom. This felt different. He was scared.

My phone beeped from my clutch bag I'd ditched on the floor on my way into the bedroom. Hastily I grabbed it. The emergency services were one call away and if I heard anything else being smashed downstairs, I wouldn't hesitate.

The beep had been a WhatsApp from Anita and I tapped at the screen to open it.

Why did Tom make you leave? The police are here.

104

TOM

The walls were closing in. Lenny had been little help. His advice was not to run, to call the police and make myself available for questioning.

'Don't you understand, my DNA will be everywhere,' I'd snapped, something I'd overlooked in my panic to get away. Eventually, I lost my rag and hung up the phone. Lenny assured me we could work it out and leaving the country would only make me guilty in the eyes of the law, but what choice did I have?

By now Savannah must have been discovered, it had to be why everyone was trying to get hold of me. Glenthorne Manor would be in uproar, but everyone would have an alibi. Everyone except me because I'd been with Savannah a few minutes before and after she'd died. She must have had some kind of heart attack or aneurysm unless someone came into the room and attacked her while I was in the shower. Was I going to hang around to find out what the coroner ruled her death as? If I did and it turned out to be murder, I'd be up shit creek without a paddle.

Chloe would have to lie to the police, but what about when they spoke to Anita, who'd give a different version of events.

Not everyone could have an alibi though – if Savannah had been attacked, then someone had done it. I'd already made myself look guilty by leaving the scene of the crime, but it was a split-second decision and I'd acted on impulse, panic overtaking any sensible thought.

My phone hadn't stopped ringing. First Harry, then Jim, followed by numbers I didn't recognise. They must have found her. It was the only explanation for my phone blowing up.

'Fuck!' I shouted into the ether, thrusting my hands into my hair.

I paced the room, adrenaline soaring through my body. We'd been back for over half an hour – almost an hour since I'd discovered Savannah. Were the police already on their way here? I picked up the decanter, drinking straight from it, letting whisky run down the side of my face. I wanted it all to go away and the only way I could do that was to run.

Bounding up the stairs, I startled Chloe in the bedroom. She backed away from me until she was against the window.

'Are you done?' I said, ignoring the terror in her eyes as I opened my side of the wardrobe and stuffed what I could grab into the holdall she'd nearly filled.

'Y-yes,' she stammered, her eyes like orbs.

I'd drive to Gatwick, it would be the quickest way and I could leave my car there. It wasn't likely I'd be coming back for it. We could get tickets at the airport, the next flight leaving ideally, wherever it was headed.

I ran to the bathroom to get my toothbrush, shaving cream and razor.

'Tom,' Chloe called timidly. Before I reached the bedroom, I could already see the blue lights flashing on the hallway ceiling, like a scene from *War of the Worlds*. The patrol car parked across the driveway, blocking my escape. Chloe looked out of the window at the two men exiting the vehicle and making their way to the front door. I crossed the room in seconds.

'You were with me all night. Don't make me repeat it,' I said, pinching her upper arm until she howled before going to open the door.

'Mr Beswick?'

'Yes?' I jutted my chin forwards, keeping my voice steady.

'Police,' the taller one said, as if it wasn't obvious. 'Could we come in?'

I stepped back, forcing a smile and let the two burly men into my home.

'Is there anyone else here?'

'My wife Chloe – she's upstairs.'

'Could you call her down for us please, sir?'

I did as they asked, catching the second officer looking directly at the passports I'd placed on the kitchen table, along with all of the cash I had stashed at home. *Fuck!*

'Going on a trip?'

'No, just organising,' I lied.

Chloe came down the stairs, carrying the damn holdall we'd been packing.

The first officer raised his eyebrow at me, but I didn't respond.

'I'm afraid there's been an incident at Glenthorne Manor. I believe you were both there this evening?'

'That's correct.'

'A young woman has been attacked,' he glanced at his notebook, 'an Orlagh Kerry.'

'I don't know any Orlagh Kerry,' I said, eyebrows knitting together.

'We believe she goes by the name Savannah.'

Chloe gasped and dropped the holdall, which thudded to the floor, her mouth gaping. *Perfect timing, the stupid bitch.*

'Mr Beswick, we'd like you to accompany us to the station.'

105

CHLOE

Another car arrived before Tom was taken. The police had come to collect me and we were to be transported in separate vehicles. Everyone had had their statements taken at Glenthorne Manor, the officer said, and were only just being allowed to leave. The place had been cordoned off as a potential crime scene, with Savannah carted away in an ambulance. We were, it seemed, the only two guests who had decided to leave early, before she had been discovered.

Tom had been reported by his colleagues as the last person to be with Savannah and they wanted an itinerary of my movements: who I'd been with, where in the house I'd travelled and at what points in the evening I'd seen Tom. My husband's parting words to me back at home throbbed in my head, along with the bruise now forming on my arm. Had he harmed Savannah?

'I thought Jim won the raffle?' I murmured, thinking out loud. I'd been delivered to an interview room a cup of coffee placed before me.

'The raffle?' an officer with kind eyes asked, his hand poised on his notebook.

'An evening with Savannah – she's the prize,' I grimaced.

'Do you mean to say Savannah was a prostitute?'

'An escort – she told me herself in the bathroom, not tonight – at the last dinner.' I was rambling, words spilling out of me with no filter.

'How well did you know her?'

'Not well, we met that night, around a month ago,' I answered, deciding not to tell them my husband was in a relationship with her. They could find out for themselves.

'Did you witness Jim leave the ballroom with Savannah?'

I shook my head.

'I didn't see anyone leave with Savannah,' I admitted, trying to piece together the stages of the night.

I didn't lie as Tom had asked me to. I owed Savannah that, but I wanted to leave the police station with a clean conscience.

A note had been found in her car addressed to me, they said, a warning of Tom's intention to hurt me.

'Does it mean anything to you, Mrs Beswick?'

I shook my head as I read the note sealed in a plastic bag.

'And does he hurt you?'

I rubbed at my arm, the pinch mark visible.

I didn't need to confirm it. As it turned out, Anita had done it for me. She'd told them all about Tom's viciousness, his domineering nature. Everyone it seemed had painted Tom's character for the police before I'd uttered a word.

I stared at the coffee rings on the table. How many people had been in this room before me, telling their stories, defending their innocence?

A wave of tiredness hit and I stifled a yawn.

'Can I go home?' I asked.

'Of course. I think we have everything we need for now.'

I was given a lift home in the early hours of the morning, yet sleep wasn't an option. My response to Anita's message sent once I'd got back remained unopened. Was she at home, asleep? How could anyone sleep after what had happened?

On the answerphone was a hurried message from Lenny, letting me know he was on his way to the police station to be with Tom. He could be out in a matter of hours, yet I was too exhausted and confused to run. I sat

at the kitchen table until my backside went numb, staring at the clock as
the minutes ticked past, trying to make sense of the news.

Savannah was in the hospital that was all the police had told me. Was it
an accident or had Tom hurt her? Nausea turned my stomach, but still I
managed a bottle of wine from the rack. She'd tried to warn me, but I
hadn't listened, I'd brushed her off, sure she was in on Tom's plan to get rid
of me and collect the life insurance.

* * *

The call came through at eleven on Sunday morning. It was the home
phone that woke me, the shrill ring a few hours after I'd curled up on the
sofa as dawn was breaking, eyes stinging from exhaustion.

'Chloe, it's Lenny. They've charged Tom with attempted murder.' He
sounded exhausted and deflated.

'When is he coming home?' I asked, trying to process what Lenny had
just said.

'Bail will likely be denied, the police are claiming he's a flight risk due
to the passport and bag he already had packed when they arrived at the
house.'

The words seemed to float over my head and I didn't know what to say.

'I'll do my best, Chloe, but it's not looking good. There might also be a
bit of a media storm coming. It might be a good idea to get away for a
while.'

I smiled. This stranger, who I knew the name of but had never met had
just given me what I'd needed to hear.

'Okay, I'll go to my mum's.'

EPILOGUE – THREE MONTHS LATER
CHLOE

Once off the motorway, Anita drove with the top down, the Indian summer breeze whipping through my hair, which had finally reached my shoulders again. The beginning of October was unseasonably warm and I was glad, not quite ready for the autumn nights to draw in.

HMP Woodhill in Milton Keynes was around two and a half hours away, and despite having had a few lessons, I was still months away from taking my driving test. Anita had offered to drive, insisting we stop for lunch before coming home. A girls' road trip, she'd suggested, allowing up us to catch up on what I'd been up to.

Since Tom's incarceration, I'd moved back to my parents', initially desperate to put some distance between myself and the cottage. I spent a month hiding away until Mum forced me to see a therapist who helped me come up with a plan to put my life back together. Eventually, I felt brave enough to return to Copthorne and pack up my things, but even without Tom, there the cottage felt suffocating. The pawn shop still had the diamond set hoops my parents had bought me for my twenty-first birthday and buying them back was the first step to regaining control.

'I can't believe they still haven't set a date for the trial,' Anita said, slowing for a roundabout.

'I know. Lenny said Tom's barrister isn't hopeful of a positive outcome.

There's so much DNA, and without an alibi for part of the evening, he's pretty much screwed.'

'But Savannah still can't say for sure it was him?'

'No, she never saw, but who else would it have been? She was tied up with his belt! Thank God she was discovered and an ambulance called in time. She got a first-class honours degree despite her stint in hospital. I'm going to her passing out parade next week.'

'Let's just hope Tom signs the papers,' Anita said after a pause, the subject of Savannah still a touchy one. Her and Jim had managed to move past his infidelity with the help of marriage counselling and she was looking forward to going on a cruise since he'd taken early retirement.

Middeon had been sold for less than Harry was hoping for due to the media storm surrounding Savannah's attack. A persistent journalist had written a story about the misuse of company funds and Harry was still being investigated for fraud. Not quite the retirement he had planned. Many of the directors had moved on, keen not to get caught in the media spotlight and become part of the headlines detailing the rotten culture at Middeon and how it had been allowed to go on for so long. The wives club had also disbanded, Anita only kept in touch with Sara and Victoria, although I hadn't seen them. I'd been spending my time with my old friends, who thankfully had welcomed me back into the fold. I was moving on with my new life, leaving the past behind but there was still one final tie to cut.

* * *

Sitting in the oppressive visitation room, nausea making me want to run, I didn't see Tom enter. I practically jolted out of my chair when he slumped down in front of me. He looked awful, thinner, with a week's growth on his chin and uncombed hair. It was a pitiful sight but I couldn't muster up any sympathy for my husband, it was his own fault he was here.

'Why haven't you called or answered my letters?' That was my greeting after not having seen him since the night of Savannah's attack.

I blew air out of my nostrils attempting to find my inner sanctum of calm. I had been dreading this visit, being so close to Tom unnerved me.

Both mum and Anita had offered to come for support but it was something I wanted to do alone.

'I need you to sign these papers,' I said, pushing a small stack towards him.

'What are they?'

'If you don't allow me to sell the house, the bank will repossess it. I haven't paid the mortgage for three months and you're receiving demands.'

'I'm not selling the house. Get a job, pay the mortgage,' Tom said coldly.

'I'm not living there, I've moved out. If you don't sign, you'll lose the equity. If we sell, I'll split the equity and give yours to your parents to keep for you.' His mother had been stoic, the typical British stiff upper lip, standing by her son even in the face of his attempted murder charge.

'Fuck off.' He laughed in my face.

My knee jiggled under the table and I eyed the guard at the corner of the room. There was always the possibility Tom would lose it, reach across the table and be on me in seconds.

'There's divorce papers in there too.' I tapped the pile.

Tom leant back in his chair, folding his arms across his chest, sneering.

'On what grounds?' he sniggered. 'You don't get to leave, I told you that.'

'You tried to kill Savannah,' I hissed.

'I didn't hurt her, I loved her.' A pathetic attempt to wound me.

'She didn't love you,' I spat, feeling the venom rush out of me. 'I paid her, Tom. I paid her to pretend she cared for you. I wanted you to let me go, I didn't realise you were going to try to kill me.'

Tom's eyes blazed, first with fear at the realisation I knew everything and incredulity I would pull off something so brazen behind his back. My lips twitched, trying to conceal a smile, I'd finally managed to get the upper hand.

'If you ever get out of here, it would be nice to have some money to start again with, wouldn't it? There's not even a date set for your trial yet. I just want my half.'

'Bitch,' he hissed, 'you did it, didn't you? It was you!'

'Sign the papers, Tom.'

He hung his head in his hands and quietly cried. It was obvious he wasn't coping well, having his liberty taken away, but he'd brought it on himself and I felt no remorse.

We sat in silence for five minutes, the chatter around us loud. Eventually, Tom signalled a guard, who ambled over.

'Can I have a pen to sign this?'

The guard walked away, coming back a few minutes later with a biro, standing beside the table while Tom signed the documents I'd brought with me before taking the pen back.

Tom didn't even bother to read them before he pushed them back across the table.

'Have you seen my parents?' Tom sniffed, cuffing his nose with his sleeve.

'A couple of times, they've been helping me pack up the house. I found the safe.' His eyes shot up to meet mine, drilling into me. 'I had a nice little bonfire once they left.' The corner of my mouth curled upwards as the vein in his forehead throbbed. Those Polaroids were nothing but ash now. 'Goodbye, Tom.' I stood, not waiting for him to answer, and walked towards the exit, where a guard waited to let visitors out. I didn't give him the satisfaction of looking back.

* * *

'Is it done?' Anita was leaning against the bonnet of her car, basking in the sunshine.

'It's done,' I replied, walking towards her but tripping over my own feet, dropping the papers on the tarmac. 'I'm such an idiot,' I said, slapping my forehead.

Anita stooped to help me. 'Here,' she said, pulling a blue carrier bag from her handbag and pocketing the papers inside.

I sighed, feeling as though the weight of the world was finally off my shoulders. Once the house was sold, I'd have a deposit to buy my own place. Somewhere between Copthorne and my parents where I could regain my independence again. I'd been too reliant on them since I'd turned up on their doorstep on that cloudy Sunday in early July, but between them and my therapist, I was starting to find my way back to myself.

I was still running but my appetite had come back and I'd put on half a stone. Reconnecting with my old friends had helped, and with Anita's support, I was almost ready to start looking for a job back in the world of publishing, which I'd missed terribly.

'Right, let's go and find somewhere to eat.' Anita clapped her hands and opened the car door.

'Speaking of eating, what time should we arrive for dinner tonight?' I asked.

'Seven is good. Jim and I are so looking forward to meeting Ben.'

ACKNOWLEDGEMENTS

Firstly, I'd like to thank the entire Boldwood Team for their unwavering support. I consider myself so lucky to be on this journey with you. Caroline Ridding, thanks for being the best editor and helping me wrangle these stories from my head onto the page.

Jade Craddock, as always you are amazing, you do a fantastic job making everything flow better and your suggestions are always spot on. I feel very fortunate to have you as my copy editor.

To my lovely mum, my first reader, who declared this was her second favourite book I'd written. Your enthusiasm pushes me to keep at the laptop, the demand for more chapters at the forefront of my mind.

Thanks to my wonderful family who have always supported me, my husband Dean who cooks and cleans and lets me spend hours in the office, always stepping up, and my two gorgeous daughters, Bethany, and Lucy. I love you more than I could ever put into words. I'm looking forward to one day, when you're both old enough, that you may just pick up one of my books and have a read.

Lastly, a massive thank you to my readers. To those who pre-order the books and read everything I write. I couldn't do any of this without you and your messages and social media posts really do make a difference on days when I'm struggling with imposter syndrome. To those who write reviews and leave ratings, endlessly promoting, I appreciate each and every one of you.

ABOUT THE AUTHOR

Gemma Rogers was inspired to write gritty thrillers by a traumatic event in her past. Her debut novel Stalker, released in 2019, marked the beginning of her writing career. Gemma lives in West Sussex with her husband and two daughters.

Sign up to Gemma Roger's mailing list for news, competitions and updates on future books:

Follow Gemma on social media:

facebook.com/GemmaRogersAuthor

x.com/gemmarogers79

bookbub.com/authors/gemma-rogers

instagram.com/gemmarogersauthor

tiktok.com/@gemmarogersauthor

ALSO BY GEMMA ROGERS

Stalker

The Secret

The Teacher

The Mistake

The Babysitter

The Feud

The Neighbour

The Flatmate

The Good Wife

THE

LIST

**THE MURDER LIST IS A NEWSLETTER
DEDICATED TO SPINE-CHILLING FICTION
AND GRIPPING PAGE-TURNERS!**

**SIGN UP TO MAKE SURE YOU'RE ON OUR
HIT LIST FOR EXCLUSIVE DEALS, AUTHOR
CONTENT, AND COMPETITIONS.**

SIGN UP TO OUR NEWSLETTER

BIT.LY/THEMURDERLISTNEWS

Boldwood

Boldwood Books is an award-winning fiction publishing company seeking out the best stories from around the world.

Find out more at www.boldwoodbooks.com

Join our reader community for brilliant books, competitions and offers!

Follow us
@BoldwoodBooks
@TheBoldBookClub

Sign up to our weekly deals newsletter

https://bit.ly/BoldwoodBNewsletter

Milton Keynes UK
Ingram Content Group UK Ltd.
UKHW042123150224
437885UK00002B/5

9 781805 494881